PRAISE FOR
THE PAROXYSM DECEPTION

"If you have the pleasure of picking up the dark world of *The Paroxysm Deception*, brace yourself for an intense read that will surely transport you inside criminals' minds! Jastrow Hill keeps you guessing and on the edge of your seat. I found myself anticipating what would happen every other sentence. It was so interesting to grasp a perspective of human desires and how far people are willing to go for them. Hill writes splendidly!"
- Quinn Jamison, author of *The Art of Time* and the sequel *The Art of Bending Time: A Forbidden Return*

"A bone chilling conspiracy! Jastrow had me on the edge of my seat the entire time. I couldn't put it down. I had to know what happened each chapter."
- Samantha Davenport, author of *Conri*

"*The Paraoxysm Deception* is a gripping story with distinctive characters. Everything feels at stake especially as the blurred lines have very real consequences. The openings of every chapter are my favourite aspect of the book as it develops the curiosity of the reader and confronts the chaos of everything that is happening."
- Charnjit Gill, author of *Pray Tell*

THE

PAROXYSM

DECEPTION

Jastrow Hill

atmosphere press

© 2024 Troy Held

Published by Atmosphere Press

ISBN 979-8-89132-469-5

Edited by Dr. Nathaniel Lee Hansen

Cover design by Kevin Stone

No part of this book may be reproduced without permission from the author except in brief quotations and in reviews. This is a work of fiction, and any resemblance to real places, persons, or events is entirely coincidental.

Atmospherepress.com

To my amazing wife, Susan who always supports me.

My mom and dad who provided for me and taught me well.

And to my two dogs, Bo and Wiggles, who are always with me.

CHAPTER 1.

THE LAW OF AVERAGES

Evil comes in many forms, and mostly without welcome. The shapes are varied, but the intent is the same. That evil can be invisible, physical, or even unfathomable. Although wickedness is all around, it will most often strike not from strangers but from those known and those known well.

*

David Deagan and Lisa Cooper met at the high school in town when they were young, corporally bound, yet free of mind. David was born and raised in the Mountain View area. Lisa moved to Mountain View in her sophomore year of high school. She and her family had moved from a city where she had principally learned how to obtain services to meet the needs of human comfort. Lisa would soon find herself in rural America, where services were few, and the necessity to care for oneself was optimal and, at times, critical.

*

Her parents were running from city life and seeking a slower, more relaxed pace—one that they discovered only occurred in life when you made it happen yourself. Lisa had two siblings. One was over eighteen and the other would be starting her senior year at Mountain View High imminently. Lisa's dad,

Ben, had sold insurance for a national brand in the city. He leaped at the chance to help open a new store as the general manager of insurance sales, claims, and staffing in rural Mountain View.

Lisa did not know what she was going to do with her life in particular, but she knew that she didn't want to move to Mountain View. She also knew that she wanted to be rich and famous. She fantasized that she would eventually marry a television or movie star...maybe even a professional musician. She had been a fan of many teen idols and learned about the fabulous lives of the likes of Ricky Nelson, Elvis, and The Monkeys, to name a few. Lisa's sister Mary was gung-ho on leaving the city and looking for new boys to tease. Lisa liked her current life just fine and asked her parents if she could stay behind with relatives so that she could remain with her friends. Her request was denied without explanation or concern, so she came kicking and screaming northward with her family. The family arrived in Mountain View at the end of the summer, and the girls were in school within a week. They had not settled in or seen the sights when the calendar and the bureaucrats of public schooling called them forward. Lisa was amazed at how easily she made friends in her first week. She also saw a couple of boys that caught her attention, contrary to plan. Since Lisa and Mary were the new kids in town, their stock was high, and they were sought after as the "it girls" to go steady with.

*

A new kid in the yard of a small school was like a new sports car at the dealership in town. Everybody wanted to take it for a spin. One of those takers was a guy named David Deagan. He was handsome and popular. David thought that Lisa was smokin' and someone that he wanted to take to the dance in a few weeks to start the school year off. David was a wrestler and football player on the junior varsity team. He was considered athletic in his realm, as his pool of competitors was thin. He saw his future wife alone and on her way to class. He stopped her and said, "Hey, the school dance is coming up, and I was wondering if you were going?"

She looked at him and smiled. She said, "Well, I would, but I don't want to go by myself. I'm new here and don't really know anybody yet."

The school bell suddenly rang its final warning. David quickly said, "No, I didn't mean it that way. I want you to go with me. Will you go—with me?" After Lisa accepted and she and David attended that dance, he asked her if she would go steady with him, and she agreed.

That summer, Lisa got a part-time job at the bank as a teller, while David worked construction with a classmate who went by the name Kool due to his smoking habit and his preferred brand of smokes. Kool's dad owned and operated a construction company. He felt obligated to employ his kid, but he really liked David since he believed that he was smart, conscientious, and a hard worker.

As the young couple navigated their way through the travails of high school, their relationship prevailed, even when they went through the late teen and early adult phases of unrealistic dreams, omnipotence, self-loathing or narcissism, maturation, and settlement. The hardest part of high school is finding out that you really can't do anything that you want. You come to realize that there is talent, drive, or the lack thereof, and hordes of people standing in your way. Both Lisa and David shared in this series of discoveries, which inevitably destroyed their worldview but brought them deeper into each other's hearts as they vowed to meet the challenges and joys of life together.

The couple married in the summer of their high school graduation in 1970. Lisa decided to make a career out of the opportunities at Mountain View Bank due to the lack of any opportunities elsewhere. David was hired by his father-in-law to work in the insurance game. The insurance venture handled home, life, and auto insurance, which was the bedrock of the responsible. The career at Mountain View Life, Auto, and Home Insurance Company provided well for David's father-in-law and would for David and Lisa. It brought respect in the community, a white-collar career, and sufficient money.

The interest rates were high in the 1970s, and a down payment on a home was a heavy lift. This made home ownership something that was typically out of grasp for the young. David and Lisa had agreed to take her father up on his offer of assistance prior to their nuptials. They were to receive a sum of cash from Lisa's dad in lieu of a costly wedding. This wedding gift was the nest egg that they built upon for three years into a legitimate fund for a down payment on a house.

*

It was just starting to snow outside as David took a break from unpacking boxes and looked out the window. Although the falling snow dimmed the immediate view, the future appeared bright. It was October 1973, and the couple was moving into their first home as owners and not tenants. The house was a nice ten-year-old, three-bedroom, two-bath home located at 725 Blumenthal Street in Mountain View. It had a decent-sized yard in the back and a small plot of grass in the front. The neighborhood was quaint, with a mixture of young families and older couples who had already been through the turbulence of parenthood, with only one other house on the street painted yellow with brown trim.

*

As winter faded into spring, Lisa had her bags packed. She had gone through the steps of what she would do when it was time. Her husband David was excited to have his first-born child on the way but was also abound in reticence. He wasn't sure that he could financially and physically care for another person, let alone an infant. The man was fighting his sudden array of fears when Lisa walked down the hallway to the kitchen and had her right hand on her outstretched stomach as if to keep the baby in place until she was ready.

Noticing the tell-tell signs, he asked, "Is the baby kicking?"

"It's time," she quickly answered.

David was taken by the seriousness of the moment, but he was ready. He had been working on placating any panic through weeks of mental preparedness. Lisa partially bent forward with her right hand on her hip as she took deep breaths. She was outfitted in a pink bathrobe and slippers to match as her official attire for such a matter. He reached out and grabbed her hand as he began to escort his pregnant wife to the doorway leading into the garage. There, David had his trusty newish car waiting. As they made their way into the garage, Lisa smelled the mixture of automobile fluids circulating in the air. Oil and gasoline fumes were the incentive to quickly get into the car to escape any further command of reuniting the breakfast from the stomach to the mouth. He could see her discomfort and apologized as he squeezed Lisa into the passenger seat of the 1970 Chevy Nova. Once the expectant mother was inside, she was semi-comfortable considering her nine-month endeavor and immediate condition. The best part for Lisa was that the bucket seats provided the support on her lower back that it begged for at that moment. He opened the garage door and started to take a seat behind the wheel when he suddenly remembered that he had not gotten Lisa's overnight bag and went back in the house momentarily to retrieve it.

David re-entered the garage and leaned down as he cracked the door open and said, "That was a close one. Hang in there,

Honey. I'm gonna put this in the trunk."

She nodded her head as she began to take gasps of breaths with the fluctuations of pain. His immediate anxiety shifted to the challenges of backing out under stress through the narrow opening of the small garage door frame. As the Nova sat idling in the driveway, he closed the garage and headed back to his current pride and joy, the Chevy Nova, for a long yet quick drive to the hospital. David rolled down the driver's window so that they could drink in the pine-scented clear breeze of the northern California and southern Oregon region of the country on the way to the hospital. He was deliberate in his desire that such a prescription would calm any further rise in anxiety. Mountain View General Hospital was only three miles away in the small town that they called home, and they were pulling up to the front of the hospital within minutes of their departure. As he stopped the car in the loading area, he jumped out and ran around the car to help Lisa out of her seat and onto her pink-slippered feet. The baby inside the bulging striped belly suddenly began to be compelled by the force of God's will to leave its protective home. The expectant mother felt the necessity for some assistance and shuffled a little faster to reach the cusp of the hospital entrance and into the maternity ward. David quickly moved the car and then re-entered to sign her in. Staff brought a wheelchair in and gently assisted Lisa into the seat and guided her feet onto the footrests and headed for the birthing room. David trailed behind and then lost his nerve as he spotted the sanity of the waiting room with comfortable chairs and reading material to safely pass the time. He veered to the right and took a seat in the waiting room as men did in his time and place in history. As he sat, he looked for and found the latest local newspaper on a table in front of him. He reached out to feel the comfort and familiarity of newsprint press back against his nervous fingers. He perused the goings-on, framed within the front page and its verso, as he then spied the distinctive attraction of the sports pages calling to him from a separate fold in the local rag. He was comfortable in the room for custom and timidity as he relaxed within its cocoon.

David had always hoped for a boy. He began to imagine the athletic heroism that his first-born son would have as he crossed the plane between sports reality and sports fantasy. The first-born son suddenly evolved into the American football hero at Mountain View High School, where all the dads envied him, to the field of the Pacific Eight Conference, where his blessed prodigy would bring glory to the University of California, at Los Angeles as they won the Rose Bowl. With that success, his son would be the first-round pick in the draft and onto the Burbank stage with Johnny Carson, and then finally into the hearts of millions. The crescendo of his fantasy brought him the soothing calm he had been seeking for weeks when he spotted another man pacing about the room. He recognized the guy from being out and about in town but did not know his name. He aggressively approached and shook the man's hand and asked, "Is this your first kid?"

"It is. You?"

"Yeah. I'm hoping for a boy. I think I'm supposed to give you a cigar or something...but I don't have any."

"That's okay. We can't smoke in here anyway."

The man continued pacing as minutes and then hours passed. Eventually, they exchanged names when David and Gary eased into a conversation about mutual friends and acquaintances, providing some semblance of comfort while they sat on the seats laid out in the waiting room like checkers on a board ready for battle. The conversation moved from the people in Mountain View geographically outward. They began to gripe like curmudgeons at a bar delving into the issues of the day and then eventually into how fucked up the country was and that gas prices were ridiculous. It was April 14th, 1974, and Watergate was in the news cycle, gas was around fifty-three cents a gallon, and the United States was still trying to get out of Vietnam. After ten cups of coffee, a full newspaper, friendly jabber, a few walks outside to exhale recycled hospital air, and periodic checks on the positioning of the clock hands, eight hours had passed. David and Gary had not seen many people in that time. Medical staff had passed through, and the fathers in waiting had ventured into the cafeteria to see others as they marveled at how populated the cafeteria was, considering the food was so terrible. Eventually, Gary left. He had arrived as a husband and left as a husband and father while David continued to wait. Eventually, another nurse entered the maternity ward waiting room as David paid her no notice. She had not seen David before, so she asked, "Are you Mr. Deagan?"

"I am," he said in a quivering voice as he arose and smiled the best he could.

"Well, congratulations, Mr. Deagan, you're a father!"

He was over-caffeinated and tired at the same time as he blandly stared back. He realized that he was unaware of the pain and intensity that Lisa had experienced over the same ten-hour timeframe, but he was sure that he would hear about it later.

"You can see your wife and your baby in about half an hour," the nurse said as she saw David's grin expose his front teeth.

"Is it a boy?" he asked as the nurse turned to walk away.

"Nope. It's a girl," she answered, turning her head back over her shoulder as she continued out of the room.

David's dreams of athletic glory were dashed. His head dropped, but then he realized that he had read an article recently about women being eligible for college athletic scholarships under a new federal law in the past year or so. A half grin re-erupted onto his face when he said, "Well, you never know. She'll be smart, successful, athletic, and a good person. That's all I want!"

David was finally reunited with his wife, and he met his

daughter with a smile and a gentle kiss. The new mom looked tired and worn out as she finished her last cup of ice chips. "How's my girl? I guess I should say, girls," he asked.

"I'm better than okay. We have a baby girl! She's perfect."

"She *is* perfect. She's a little angel...well, maybe one of them cherubs, I think they call 'em. But still, an angel."

Lisa relaxed as she realized she was now part of a precious process that had gone on for eons. The cycle of life had made an appearance between her and David, and she was now part of a family unit made of divinity.

She then said, "That pregnancy was difficult, and the delivery was long and painful, but when the nurse laid her on my chest, it connected my heart to our gift."

As she eased back, she was wrecked, but she never felt so good. The new parents cooed and coddled their fragile little newborn when he said, "I love you. I'm so grateful to have you and our baby girl. Thank you for marrying me," as he caressed her hand with his.

Lisa began to cry and said, "You're the best husband a woman could ask for, and I love you too! Look at her; she is us," as they looked into the squinting eyes of the new member of the family.

The maternity nurse who had helped the doctor in the delivery had left the room, now walked back in among the new family unit and asked a few questions for the birth certificate that she had been trying to complete at the nurse's station. She wanted to double-check the information provided to her by David's initial paperwork, and to ascertain the name of the baby. The information seemed correct to the new parents. They were prepared with first and middle names for either a boy or a girl long before this day, as they said, "Camille Elizabeth Deagan." They then spelled it out "C-A-M-I-L-L-E" for surety's sake. Both parents eagerly signed the completed birth certificate when it was walked back into the room a while later. Those signatures made it official! Camille

Elizabeth Deagan was in the world.

Soon, mom was asleep in the hospital bed while Camille suckled the life-giving milk from her mommy's swollen breasts. The two were to spend the night, according to the hospital and Lisa's physician. Dad took a break and drove home to make himself some semi-palatable food and watch the news on television. As he did so, the anticipation and anxiety took its toll, and he was fast asleep. He awoke to find the television still on but covered in "snow" as the station stopped broadcasting from midnight until six o'clock in the morning. He looked at the time and realized that visiting hours were long over, and he had never made it back to the hospital to bid his wife and daughter a good night. He knew that his wife would eventually understand, but he was somewhat ashamed of his weakness and inability to come through for his wife and child—already.

The next morning, David made the short trip back to the hospital to see his wife and child and to bring them home, though he detoured and stopped at the hospital gift shop to buy some flowers. He hoped that this would be his segue toward an apology for his failure to return the night before. As he entered the stark eggshell-colored room littered with machines, other doodads, and one mass-produced painting on the wall of a lone flower in a stark field, he saw Lisa smile as the nurse was helping her get out of bed and prepare for her departure. "Perfect timing, Love," Lisa said.

David smiled on the inside as he sat the flowers on the tray table near the bed and stepped in to kiss his wife, apologize, and relieve the nurse from her duties.

She quickly said, "I knew you fell asleep, well, not really. I fell asleep too and only realized that you weren't here when I woke up after midnight."

"Did you get some sleep? How's the baby?" he asked as he smiled back in relief. Suddenly the room door opened, and a nurse was bringing baby Camille into the room. Lisa was just finishing changing into her clothes when the nurse attempted to hand the baby to him. David reached out slowly as if he was stealing honey from a beehive. His reluctance and unassuredness were in bad taste, but his instincts quickly took over when the nurse giggled and then proceeded to give him instructions. She laid the infant into his arms and said, "Now, Dad, don't drop her," while she positioned his hands onto the blanket holding the infant. David was a dad, and for the first time, he felt like an adult.

Lisa held Camille in her arms while riding home in the passenger seat, feeling the glow of motherhood. Once at home, the trio was suddenly a real family. The Deagans had the American Dream. A marriage, a child, a car, a house, and steady employment. It was conventional wisdom that such an achievement came with the ability to rest on a person's laurels after the acquisition of the big five, but alas, it was not true. It was a time to converge into parenthood and commitment. It was time to apply the gas pedal, not the brake.

David blended marriage, parenting, and work into his daily mainstay. Since he was the major breadwinner now that Lisa had quit her job at the bank to stay home with Camille, he felt more pressure than ever. The joyful holidays, family events, and baby's firsts came and went with the news cycles, television shows, college football bowl games and the months torn from the calendar as life passed by like a parade. Slow to start, exciting in the middle, and almost no one present at the end.

*

Over the next several years, Camille got through the elementary and junior high school grades, making C-average grades and finding it difficult to make lasting friends. Camille wasn't smart, and she wasn't cute. She wasn't athletic or musically inclined, either. She was just "average." In fact, every teacher who taught her along the way made sure to declare in the parent-teacher conferences that Camille did "average" work. Camille never viewed the evaluation of her soul, physical embodiment, and capabilities as a compliment. She generally received such a review from almost everyone she encountered. Sometimes, that projection amounted to the acceptance of being less than average, which became the weathervane of her diminishing academic career.

Her parents, especially her dad, had always tried to present the bright side to the evaluations and the evaluators. He would tell his daughter something like, "It's okay. It's what you think of yourself that really matters. Sometimes, though, these evaluations can be an opportunity to improve yourself. You should at least consider each one honestly and without taking it personally. They are trying to help, you know." He would end with, "You will always be special to your mom and me."

Camille was never in the mood to hear such nonsense and either ignored the repeated lesson or just presented her mean teenage face to rebuke the gesture outright.

*

David was still working at the Mountain View Life, Auto, and Home Insurance Company with his father-in-law. Lisa had gone back to work at the bank part-time and was enjoying some variety in her life. The fall of 1988 inevitably found its way into the timeline of human existence, and Camille was ready for high school. She was not ready because she was enthusiastic about school; she was ready because she was closer to getting it over with than she had ever been before. By this time in her life, she was beginning her rebellious phase, making life more difficult for those around her. It wasn't cool to be hanging out with one's parents or listening to their rules, or really anything that came out of their mouths. Kids in Mountain View did not have parents who were rich or famous, and those parents clearly didn't know as much as the new teenagers of the modern era. According to the unusual group of kids that Camille hung out with, they were already smarter than their parents, the teachers, and any other dill weeds on campus. They already had it all figured out.

Lisa and David still loved one another but chose to keep their progeny numbers in the single digits. Actually, in the single digit of one. Money was already hard to keep, and they were not impressed with their daughter's zest, nor their own ability to parent her into enthusiasm and the stick-to-it-iveness that was needed to get beyond the welfare line. To put it succinctly, they had all they could manage themselves. They were sure that any more children could produce displacement, ending in further failure of their family structure. They decided to save all of their resources for the child they did have. This idea included family vacations, tutoring, counseling, a car depending on her progress at school, and her attitude.

*

Ninth grade was a transition year when Camille hoped to make it into the popular group or at least date a guy who was kind of popular. She was also physically maturing into a young woman with features and curves, making some male eyes pause, although the developing lures of femininity were still insufficient in helping her find a more collegial life. All that seemed to happen, aside from the prolonged stares and the boob jokes, was the occasional guy trying to rub them surreptitiously or a dude blatantly asking to see them. Camille was definitely annoyed by the boobs looking at her breasts. She was pudgy for her age, and her maturing endowment was more of a curse than a blessing. As a single child, she had learned to bring her worst problems to her parents. This one she brought to her mother. Camille had seen other heavy-breasted girls get out of physical education class with a doctor's note, and she wanted the same thing. She had asked a girl named Stacey who her doctor was. Stacey was reluctant but was proud of her ingenuity and gave Camille the name and location in town of her prized, saintly, and cool physician. Camille was living in that terrible, youthful time where peer pressure and bullying were something all endured, especially for the maturation of one's mammary glands and/or their dorkiness on the gym floor.

Lisa understood when Camille brought the problem to her, and as her mom, she wanted to fight her battles for her or at least provide a break from them. Lisa picked up the phone in the kitchen and made an appointment with the saintly doctor. It would be a week before Camille could see Dr. Johansson, but it was a fait accompli.

David did not find out until the end of the first semester when he noticed that Camille's report card did not mention P.E. and Cami's changed physical appearance. "Why don't I see P.E. on this report card?"

"Okay. Don't get mad...Her breast size caused her problems in the class, so we went to see Doctor Johansson. He agreed and wrote a note."

"What the Hell! Why didn't you include me?"

"I'm sorry that I didn't tell you. I should've, but I knew that you wouldn't understand. I didn't want to argue about it. It was the right thing to do!"

"I know I'm not a teenage girl, but I have an open mind, you know. You should've talked to me first! This will ostracize her from the other kids even more, and she'll get zero exercise now."

"I'm having a hard time dealing with her, David! I wanted to help her and see if this made things better for her and for all of us."

"Oh, I get it. I see why you did it. Look, I don't blame you for that. My concern is that if we give in on things, it may embolden her and cause her to become worse. She does need a break, though, and she doesn't really need P.E, I guess."

CHAPTER 2.

CASTAWAY ISLAND

It takes all kinds, but to seek a friend, one must be friendly. To keep them, one must also be a friend.

*

Ninth grade brought social pressure into Camille's life. As she started tenth grade, she still had a tough time fitting in. The group of people that she did hang out with was comprised of kids who really didn't belong to the generalized high school structure. The usual remedy for this issue was a move to a continuation high school, and there happened to be one in town. This was the place for those who could not adapt to the social structure, the less rule-focused, and some of the more violence-prone students after not meeting the standards of the high school administration.

Camille and those that she associated with were not welcome with the counter-culturists at the continuation school because they were not "bad enough," nor with the generally accepted kids in their high school because they were considered nerds, weirdos, and independent of the normal.

Camille was never sweet on the idea of seeing a counselor to help her with her congenital unhappiness, so it was difficult for her parents to get her to comply. The family vacations were successful, though, as a great getaway for all three members of the family. The group of three seemed to enjoy themselves on their summer trips and came back closer as a family unit. Although once back in Mountain View, Camille would soon fall right back into the usual difficulties that plagued her before the out-of-town travel. Yet, for a few weeks every year, the Deagans were reformed.

The pressure to be accepted for who she was, was all that drove her. She wanted to love and be loved by people, including her parents, but such a thing was considered foolish, childish, or both among the other kids her age. She also knew that her biggest difficulty was her barrier to feeling emotion for others and the enjoyment of the infliction of emotional pain upon them. With those challenges, Camille couldn't seem to catch a break in her personal life in order to change her popularity—or lack thereof, either.

After school, she and the group that she hung out with would cross the street from Mountain View High to the smoking alley so that some of the kids could smoke cigarettes and some occasional rag weed if they could find it. Camille carried her own weed and started smoking it on occasion, but she was not hip to cigarettes. Next door to the smoking alley was a burger joint. The kids would typically go in there after smoking, bullshitting, and trying to be cool in order to get a bite to eat before they ventured homeward. Camille had an allowance, so she usually got a milkshake and fries after the meeting with the angry and downtrodden before she had dinner at home.

Eventually, one of the supervisors of the restaurant said, "Hey, Camille, can I talk with you for a second?"

"Yeah, what's up?"

"We need some help around here, and I was wondering if you wanted a job after school?"

"No thanks," Camille quickly answered, even though she had wanted some additional money. At this point, her paltry allowance of ten dollars a week wasn't enough, so she would steal some of the things that she wanted and couldn't afford from various businesses in town and from others at school. Sensibly, Camille knew that she needed more money, as she couldn't steal her way to wealth one item at a time. She also thought that if she had more money, she could become popular with other kids.

As the group of castaways from various grade levels began to dissipate and head home, she went back into Rusty's Burgers and said, "Hey, Kimberly. I was wondering. What do you guys pay per hour anyway?"

"Are you interested after all?"

"I dunno. Maybe. Depends on how much, I guess."

"How about $4.25 an hour? Tips are split among the shift, and you would work three days after school and three-hour shifts on Saturday and Sunday when we are slammed. What do you think?"

"I dunno. I'm not sure." She dropped her head forward and stared at the floor. She continued, "I'll be back tomorrow and let you know what I decide," as she finally looked back at Kimberly.

"Fair enough. I'm not working tomorrow, but I'll come in special in order to bring you onto the team."

"Oh. That's nice of you. Alright," as she turned and headed for the door.

"Don't make me come down here and have you blow me off," she said in a louder voice.

Camille turned and looked at Kimberly and nodded in the affirmative then turned again for the door and walked out.

That Friday night was movie night at the Deagan house. They were going to rent the latest hit movie of 1989. The three left the house to pick up a pizza and a VHS tape. They ended up with two movies. *Major League* and *Pet Sematary*. David and Lisa wanted to watch the sports drama/comedy, while Camille dug in for the latest King movie and said, "Why can't we watch what I wanna watch for once? It's bullshit. You two can be such self-centered assholes."

"Watch your mouth, and don't talk to us like that," her dad said as his reddened face glared back.

"I wouldn't have to if you both treated me with respect. You know, like Aretha Franklin. I shouldn't be stuck here with you two, but since I am, I should get to watch what I want."

Youth and aggressive behavior prevailed. By the middle of the movie, she was engrossed, and her parents had drifted off to other ventures. Her dad was reading the newspaper, while her mother was working a crossword puzzle still pretending to watch the movie.

Late that night, Lisa and David were in bed. "We need to stop enabling poor behavior. It makes us feel like shit, and it makes our daughter into an emboldened asshole," David said.

"She's a teenager. We need to make more attempts to meet her likes as well, or we will only alienate her even more."

"Yikes! That sounds like a terrible idea."

"Try it my way. Please."

"Alright, alright, I guess if we have a once-a-week family event that she enjoys, I guess that's a good thing. But we need to agree on the movie choice that one of us makes so we have a majority. If you take her side, you'll be sleeping on the couch that night!"

She laughed and said, "I'm not sure that is a good idea, but I'll try…by the way, you would be on the couch and not me!"

*

Camille had pulled her grades up above a C average as she closed out her sophomore year. It was a C-plus, which was nothing to get overly excited about from her dad's point of view, but it was progress. She was less trouble for her parents—or she was better at hiding her issues and anger.

About two months before her sixteenth birthday, and just before she was about to leave the house to catch the school bus, Camille told her dad, "I want a driver's license and a car!"

"And what have you done to deserve a driver's license and a car, my dear?"

"Oh, Daddy, you know I'm doing better. I promise to help Mom with the chores and be home by my curfew at ten. Plus, it'll be easier for me to be able to make my curfew with a car you know."

"You're doing better, and you're a good kid. I'll talk it over with your mother, but don't be disappointed if you don't get a car."

"What? Oh, I'll be disappointed. Actually, fuckin' pissed!"

"If you don't get a car on your birthday, it *may* come later. If you throw a tantrum, you'll never get one from us. Understand?"

"I understand." She sighed and looked into her dad's eyes.

"And how did you arrive at a ten o'clock curfew when it's currently nine?"

"Dad, I *am* going to be sixteen."

"You know what? I'm going to take you to the DMV this afternoon to get your learner's permit. What do you think of that?" he said after momentary reflection.

A rare smile arose upon her face as she let out a little shriek and briefly jumped up and down. When she recovered from her enthusiasm, she hugged her dad and thanked him, as she repeatedly said, "What time will you get me?"

"Uhm, let's see. I'll be there at two," David said as he smiled and watched for his daughter's response.

Camille paid little attention to any of the teacher's lessons that day as she fantasized about being cool and having some independence zooming toward adulthood. Two o'clock finally came, and Camille got the nod from her teacher after a note was brought into the room directing her to go to the administration office. She packed up her things and headed for the classroom door. As she walked out, she slyly turned her right hand upwards behind her skirt and displayed her middle finger to the class. She walked the vacant indoor and outdoor hallways of the high school on her way to the admin office to meet her dad. David had already signed her out and was waiting in the hallway when she arrived. They quickly exited the administration building and headed for the parking lot. "We'll get some shakes at Snowy's after you get your permit," David said.

Camille smiled back at her dad since that meant that she would probably not be going back to school after the DMV. As they pulled into the Department of Motor Vehicles parking lot, she asked, "What if I flunk the test?"

"Here's the good thing. You don't need to take a test today. You're just going to get your learner's permit."

"Whew!"

"But to get your actual license, you'll have to study the driver's handbook, take the high school's driver safety class, take the written exam, and then a driving test, and pass them all."

She gulped at the thought of the incredible endeavor before her. Since those things were for another day, she then let them fall from her ears before they penetrated her mind with more noise.

The pair crossed the parking lot while closely watching for vehicles in the second most dangerous parking lot in any town, the first being the one at the traffic court. As they reached the safety of the sidewalk next to the dreary and despised building, they went through the doors and entered the famously infamous DMV. There were few, if any, people inside and so the father-daughter duo walked right up to the lady at the open window. David filled out a few forms at the window and the learner's permit was issued for the girl with dreams of independence. David paid the demand, and they were soon out the door and headed to the fairgrounds parking lot so that Camille could start to learn how to drive.

"Where're we going? I'm supposed to go back to school... right?" she asked, intently looking at her dad as she hoped for the right answer.

"I was thinking of driving practice, but if you wanna go back to class...."

"Am I really going to drive your car right now?"

"Yep. No time like the present. Unless you don't think you're ready?"

"I was fuckin' born ready."

"You were, huh? Why don't you apply that overused philosophy to your schoolwork? Let's see how ready you are."

The car came to a stop in the wide-open spaces of the parking lots adjacent to the rodeo arena at the Jefferson County Fairgrounds. He turned the engine off and got out as he leaned his head back down into the door opening and said, "Okay, your turn."

She jumped out of the car and moved rather quickly to take command of the Nova's cockpit. Once inside, she realized that she felt ready but didn't really know what to do. She sat there staring at the wheel and then asked, "Okay. What do I do first?"

"Start with holding the steering wheel at ten and two." He then brought her through the sequence of ignition. Lastly, he talked her through the steps of driving a manual transmission, braking, and turning off the engine. After some practice going through the motions described with the car engine off, David finally said, "Okay, put your foot on the clutch and press it to the floor. Okay, now turn the key in the ignition... STOP. STOP! Turn the key off!"

"What was that screeching noise?"

"You! You were destroying my ignition. Just turn it until you hear the engine start, then let it go. Okay?"

"Got it. Sorry."

"Okay, make sure you keep the clutch down and gently press down on the gas pedal to get the car running."

The engine roared to life as its revolutions per minute redlined. David screamed over the loud motor, "Let off on the gas! Take your foot off the gas!"

Camille heard the instructions and let her foot off of both the clutch and gas pedal as the car shot forward, lurching to and fro until she found the brake. The Nova immediately came to rest as the engine stopped, and the car ceased its rendition of a breakdancer doing the quake. David laughed inside as he said, "Don't worry. You're doing great. This happens to everybody...a lot."

Camille started to sweat as the gravity of the situation enveloped her. She now knew that it was not as easy as it looked.

David summoned all of the patience he could muster as another hour rolled by. Eventually, on that spring afternoon, the girl tied to youthful boundaries was now making laps around the fairgrounds and could use the clutch and accelerator, even in unison. She used her turn signals and even stopped and restarted the car numerous times. As Camille improved and David's nerves eased, she then obtained a small amount of training on how to back up into the place that you wanted to go.

After the intensity of learning and the concerns for life, limb, and vehicle damage lessened, the training for the first day came to an end. David retook the driver's seat and headed for the promised milkshake at Snowy's. As David left the parking lot of the fairgrounds, he decided that he would purchase his daughter her own car so that his would not be demolished by the developing skills of a teen driver.

As father and daughter sat on the benches outside of Snowy's to sip their milkshakes and talk, she said, "Thank you for today. You're a good teacher, and I want to do this again. When can we do this again?"

"How about another afternoon later this week and Saturday morning if we have time."

"Wow, yeah. That'd be good."

"You need to read and re-read the driver's handbook. If

you do that, you'll do well in driver's training class, and more importantly, you'll pass the written exam at the DMV." After a pause, he said, "I want you to understand that I'll have you ready to pass the practical driver's testing component of getting a driver's license, but the written test is on you."

"I can see that driving is serious. I really understand this time, and I learn better by doing something, and especially by someone like you who has the patience to teach me," as she carefully watched for his reaction.

Her dad felt the rare showering of praise from his daughter as he leaned over and hugged her as tight as he could without smashing their milkshakes, as she thought, "He's so easy to hustle. What a moron."

Camille was able to get a spot in the driver's safety class during the Easter break from school in March and continued to practice driving with her dad. She even had numerous occasions to drive with her mother, whose car had an automatic transmission. Her real goal, beyond just fitting in with others, was escape, and escape would help her spread her wings. Yet what she didn't realize was that although she wanted some semblance of freedom, she also wanted to be a cool kid with a car who could drive her "friends" around. Those two things were mutual and mutually exclusive.

For once in her life, Camille was prepared for a task. She completed the driver's training course at her high school. When her dad came by to pick her up, he said, "How was your day?"

"It was good, I guess."

"Did you finish the training class?"

"Yeah."

"Well?"

"Dad, I did it! I passed the driver's training class!"

After she got home, her parents tried to reinforce the unusual feeling of success for their daughter, and she ate it up.

The treasured sixteenth birthday arrived, with her parents waking her to wish her a happy birthday. She walked down the hall with a face that was rarely filled with a smile and said, "Do you have my favorite breakfast ready? 'Cause ya know, it's my birthday!"

Her mom was quick to say, "Of course, a Denver omelet with lots of cheese and ham, *with* orange juice!"

As she sat at the round-shaped breakfast table, her fingers fumbled at the doily-styled tablecloth laid over the small oakwood table. As she worked her nervous energy and tried to subdue any hope of a car, she watched her mom look at her with a smile while her dad sipped his coffee. "Are you about ready to leave for work?" Lisa asked David.

"Yep, as soon as the birthday girl opens her card."

"Cami, here's your birthday card," her mom immediately said with a smile while she produced an envelope and laid it on the table.

This was a tradition that her mom started more than a decade ago. It kick-started the birthday while postponing the culmination of the celebration for after school when presents were opened and a birthday dinner took place early in the evening. As her dad paid careful attention, Camille picked up her birthday card. Her parents waited in silence for the revelation of good or evil as a result of the contents therein. Camille quickly opened the envelope and removed the card as its contents fell away into her lap. She then said, "Forty dollars! Thanks, you guys."

"Read the card, Cami, read the card," her mom cheered as she smiled in delight.

The card read, "Happy Sixteenth Birthday to our dearest Cami. We love you with all our hearts."

As the gift-givers didn't see any emotional change, their daughter nodded and put the money in her pocket and the card back into the envelope. Upon making it through an attempt at an emotional sweet sixteen event, they slid into the neutral zone instead. Her mom said, "The bus will be here soon. Have a good birthday."

Dad echoed the sentiment.

Camille tried to hide her anger as she recalled the warning from her dad about not getting a car on her birthday and heeded the admonishment. It was still early in the drawn-out birthday that her mom enjoyed. Camille's mind started to play the scenes of terror and abuse that she would release upon them if she was not the recipient of a license and a car.

"By the way, I'll be taking off the afternoon from work so that I can take you to the DMV for your driving test. I'll be there after lunch at one," her dad then said.

Camille cracked a smile and then hugged her mom and dad before she headed for the bus stop.

David went through the same steps as he had done a month before in order to get his birthday girl out of school for the afternoon. Once again, the father-daughter duo walked through the high school parking lot toward the Nova as Camille skipped along. "Are you prepared for your test?" asked her dad.

"Oh, Hell yeah! I'm gonna show 'em how it's done."

They arrived soon thereafter at the California DMV parking lot. Camille casually noted that the lot was empty, except for a new red 1989 Acura Legend and a gun metal grey 1986 Honda Accord. "Oh good, there aren't a lot of people here."

They went inside to seek the delivery of the two tests that measured acuity and basic skill. David had Camille complete the paperwork this time as he provided her social security card for approval by yet another overseer of freedoms. Soon, Camille was alone along the back wall of the DMV, taking the written test to get her license. She was alone with no one to cheat from, but she felt like the test was easy, and within minutes, she was back at the window with her completed exam. David's head dropped after seeing her come back so soon, and then he arose to meet her at the DMV window. On the way, he prepared himself to deal with the aftermath of his daughter's failure with another of life's roadblocks or detours.

The lady quickly scored the test and Camille missed two and passed. She could not contain her enthusiasm as she high-fived her dad and said, "I told you so!"

After about a ten-minute wait, Camille was soon out with a DMV employee working the practical component of the test in the stick-shift beauty.

After taking the DMV-assigned route, she was back in the parking lot, whereupon the DMV employee said, "Congratulations. You passed." Camille was holding her excitement as the man then told her, "You need to work on remembering to use your turn signals sooner than your turning movement and to concentrate on applying your brakes sooner before a stop so it's not so sudden. You can now go back inside to get your temporary license."

Camille didn't hear a word that was said. Her inside voice screamed, "Dude, you are such a loser. Please, just shut the fuck up, would ya?"

As she got out, she was all smiles like the rest who got their ticket to ride while in high school. She fluffed her hair and presented her best smile for her driver's license photograph since the DMV never did retakes.

Within minutes Camille had her temporary license for immediate use in the form of a piece of paper. "When do I get my real one?" she asked.

The woman answered, "We mail it to you. It'll be in your mailbox in a couple weeks."

As they walked out of the DMV office, Camille kept saying, "I bet you're surprised, huh, Dad. I'll bet you didn't expect that, did you?"

David remained mute and showed no expression. She then looked across the parking lot and spotted her mom standing outside of her car, waiting for them. She ran to her mother to brag on her success. Camille then said, "Can I drive either one of you anywhere?" as her mom handed her a set of keys. Camille read the key fob, which had the word HONDA printed on it. She looked toward the Honda Accord sitting nearby when both parents said, "Happy Birthday" in unison.

Camille rushed to get inside and look it over. She got out screaming and kissed them both and said, "Can I drive it? I wanna go back to school."

"Sure, you can. Come home after work by seven," her mom said, while Camille and David shared a mutual look of surprise upon hearing the shocking revelation.

*

Camille was once again reunited with her new car and headed back to school, where she would park her Accord prominently for those who were keenly astute.

Camille told all of her loose set of friends in the clique of misfit boys and girls about getting a car for her sixteenth birthday. Some didn't care, while others were jealous. Only a couple in the group were actually happy for her, especially the skilled manipulators, who immediately saw a new asset to use.

Camille had to work at Rusty's after school that day but still took time to give a couple of kids in her class a ride home. This would be the first of many rides that the girl seeking acceptance would provide. Due to Camille's narcissistic fake altruism, she arrived late to her job.

"I'm sorry I'm late, Patricia. I was taking a couple kids home from school on my way here."

"How did you do that?"

"It's my birthday. I got a car! Wanna see it?"

"Maybe later. Congrats girl. In that case, I won't write you up but get to work. Oh, and happy birthday," Patricia said as she headed off to check on the inventory.

"Thanks. It won't happen again."

"Hey, I was a teenager too. And not that long ago, either."

That evening Camille was home at seven as requested and feeling unusually hopeful about her life and immediate future in Mountain View.

*

The excitement of having a car continued through the remainder of that school year, the summer, and into the fall semester of her junior year. As high school football arrived back on campuses nationwide, the Mountain View High School Miners were awash in pride and excitement. Camille could attend games if she wanted to, and usually did. She was not a sports fan nor a prominent supporter of her school. The reason for attendance was so that she could hang out and provide rides to her "friends" after the game was over. Since there were few takers in her immediate semi-social circle, Camille opened her heart and decided that she was now alright with giving rides to most kids in her class, as long as they were popular, and to any senior who needed one. The former happened frequently, but the latter never did.

Camille was still ambivalent about her grades, learning, and school in general. One night, while the Deagans were watching the latest television sitcom, Camille said, "Just so you know, I've decided that I'm not going to college." The surprise delivery was due to her continuous need to hurt her mom and dad, so she waited to see the damage. Her parents pretended that they were surprised when they were actually relieved since their daughter wouldn't feel the pain of college rejection.

"Whatever you decide to do to make you happy is what we support," her dad finally answered.

"I knew you didn't fucking believe in me!"

As Camille proceeded onward at Mountain View High, her grades continued to slump, keeping her at her word. To her parents, Camille was doing the best she could. To other people who knew her, Camille was a fuckup and going nowhere fast.

After one of the home football games, Camille saw a couple of acquaintances who begged her for a ride. She could smell the alcohol on their breath and asked, "I'll take you home, but do you have any of the hard stuff?"

"Oh, man, thanks. Nope, we drank it all."

"That blows. I'll drop Jenny off first since you're close."

"That's cool," Jenny answered.

She left Jenny on the sidewalk in front of her house. As she pulled away, she said, "Am I taking you home too?"

"Yeah, sure. I'm in no hurry."

The Accord headed out of town with Sam to make the short drive to his house that was on a small piece of land where his parents ran a small cattle operation. Sam was a handsome guy with whom she had been interested in for a couple of years. As they put the lights of town behind them, he suddenly said, "Pull over. I gotta puke!"

As Camille pulled over to the side of the road and neared a full stop, she could see that Sam was pretty hammered. As they came to rest, the interior light came on in the front cabin of the car as she saw Sam trying to work his way out of the door and onto his feet. Once he was standing on his feet, he said, "Hey, you gotta help me. I'm not feelin' too good," as he swayed back and forth on the blacktop.

It was warm and dark along the country road. The buzz of mosquitoes and the echo of pond frogs broke the silence at the illuminated car and its surroundings. Sam stood a little firmer on the edge of the road in tall grass with a half-cocked smile as he stared at Camille and her big boobs. Nature's sounds were suddenly broken as Sam asked, "You got a blanket?"

"I don't think so. Wait, I have a large towel in the trunk. Will that work?"

"Oh yeah, totally."

"What do you want a towel for anyway?"

"Sex, baby."

Camille was suddenly eager as she wanted that too. She started moving toward Sam with the towel in her hands when truck lights illuminated her and her car. She cast her head away from the beams and set her gaze upon the ground to shield her eyes and face. She expected it to be a Jefferson County Deputy Sheriff as the truck eased up next to her. The window came down as she faced the opened passenger window, and a man's voice said, "You kids having a problem?"

"No. My friend doesn't feel well. He's almost home, though. Thanks," she quickly answered.

"Sam? Is that you?" the man asked.

"Yeah."

"Do you want me to get your dad?"

Camille could feel the intrusion starting to disrupt the end of her celibacy and venture into adulthood. Camille said, "Hey, old man, why don't you mind your own fucking business and leave us the fuck alone."

The aspiring Good Samaritan was shocked and dismayed. The truck window rose up, and the truck barged down the highway in synchronous anger with its pilot.

"That was fuckin awesome! I always wanted to tell that guy that," Sam yelled.

"Do you know him?" she asked with a smile.

"Oh, that nosy bastard? Yeah, that was my uncle."

Camille began to laugh, and Sam joined in. Camille said, "C'mon," as she took Sam's rough, calloused left hand with her right and led him down the grassy slope of the hill below the car as they neared a small grove of leaved trees.

"This should make it comfortable," she said while she laid the towel down on the shorter grass under the tree. She removed her clothes and hung them on the top strand of barbed wire strung along the wooden fence posts behind them. As she looked back for Sam, she felt a sudden burst of air meet her skin from her right side. Sam was already naked and throwing his clothes onto the fence wire, too. Camille lost her virginity and entered the long road of frisky business. They didn't use a condom, nor was Camille wearing an IUD. It was dicey, but she finally felt what it was like to have a boy who liked her. Even if it hurt and was only about three minutes long...it was worth it.

*

Word had been out for a while that Camille was a sucker for giving free rides. The people who participated in her sad and weird taxi service liked being chauffeured. For the others, they knew that she would give rides so that she could brag about having a car instead of being a good friend. She saw her ride service plan fail as the people that she wanted to impress realized that she was still a lost soul who did little for herself and nothing for anyone else without a motive. Camille was fat, she dressed poorly, was unkept at times, her hygiene was suspect, and she could have used some tips on hair styling. Eventually, those rumors and shared feelings made their way to the castaway. She wasn't pleased, but she could not see the depth of what was being said, only that others were jealous or that they were just losers.

*

The rest of Camille's junior year was a bust. She was still unpopular and did not have a boyfriend. She was miserable and wanted out. As the summer before her senior year came to pass, Camille told her mom, "I want out of school. I have talked to a couple of people that go to The Peak, and it's a lot better."

"The continuation school? Why's that?"

"You know I fuckin' hate school, Mom. You know it's the shits."

"I hear you complain, but no, I really don't know what's going on."

"I'm tired of being beat down every day and being angry about it. I'm going to The Peak, or I'm dropping out!"

Her dad was reading the paper and enjoying some suds when he overheard the conversation. He damned near choked on his beer. With disbelief and discomfort, he walked into the living room to assist his wife in calming the Cami storm. He asked, "Why would you want to leave your classmates for your senior year? You've been there for three years. What is another nine months?"

"You two are so clueless. I'm not having the same fucking high school experience that you had. I fuuucccking hate it! It blows. I don't fit in there, and I have no friends," she said as her face reddened with anger.

"High school is hard on everyone at times. Everyone has gone through what you're feeling. You don't have much time left. You need to stick it out," her dad answered.

"I've tried to make friends and help others, but I still don't have any!"

"Nine months. Only nine months left."

"I'll just drop out of school then!"

"Look. Like I said, high school ain't for everybody. Lots of kids have a hard time with it, but they do it anyway."

Lisa jumped in and said, "You can make it through. It's only nine more months out of thirteen total years! Think about that! Plus, you might regret not graduating with all the kids you grew up with."

"Mom, you're not getting it! I don't like these people, and they don't like me. Fuck this, I won't go back!"

The battle for keeping Camille in high school was now lost, and they knew it as they once again felt parental guilt, remorse, and failure. David and Lisa talked about their daughter while lying in bed later that night. David consoled his wife and said, "Hey, we took her to therapy until she wouldn't go anymore."

"I know."

"We took her on vacations, gave her presents, spent time with her, and bought her a car, for goodness sake. What else can we do?"

"You're right. I am to the point that I just want her done and out of the house."

"I hate to hear you say that, but I feel the same way. Maybe she could graduate a little early and go somewhere where she felt better."

The next morning, Lisa was at the high school causing the transfer of Camille Deagan to the district's continuation school. She was assured that the transfer would be wrapped up before school started in two weeks.

Once she arrived back at the bank, she called her husband and said, "I got the transfer done. She's going to The Peak, David. To the fucking Peak!" She began to cry as she saw the hopes and dreams that she had for her only child rapidly narrowing or completely disappearing into the ether. She was worn out from age, a lifetime of employment, and the constant difficulties that she had to deal with from her own daughter. Her once beautiful black hair was streaked in premature grey, and the lines and wrinkles on her forehead and around her mouth were sculpted in by Father Time—and the crazy girl down the hall. It was certainly a testament to resiliency but also to submission, as the demands and pressures in life eventually cause one to crack or break altogether.

David waited and then answered, "Nobody's gonna care except us. Like I said before, a GED and a diploma are viewed the same, so it'll be fine."

Although David was correct, Lisa was concerned about the influence that the kids at the new school might have on their daughter or vice versa.

CHAPTER 3.

RIDE THE LIGHTNING

Confidence and arrogance are not synonymous, but arrogance and attitude are. The latter makes for leaders and inferiors at the same time.

*

Camille started her senior year at The Peak, the only continuation school in the Mountain View area. It was small in size and loaded with attitude and rebelliousness. Some of the kids were there because they did not learn well among large groups, while others had difficulty with structure. Still, others were in continuation school because they had problems at home. Lastly, there were the few and the extremely difficult, who were just demon seeds. Those few were a part of the California juvenile justice system or were about to be. Together, they all struggled in life as they received an education from continuation school, juvenile hall, and bad influences.

Since Camille had lived in town her whole life, she knew or knew of, almost everybody in the school. Sure, there were still cliques and groups of mean kids, but they were thinly held due to the meager student population and the need for social crossover in such a small environment.

The structure of the schedule, classes, and lowered expectations were easier to deal with for everyone enrolled, including Camille. Most importantly, the classes were easier and the time constraints for moving through them were expedited. Camille could take and pass classes faster and with less effort than at Mountain View High. This benefit would ensure that she graduated on time and without the pressure and pain of dealing with the subjects and social hierarchy of a traditional high school.

The school had thirty-nine kids in it, and twenty-eight of those were boys. That left a small minority of eleven girls. Some of the kids were sexually active, especially the juniors and seniors. The full complement of students at The Peak was a close-knit group after only a few months, and most of the eleven girls were prepared to have intercourse with some of the boys, especially Luke Johnson. Luke was another lost kid who had been abused by his grandparents after his mom and dad were incarcerated. He had been living in the foster care system or the juvenile justice system since his early teens. His current foster parents were, like most, a couple who had big hearts and could exert little to no control over their foster gifts, especially with the likes of Luke Johnson. Every deputy sheriff and city cop around knew him.

Luke was tall and lanky, with a James Dean face and look to match. That is where the similarities ended. James Dean was a presentation, whereas Luke Johnson was authentic and an aggressive manipulator. He had been in a lot of physical fights and the scars on his face provided the evidence. He usually carried a weapon, typically a knife, but he also owned a pair of brass knuckles. Luke was a heartbreaker who liked a stable of women to have intercourse with, even when they didn't consent. Because of Luke's tough guy persona and his lack of care when it came to other's feelings, he had followers. He also had steady girlfriends that were loyal and giving. Camille was one of his girls, and because of it, she was finally somebody. Camille was almost always open to intercourse with Luke, even though she was one of three girls attending The Peak at that time involved with the same bad boy. Camille was not on the pill and never "had the talk" with her mother and didn't care to do so now. She stole condoms when she needed them and was finally able to get an IUD through a friend in order to double up on protection.

Camille never got caught shoplifting, and she had zero contact with the police. Since she was so average-looking, she had the good fortune to blend in with the crowd. Of course, Camille didn't understand the value of this gift and instead made it her life's work to try and be seen.

At The Peak, she was able to pull it off due to the small amount of people in attendance and her occasional verbal aggression. Once she was noticed, part of a group, and was seen as a woman by the popular boy for mature activities, she started to blossom. She was more outspoken and seemingly more effective and was frequently able to take charge of herself with others in certain circumstances. The nuance to her slight metamorphosis was that she always gained ideas from others but was never in a place of power to push them into mob rule. Now that she was popular and a big fish in a small pond, she could add her voice and position as a senior to eventually move it into conventional wisdom, thereby achieving her majority-rules utopia.

*

Camille's eighteenth birthday was coming up in April, and she was going to graduate with a credential certifying high school equivalency the same month. She would get out of school earlier than if she had stayed at Mountain View High School by a month, which she was certainly happy about. As legal adulthood came rushing in, Camille needed to strike before she was considered an adult. She had always disliked one of the other girls at The Peak who was having sex with her shared boyfriend, Luke. Her name was Sherry Burns. Sherry was smart, popular, and hot. She had black hair, a nice shapely physique that was a head turner, and a matching eerie but sultry stare that secured the immediate sexual desires of the boys who wanted to tame her. Camille told a friend, "I'm going to kick Sherry's ass today after school. Pass it on. I want an audience. Everybody in school."

Her friend nodded in the affirmative and left to spread the news.

The possibility of violence spread like wildfire, and by that afternoon, Sherry was notified. When she was given the message by the latest courier of information, she said, "Oh, I'm not taking any shit from that fat bitch! Tell that cow to meet me in the alley behind the school at three."

Neither girl was reluctant, and at three, they stood facing each other in the dirt alley. The alley was a good place to throw down since the backyards of the houses abutting it all had solid wood fences. In addition, large garbage cans and some bushes obscured the alley from passing police cars. The student viewership was high, as kids stood in a circle and waited for mayhem. Sherry ran up to Camille and pulled her hair from the top, trying to pull her to the ground with the move. Camille reciprocated and got Sherry's head low enough to knee her in the face. They stood and faced each other as the slap fighting commenced, and to accentuate the gravity of the situation, scratches were applied, and blood was drawn. Both of the girls tired out quickly, but Camille wouldn't stop until she made her point. She did just that as she pulled Sherry's head to the ground and then jumped on her back, riding the rest of her to a full stop onto the dirt. She pushed Sherry's face into the dirt and rocks occupying the alley floor as she leaned into her ear and said, "Bitch, stay the fuck away from Luke or I'll kill you."

Camille found her way to her feet once again and then kicked Sherry in the back of her head with all she had while Sherry was trying to get up. Camille said, "Ooh, that had to hurt!" Sherry hit the dirt once again as Camille turned and walked away.

The crowd stood silent as she walked by. Some could not believe that this once timid girl could be so ferocious. No one helped Sherry to her feet as the guys headed out of the alley and off to other things. The girls in attendance low-fived Camille's hand as she passed them and said, "You kicked her ass!"

Luke watched from the end of the alley. He approached Sherry after it was over and said, "Hey, it don't matter what happened here. You and me are still a thing."

"Oh, go fuck yourself. You're such a piece of shit! I'm leaving this shithole for LA in a few weeks, so just stay the Hell away from me," she said while stepping closer to look into his face.

"Yeah, sure ya are. You ain't goin' nowhere. Call me when you get over this ass kickin'," he said while looking her up and down. Anger suddenly filled his emotional space as he realized that he had just lost a piece of ass in a girl fight over petty jealousy. He recovered quickly, though, as his immediate thoughts then moved on to other candidates around town who could be replacements in the love scene of life.

*

Camille was asked by her mom if she was going to be walking at graduation. Camille instantly answered, "I'm not waiting around for two weeks to do somethin' that lame."

"You don't want to get your credential with your friends? I thought you liked it there."

"Why are you so dense! Remember? I hate school...You should fucking know that by now! One more time, do you remember high school?"

"Mostly."

"Well, I don't want to remember it at all! Besides, I'm moving out before then anyway."

"Your dad and I kinda expected you would move out after graduation, but why so fast?"

"I got a full-time job."

"Here in town?"

"Hell no. I'm moving to Benton. I have a management job there, and so I'm blowing this shitbox."

Benton was south of Mountain View by about ninety miles. It was a big city in comparison, and it had big city problems. It lay within Cassell County, which contained the highest per capita amount of prison parolees in the state, and a significant percentage of those were registered sex offenders. Not the best choice for a young woman, but it also had two shopping malls, a long strip of major box stores and outlets, movie theaters, parks, a river, a lake nearby, and a plethora of food styles and choices. Camille had been to Benton many times with her mom over the course of the past eighteen years, as it was a shopping destination for the regional area.

Lisa understood the draw to the big city and hoped that her daughter would find peace and happiness there.

"What job did you get there? Tell me about it," her mom said.

"Rusty's is going to open a restaurant in Benton in the parking lot of the mall, there on Hilltop Drive."

"Oh wow, yeah, I saw that in the paper. YOU are going to manage that store?"

"Yep! The owners asked Patricia to take it over, but she didn't want to. She said she'd help start the store but then would come back here after about a month or so. They offered it to Kimberly, but she wanted to stay here, too. I was the only other choice, I guess, so they asked me, and I said, 'Fuckin' A!'"

"Oh my gosh, Cami—that is wonderful news! Do you need any help in finding a place?"

"No, I don't think so. Patricia and I will be living in one of those hotels that you live at temporarily and Rusty's is going to cover the rent. I'll look for a place there that I can afford in my free time so that I can be ready when I get kicked out of the hotel."

"I'm so happy for you and your dad will be very proud as well."

Camille smiled as she felt the rare feeling of success.

David was so happy with the news that he took the family out to dinner that night to celebrate. They went to the swanky new El Caballero in town since it was the trendy place in Mountain View at that moment. Five days later, the proud parents were bidding their daughter goodbye as she had her Accord loaded with her immediate needs for the next few weeks in Benton.

Patricia was leaving Mountain View a few days later on Sunday night, but Camille wanted to get there earlier and get situated while also getting away from her hometown. As the Honda Accord drove away, the empty nesters hugged each other with a fresh perspective that hadn't been present in years. A shift in hope and maybe even the belief that their daughter was capable and could even be suitable for continuous success through longevity.

"Maybe she was right all along, and she just wasn't meant to grow up in this town," Lisa said.

"Perhaps she was."

Camille arrived at the Benton Extended Stay Hotel near the site of the new restaurant in a couple of hours' time. She parked in front of the hotel and headed into the lobby to the front desk to check in and get her room key. She immediately noticed that the hotel was nicely appointed with beautiful beige carpet enclosing a strip of red that took the guest from the entry door to the front desk. As she looked about the large room, she saw three chandeliers hung in the lobby. The latest national news barked from the television screen at the back of the room, while a smaller screen revealed the services and benefits that came with staying at the Benton Extended Stay Hotel.

She couldn't believe it as she slid the key card into the door and opened it. She blurted out, "Holy shit, this place is

NICE! Wow, I can even see the river. Oh yeah, I'm gonna like it here."

Eventually, Camille got her belongings from the car and into the room. She either put them away in the chest of drawers that were part of the room décor or displayed them for a permanent residential feeling. She had limited phone call privileges through her work, and when she was satisfied with the immediate conditions, she made her first call to meet a commitment. "Well, I'm moved into my new home. Yep, already. Yeah, it's really fuckin' nice! No, I'm good. Tell Dad, and I will call ya later."

She then made a second phone call. "Hey, baby. How's it goin'?"

"Camille? You haven't left yet?"

"No, I'm in Benton at a sweet-ass hotel, and I wanted to talk to you and let you know that I was okay. I miss you already."

"Well, good for you. What else do you want?"

"Do you wanna come down next Saturday and stay for the weekend?"

"Hey look, baby girl, if you come up and get a hold of me, we can do the dirty, but I ain't driving all the way down there when I got way better ass just around the corner. You know what I'm sayin'?"

"Don't say that! Don't you want to see me? I'll make it worth the trip."

"C'mon, you know we're done...But listen, if I'm ever in Benton, and I have some time, I'll stop by for a piece, you know, a sympathy fuck for old time's sake."

"Sure, I guess...You know what? Just forget it. Fuck you! You're gonna regret this."

"Oh yeah, I bet...Not." and then the line went dead.

After Camille hung up, she told herself, "Fuck him! I'm moving up in the world, and he ain't. There has to be more options in this city than in that tiny ass town."

She stayed up late that night watching movies on the television in her bedroom. The hotel didn't have room service, but pizza delivery was an option and there was a good pie place that was close by. She called Tom's Pizza and ordered a pepperoni and sausage with some soda for a celebratory binge night of television. Soon, the pizza delivery was made, and Camille was living the good life. She was in her own hotel room and eating pizza in bed while watching HBO.

The next morning, she was ready to buy some new work clothes and headed up Hilltop to the Benton Mall to do some shopping. She loved going to that mall and was excited to go by herself for once. The mall had the big chain anchor stores around the corners with other noted stores throughout, a smattering of niche shops, a food court, and specialty clothing options. The trip was a success, and she was leaving after a couple of hours of looking and trying, with a few pairs of work pants and tops, along with some thick-soled shoes for long days on the hard floor.

She wanted to take advantage of her newfound freedom and took a drive around town, and even spotted a couple of boys that she thought were hot.

*

The weekend of freedom sped into Sunday night, and soon Patricia was knocking at the door as she opened it with her key card. Camille was happy to see her even if she really did not want a roommate. She had always liked working for her, and Patricia always treated her well.

"Hey, let's get some food delivered. Whaddya think?" Patricia asked.

"I'm in. They got good pizza on delivery."

"How about that Chinese place down the street?"

The delivery arrived, and as they started to fill their plates with the choices, Patricia said, "I'm gonna be here for the whole week this week and the next. I'm still going home for the weekends, though."

"Uh-huh."

"New plans. The following week, I will only be here three days for a couple of weeks and by then, you gotta be on it."

"Okay. Kinda figured that. Hey, I just wanna say that I appreciate the trust. I'm not used to that from most—well, anybody, really. You've always supported me, and I appreciate it. Okay, enough of that, so what are we going to be doing tomorrow morning?"

"No problem. You know, you need to work on your confidence, girl. You're gonna do well. We'll need to be there at eight, and we'll do a walkthrough at nine with the contractor to go over the punch list, hopefully for the last time."

"That sounds good to me. I gotta tell ya, I'm a little scared, ya know?"

The ladies worked hard those two weeks, as Camille had no time for the hobbies that she enjoyed. No alcohol and no weed made her a little edgy, but the busy schedule and fast pace were good for her. Without a roommate on the weekends, Camille rested and watched television.

The Benton Rusty's finally opened to the public to some media fanfare, and it was instantly busy. Patricia was present for the initial opening of operations, and it went smoothly since both she and Camille were seasoned in the operational aspects of the business and knew the owner's expectations. That first month required Camille to manage and operate the food stations and work the front counter when needed. It was coming together, and starting to smooth out a couple of months in. During this time, Camille had met a few people her age around town and through work, to her delight.

Her time was running out at the Extended Stay Hotel, although she was somewhat prepared for that event. She had watched the local newspaper for apartment rentals in the area and talked with her new acquaintances about sections of the Benton area with less expensive rents. She had met a guy who was a customer in those early days when she was working the register and taking orders on occasion. The guy was twenty-one years old with dark hair and brown eyes. He was tall and thin and seemed tough. His name was Shane Summers. Shane took an interest in the new manager of Rusty's, especially since she was eighteen years old and already managing a restaurant.

Shane lived in a suburb of Benton called Happy Valley. Happy Valley was far less expensive to live in for a reason. The area was part suburban and part rural and, at one time, enticed folks who were looking to be more isolated. Not always because they were seeking solitude, but because they were doing sneaky shit. This was a dusty, brushed-in area of Cassell County that had modest older homes or mobile homes on small tracts of land. Most of the places were several decades old or older, and the people who lived there did not like intruders or nosey neighbors. Shane grew up in Happy Valley and knew most of the people who lived there or knew of them. He liked that he could live his life there without much law enforcement interference. If law enforcement was present, it was normally due to a warrant or an unusual 911 call. Not that crime was low, but rather that calling the police to settle your problems or disputes was frowned upon.

*

After befriending Camille, Shane stopped by one afternoon to tell her that he had some leads. Camille spotted him in the lobby and went out to greet him. "Hey, what're you doing here? Did you come back for another juicy burger and shake," she asked and then giggled.

He smiled and dropped his head as his left foot moved about on the floor. He looked up and answered, "I don't know. Maybe. Can I get that?"

She smiled wide and stared him down as she said, "Maybe so, if you work it right. So, really, what are you doing here?"

"I found some places that you might be able to get. There are a couple mobile homes near me that are up for rent."

"Thanks. I'd like to see 'em. I need something cheap to start if you know what I mean."

"Yeah, I do. I can take you when you want."

"How about Friday afternoon at three? How does that sound?"

"Good. That's good for me. I can meet you at the Liquor Mart on old Highway 42."

"Hey, that would be great. Thanks for stopping in. Can I get you lunch on me?"

"Sure, I will have that juicy burger and that shake...vanilla, please. Wait, can you put a cherry on top of that?"

Camille blushed a little, and Shane said, "I'll wait and take that after we find you a place."

"Promise?"

"Oh yeah. I don't need to promise. I always come through."

*

They were set to meet in front of the happiest place in Happy Valley, the Happy Valley Liquor Mart. The store was located in the middle of the small area of Happy Valley among a few other small stores that also provided the essentials for the locals. Camille arrived on Friday at the appointed time and had Shane get in her car. Surrounding the measly downtown were acres of rolling hills filled with green grasses for about a month or two in spring, which abruptly turned in color to that of coyote tan for the remainder of the year. Spread among the tick-laden dry weeds were manzanita bushes frozen in the look of agony and despair, along with the acres and acres of yard cars that seemed to always surround every dwelling. Valley oak trees provided the only respite from the summer heat as they stood juxtaposed against the backdrop of the blue sky. When one looked past the occasional canopy of green into the sky overhead, all that appeared under the contrails of passing jets were the buzzards circling for carrion as the rays of the sun punished the onlooker's eyes for being brave enough to take the chance.

Camille was a little turned off by the environment that revealed itself as it bore into her corneas, along with the less-than-cordial faces of the people who inhabited it.

Camille hung out with Shane after they looked the area over and saw the places that were available for rent. The tour did not take long since the inventory was limited, while the abuse was not. They stopped at Shane's apartment, where the constant humming of window-installed air conditioning units made the insane keenly aware and the sane maniacal. The cool air blew across their faces as they sat on the couch and drank a couple of cold beers. Shane made his move but was unsuccessful. Camille was interested, but certainly not at the moment. As she excused herself and headed for the door, she said, "Maybe we could see a movie or something," as she did her best to present a look of sexual appeal to keep Shane hooked.

Shane nodded his head as he answered, "Yeah, that'd be good."

"Okay, it's a date. Well, thank you for the tour and for goin' with me to see all the places. Call me at the Extended Stay."

In some ways, Shane was intrigued by Camille but not pleased about the rejection. As she walked out, he said, "I'll call you."

*

Camille hit the road on Saturday morning looking in the downtown area of Benton and some of its suburbs for available and affordable housing. Some of the places were nice, but then over her budget. Others were crappy, but those she could afford. She was at the crossroads of most young people in the world, or at least in America. You could rarely afford what you really wanted, while on the other hand, you could generally afford what you didn't. This is where a soul learns to settle through attrition.

On that Saturday afternoon, she set out in a bigger circumference around Benton to the south into the lands that only bordered Happy Valley. She visited a lot of apartment complexes that day. She looked at studios, as well as one-bedroom and two-bedroom apartments, in case she could find a roommate. She was tired and once again frustrated by her lack of success. As she was heading further away from Benton, nearing the edges of Happy Valley, she decided to turn around at the next available spot in the road. As the turnaround revealed itself, she noticed a sign that said, "Valley Oaks Apartments," with a banner that read, "Apartments Available." Since she had already made the right turn into the entryway to the apartments and was preparing to make the left turn back into the roadway, a feeling took over, and she spun the steering wheel back to the right and into the entrance to the apartment complex.

Camille found her way into the leasing office and made an inquiry. She was met by a dark-complected woman named Samira. Samira was used to people coming in day in and day out looking for something that they couldn't afford but always hoped for an exception. As she met Camille, Samira reached out and introduced herself as she shook Camille's hand. She instantly knew that she had another one wasting her time as she read Camille's facial expression. "Do you have any apartments available, and if so, what is the rent and the deposit?"

Samira laid out the pricing and showed the floorplans to the visitor at her desk. Camille quickly pointed to the single-bedroom unit and asked if she could see it. Samira reached out and touched the back of Camille's hand as it still lay atop the floorplan document with her index finger pointed to her anticipated home and asked, "What's your credit history like, and if it meets our criteria, when do you need it?"

"Oh, uhm, I don't know. Soon, I guess. Do I need a credit score or something?"

"Yes, a credit score. It shows your credit history and whether a person pays their bills on time."

"I don't know what my credit score is."

"Give me your driver's license and fill out some paperwork, and I'll run it for you, and then we'll know. How does that sound?"

"Okay, here you go," she said as she slid her license across the table to Samira.

"Let me make a copy of this while you complete this application form. Any questions?" she asked after seeing some confusion.

"The whole thing?"

"As much as you can."

As she ventured into the depths of the rental application, she felt overwhelmed as she provided the phone number for the Benton Extended Stay Hotel and then gave the mostly completed form back to Samira. Samira gave her driver's license back to her and said, "I will call you on Monday to let you know whether your application was accepted."

Camille was suddenly thrilled since she had not been instantly defeated. Although she was naïve enough to think that she had a chance because she had a job and the money to make the rent.

*

When Camille came back to the hotel during her lunch break on the following Monday to check her messages, she was given a note by the front desk that Samira had called and left her number. Camille made the call immediately, and Samira answered. Camille expected good news, as Samira spoke over her and said, "Your credit history was found to not be a good risk, and your application was denied. I'm sorry."

"Is there any way around that?"

"Not really. However, if you had someone with good credit to cosign for you. Someone like your parents, then maybe."

"Oh shit, really?"

"That kind of thing is done all the time. In the long run, it would help you obtain credit history by renting an apartment even with a cosigner."

"Oh. Okay. I'll call my parents and get back to you tomorrow and let you know."

As the call ended, Camille was sure that her parents would do this for her, although she could hear them say the word no, just as easily. After work that evening, Camille made the call for help and said, "Hey, Mom. I'm trying to get an apartment, and I need a cosigner. Can you or Dad do that?"

"I'll talk with your dad tonight. We need all the details. You know, like the deposit, the monthly rent, and some of the terms of the lease first. So, what are they?"

"I don't know, Mom. I've looked at so many places. Please help me! Please?"

David was listening and then got on the phone, "We'd like to help, but you don't have your ducks in a row. You're asking too much under the circumstances."

Camille pretended to cry and said, "I can't do this alone. What do I do, Dad?"

"Well, you need to find a person who has a place and needs a roommate."

Camille yelled at her dad in a string of vulgarities that would even make a pimp turn his head and then hung up. She slammed the phone down in the hotel room as she shouted, "Fuck you, David. You're such a prick!"

Camille called Patricia next and told her about her situation. Patricia said, "You know what I would do? I would take a look at the message boards at Benton Community College or at that private college in town. Or both of them and see if someone is looking for a roommate."

"Oh, that's smart."

"Make sure to check it first thing in the morning. Have your shift supervisor take charge of operations until you get to work. And I mean, hit those schools at seven or eight in the morning."

"I will. Thank you for always being good to me and for being so smart. You're always there for me when I need it."

She was sure to follow through on Patricia's advice and was successful at her first stop at Benton Community College. She found five notices looking for roommates and tore off the phone numbers and details for each. Once at work, she started making calls to see if she could be homed by the afternoon. Camille found a guy and a girl who each needed a roommate to share expenses and they wanted to meet her. She made a mad dash to meet with both of them that afternoon in order to put this problem to bed.

The first person was a guy named Tom Pratha. He was in his mid-thirties and enrolled at Benton College. He was seeking a new career path after several turns in the military and had a pretty nice two-bedroom apartment northwest of town. They seemed to hit it off. Tom said, "You look nice enough and have a full-time job, but are you clean?"

"Clean?"

"You know, organized or a mess?"

"Oh, I'm clean. For sure. Clean."

"Okay. Good. Good. So, when do you want to move in?"

"I got one more place to look at in a few minutes. I'll get back to you in a couple hours...."

"Oh, wait. Do you have a boyfriend or, um, date a lot?"

"I don't know why you asked that. Kinda weird, but neither one."

"Sure. Sure. Well, havin' a man around might be helpful sometimes. You know, protection and stuff," he said as he smiled at her and pointed to a framed shadow box on the wall that displayed some military ribbons and medallions.

"I guess that could be."

"Convenient, too. If you, um, like the occasional pleasure of a man...Am I right?" he said while he looked her over one last time. His eyes then rose to meet Camille's, and he said, "Well, please don't leave me hangin'. Would be cool to have you as a roomie."

*

The next place was south of town and the girl was nineteen and also going to the local junior college. Her name was Missy Coulette, and she was also desperate to share expenses, except her parents were picking up half of the rent until she obtained a roommate. Camille instantly thought, "This chick seems pretty cool."

"So, Camille, what do you think?"

"I like it a lot. I'd like to live here with you."

"Oh man, my parents are gonna be so happy. When do you want to move in?"

"As soon as I can. Is it a deal?"

"Yep. Awesome!"

She gave Missy the money, and in exchange, she received a key. Camille held that key and felt the pressures of life dissipate as she informed her new roommate that she was going to get her stuff.

Camille was reluctant to leave the hotel since she had maid service, and it was free. But life goes on, and with this move, she would be a real adult. She had gotten good advice from her dad, but she was bitter about the hard road he put her on, and the bitterness continued to metastasize.

CHAPTER 4.

THE NETWORK

Networks abound. Here, there, and everywhere. TV networks, computer networks, movies, domain names, and those of people. The latter either builds a web of joy and support or that which is akin to the dark web.

*

Missy Coulette was busy with school, working a job, and making her way in life. She, too, was from a small town and had moved to the big city, but she was not looking for complacency and mediocrity like her new roommate. This one wanted to be a businessperson and an entrepreneur. She was taking general education classes at the community college and was putting everything on the line to reach success in her chosen field. The two young women were about as similar as good and evil, but they got along pretty well considering the diametric.

*

It had been a couple of months since Camille had seen Shane or talked with him after the epic day of failures. She was just about to get off work when he walked in the door at Rusty's. As their eyes met, she waved, and he tried to act cool as he walked in her direction. She said, "Long time no see. How you been?"

"Good, really good. Hey, did you ever find a place?"

"I did. Yep."

"Oh wow. Glad it worked out. Where at?"

"I'm halfway between here and Happy Valley. Do you know where the River Bend Apartments are?"

Shane paused and then said, "Uhm, yeah, yeah, it's by, um, Jim's Auto Sales, right?"

She nodded her head in the affirmative as she waited for his approval.

"Hey, look at that, we're living near each other after all. You should've stopped by and said hi," Shane said.

"Yeah. I was gonna, but I've been busy. Really busy."

"Do you wanna get something to eat and have a beer or something?"

"Yeah, I'd like that." She moved in close to Shane's ear after looking around the room quickly and said, "I got a fake ID. I'd like to give it a try down here. Where can we go?"

"A fake ID? This oughta be fun," Shane said loudly as he pulled away from Camille to look into her face.

"Yeah, I got it in high school, but it didn't work in my town. Too small, ya know."

"I like this place that has good sandwiches, and they serve beer. Wanna go there?"

The fake ID worked like a charm to the unfamiliar. Soon, they had eaten their dinner and drank enough beer to feel the chains of modesty and restraint fall away. As they left the bar, they hit the road in separate cars, taking their chances on a DUI, while heading to the River Bend Apartments. When they arrived, Missy was studying at her workstation in the small living room. Camille said, "Hey, roomie, this is Shane. Shane, this is Missy."

Missy looked up from her books and said, "Nice to meet you," as the pair headed past her and into the hallway that led to Camille's bedroom.

*

Shane kissed Camille on the cheek as he got up and put on his clothes around one-thirty in the morning and headed for home. He enjoyed himself, and he liked to get laid without much effort. He was a fan of the humdrum girls. They focused on their man, took direction well, and they typically were not going anywhere since they had few options. In this regard, Camille seemed perfect. To her, sex was the acknowledgment of desire. A desire for her as a person as well as a physically attractive woman. More importantly, it was a tool. One that controlled the majority of men.

She realized that Shane was perfect after she replayed the events of the night before in her mind. He was like her last boyfriend in Mountain View but a lot more capable. He also had some attributes of a pleaser. Something that she wanted. As a result of that night, they had two options in front of them. That night of inclusion would either produce their immediate exclusion, or they would be drawn back to the well of desires as they worked from the physical into the lottery of a meaningful relationship. The pair was pulled back to the well, and either reliving perfection or seeking to perfect the activity that initially drew them together.

As their relationship moved forward, their circle of friends grew slightly larger. Camille was living well for her age. She had a job, an apartment, and a boyfriend. She had spent little time talking with her parents since the phone call of rejection and advice. Her parents still worried about their girl and would call or try and stop by when they were in Benton. On occasion, it resulted in a short visit.

*

Eventually, Camille told her parents that she was going to come up and visit them and that she would be bringing her boyfriend, Shane.

On arrival, Shane introduced himself to Lisa and David. The couple approved of him generally and liked that he was employed full-time and seemed to enjoy the company of their daughter. Camille took him out on a tour of the town as she drove the streets and coupled the tour with stories about people, places, and things. He took it all in with interest, as manipulation requires connection. The more information, especially attached to human emotions, the better.

David would not let his little girl and her boyfriend sleep in the same room that night, so the young couple stayed at a motel in town. They visited again on their second day for a couple of hours in the afternoon before they headed back to Benton.

On the drive home, Shane said, "So what's the real deal between you and your parents? How did it get so bad?"

"What do you mean?"

"You don't all get along. Why?"

"It's a long story. Well, actually, it's not," she said as her jaw clenched tightly and her hands gripped harder on the steering wheel.

"So?"

"Well, my parents are assholes!"

"Assholes? Huh. I didn't really get that, but we weren't there very long. Didn't you all go on trips when you were younger? They got a nice house, cars, and all that kind of stuff."

After a long pause, she answered, "Yeah, we did. That's the exception, though. You think they have nice stuff?" she asked while displaying a smirk of arrogance.

"You know, as an only child, you're lucky."

"How's that?"

"Me? I have to share nothing from my dad with my two brothers and sister," he professed with complacency and defeat.

She smiled since her boyfriend thought she was rich, and she wanted that belief to continue. She suddenly felt important and that there was a shimmer of hope....

*

The lights of Benton were glowing in the late evening hours as they headed down the freeway toward their offramp. Since they had shared a trip and a couple of days together, Shane wanted to be dropped off at his place so that he could get ready for work in the morning at his landscaping job with Valley Landscaping. Camille was clingy, but let her man do what he needed as she left him at his apartment that he shared with a friend from high school and a coworker.

Joe Jenkins, who went by Slob, had been a close friend of Shane's since they were in elementary school. Slob did odd jobs, including a little drug peddling. Mostly marijuana, but sometimes he could get the "good pills" and the occasional cocaine. Slob was a guy who barely got by, and that was good enough. He had no family to speak of except Shane.

The other roommate was Jake Angelo. He also worked for Valley Landscaping and was trying to get into the construction trade. He was taking a couple of classes in the trade when he could find the time. He had a girlfriend from Benton who was good looking and going places. She had brunette hair cut to shoulder length and was 5'8" and thin. Her name was Angie Sparks. She was currently working at the mall for a lingerie company selling satin, lace, and the American Dream. Jake and Angie had similar goals but separate paths. Jake was going to have to scratch and claw his way to success over a long period of time, while Angie could achieve the same within the next few years with the correct presentation that resulted in the exchange of blah, blah, blahs, presented as vows and the swapping of rings.

CHAPTER 5.

ENTER CENTER STAGE

Life is a collection of memories. Memories received, adjusted, and lost. A sequence of the highs and lows accounted for by the circling of hands and the appearance of light and dark.

*

It was 1995, and time had passed quickly in the prime of life as people came and went from view, except for the circle of trusted associates that had developed through the relationship between Camille and Shane. They were a rag-tag group of thieves, drug users, and manipulators living in static desperation, but for now, they had each other.

Camille was twenty-two years old. She still had it fairly good as the manager of Rusty's in Benton. She had not yet succumbed to the lure of taking from the drawer or through embezzlement by way of ledger or diversion. She had competent staff, and the paychecks were pretty nice as well for the young who lacked the experience to make the contrast. One early afternoon she was walking out into the dining area to check on guests and to see if anything needed to be restocked when she heard, "Camille, I can't believe it! It's like déjà vu."

As Camille turned to look at the speaker of those words, she saw her former archenemy, Sherry Burns.

"Sherry Burns! It's so great to see you. Are you up visiting from Los Angeles?" she yelled as she quickly walked up to her.

The two young women hugged as Sherry answered, "Oh no, I never moved to LA. That all fell through."

Camille stepped back from the embrace in the crowded lobby and said, "Where you been living at? I haven't seen you around Benton."

"Well, I ended up moving to Sacramento instead of LA. I lived there for the last four years. I just moved to Benton. I take it you live here too, huh?" she asked as she pointed her finger toward the floor.

"I've been here since we got out of school. You can see I still work for Rusty's. I bet you would have never thought that, huh? Hey, where you working at?"

"I was working in the entertainment business in Sacramento. I moved up here for the same kinda work."

"Entertainment? Wow, that sounds amazing. Doin' what? Acting or something?" she asked while feeling the conflict of pride and jealousy together as her shoulders sank.

"Yeah, I'm acting and dancing, just like I wanted. Well, kinda."

"That's awesome! Where do you get to do that in Benton?"

"I work my own business dancing for parties. I mainly work at Prancers. I'm a dancer there too, and I act like I give a fuck."

Camille laughed as she shook her head in affirmation and put her open palm in the air for a high five. She then said, "So, where are you livin' at?"

"Right now, I'm sleeping on a co-worker's couch and lookin' for a place to live."

Camille had taken over the lease two years ago when Missy left to attend a university and had been through a roommate a year since. She said, "Hey, I need a roommate. I would like to live with someone I know and who is my friend rather than look through a field of strangers once again. What do ya say? It's $200.00 a month. No deposit, and we get to live together and talk shit about everybody in Mountain View."

"Wow, I didn't expect to see you here. I stopped in for nostalgic purposes and was amazed when I saw you!" She paused and then said, "Hey, um, when can I move in?"

"Tonight, if you want. I'll write down the address on my business card. Just let me know when you're coming. How's that?"

Sherry hugged her former foe with joy as she was handed her takeout order by another employee of Rusty's.

"Okay, well, I'll call you around six, before work," Sherry said while the two hugged one more time to reinforce the feeling of actual friendship from that which was previously entangled in the vernacular called frenemies.

Sherry called just after six that evening and said, "Hey, girl, I've thought about it. I would like to move in tomorrow morning. Does that work?"

"Awesome! Fuck yeah, it does. If I head to work, I'll leave the door unlocked, and your key will be on the table." Camille stopped abruptly and then said, "If you need help, I can go in late, and help you move in the morning."

"Thank you. That's so nice. I think I can manage; I don't have much. I don't even have a bed, but I'll get one after I get moved in there, and I can have that delivered, so go to work."

Camille then realized that Sherry was running from Sacramento but didn't care since she liked knowing her roommate for once, and especially the feeling of cutting her rent in half.

After another long night of stripping at Prancers, Sherry had made another sizeable chunk of money. She left work at two fifteen and headed to her current place of residence to sleep on the couch for one last night. Sherry awoke after nine that same morning, brushed her teeth, and left a thank you card for her roommate, who was working the day shift at Prancers. She drank some orange juice from the refrigerator and then realized once again that the vengeance of toothpaste and orange juice is part of the hard laws of life where two inconsequential things can come together to loudly pronounce their hatred for the other. She quickly spit it out, filled her car with her belongings, and headed for a drive-thru coffee.

    Sherry liked the new apartment, and she had a bedroom once again. She worked casually to get organized as she built a list of things to buy. That list revolved around furniture and bedding.

*

Two evenings later, Sherry was off of work for the night and was at her new home waiting for an impending meet and greet with Camille's friends, who were coming over under the auspices of a social activity. After repeated knocks at the door and a welcomed arrival, Sherry was introduced to the circle. The room had the following people filling up space in the small apartment: Joe "Slob" Jenkins, his girlfriend Erin Doubleday, Shane Summers, Eric Larson, and Camille, of course. Jake Angelo and Angie Sparks arrived a little later to round out the crowd. Sherry told a few stories but mostly listened intently to the people she had just met in order to attach their stories to names and to determine whether they could be trusted or not.

    Since Sherry was a stripper, the boys were gaga over her, which made the observant girls feel even more unsatisfactory than they had before they arrived. That night, Shane stayed over after everyone else had headed home. He, too, was curious about the stripper friend who was at the same continuation high school with his girlfriend and who had also grown up in Mountain View. He was intrigued, and he hoped that he could pull off a dually independent sexual relationship with Sherry or otherwise.

    After the trio retired from drinking and headed for bed, Shane told Camille that he wanted to talk with her about something. She quickly agreed, and once they were both in bed, Shane turned toward Camille and laid his cheek into his open hand and said, "We need some more money."

She scooted in toward him and said, "Yeah, I'm tired of these bills and having to wait to pay them and then not having enough damn money. I want to live the life I should've always had. You know what I'm talkin' about?"

"Yeah, I do. Would your mom and dad help us out if you asked?"

"No, I don't talk to them much, and when I do, it's about nothing. And I don't want to ask either."

Shane laid back and stared at the ceiling and said, "I gotta get a better job or somethin'. I just need more money."

"Whaddya thinkin' about? Do you know of any jobs that pay better than the one you got?"

"Yeah. They say I don't qualify for them. I don't know. I just need a better life than this shit existence."

"How about we take that money from my parents," she said as she sat up in bed.

"How in the fuck are we gonna do that? That's not gonna work, and you know it."

Staring intently at Shane, she said, "Look, it's their fault for not providing me the life I deserve. We'll just kill them. You will do it for me, won't you?" She reached out and held his hand.

"Holy shit, girl! What the fuck!"

"Calm down. Don't be a little bitch about it. I'm not sure how we'll do it, but we need to kill them to get my inheritance. Maybe a home invasion or somethin' and take the money and valuables to sell."

"I dunno Camille, that's some heavy shit right there," he said in angst.

"Then you could have less stress, and we would stay together forever. Are you in?" she asked while staring intently into his eyes.

A premonition swept immediately over Camille as she could suddenly see her mom and dad through the window in the door from the backyard into the kitchen in her mind's eye. She was much younger in her appearance as she envisioned their scared look as they spied pure evil. She was peering through the glass when she observed an expression of safety sweep over them upon recognizing her before they were to be slain. As her mom opened the door with a smile, she and Shane came over the threshold with bold ambivalence and shot them both in the head. As her mom and dad both folded into the floor and then oblivion, she and Shane pillaged the home and set it on fire. Camille's mind easily shifted back to the reality that she was in and asked, "What did you just say?"

"I said that's heavy shit. I just saw that you went somewhere. What was that about?"

"You and me went to their house and killed them."

The pair talked it out for a while longer and then fell asleep.

In the morning, Camille waited for her boyfriend's full attention and said, "Were you serious about what you said last night? About needing more money?"

"Sure, I guess," he mumbled while looking down at the floor.

"Look, either you are in or out. This is how we get money. Real money."

"Damn, Camille! This is really heavy shit. Do you really think we can do it without getting caught?"

"Yeah! We're not getting caught, okay? Don't tell me you're scared. You need to man up to get what you want."

"Shit! This is fucked up. Why do women get me into such fucked up places!"

"Calm down, dude. Do you want money or not?"

"Okay! Fuck! Okay! If we do this, we need some help and a real plan then. Maybe Slob and this Sherry chick could help."

"I don't know if we can trust Sherry, but I'll see if she's cool with it."

"If you do that, I'll talk to Slob. If he's on board, we'll have a little meeting. Maybe we should run it by the group to see if any of those fuckers have any ideas and then work out a plan."

"Okay. Now we're talkin'! Hey, I can get some pizza, beer, and some wine coolers for Wednesday evening."

Shane left Camille's after eating some breakfast and headed off to get a few things done on his day off from work. One of those errands was to see Tania Davenport, the main woman in his life, as he wanted to let her know that a plan to get some money was now moving forward.

Tania was twenty-five years old and had two children from two different men. She was still hot, and stupid greedy. They wanted to get married and to be able to have a place to live of their own. They were anxious to move on in life instead of waiting to achieve through time and hard work. Tania had never produced a drop of sweat in her whole life except when she birthed her two babies. She had an order for child support for both kids, but it wasn't a lot, nor nearly enough.

Shane met with her at her mom's house where she was currently living along with her kids. As he walked in, he said, "Hey, baby, I might have some good news that I couldn't say over the phone. Camille has come up with a way for us to get some money."

"She has? It's about fucking time for that bitch to come through. What did she say?" she asked intently.

"She wants to kill her parents for her inheritance. We're having the group over to talk about planning it."

"Group? What do you mean by group?"

"You know, Slob, Sherry, Eric, and Erin. They might have some ideas."

Tania's face reddened as she turned both palms upward and said, "That's fucking stupid. You're an idiot! You understand that means less money for us and more chance that one of those dirtbags will talk. Right?"

He cautiously looked away and then turned back and softly said, "Sorry, baby. I need their help. They won't talk, and we'll still keep all of the money for us."

"That's more like it. Trust me, though, you can't trust them!"

Feeling the pressure lessen, he casually said, "You worry too much. These are my homies. They'll do anything for me."

"How much money are we talkin' about?"

"Three hundred thousand. But it's not a swindle. It's a murder. Two murders, actually. I'm not sure I can do that. I don't want to kill anyone. Right? What do you think?"

"For three hundred K, you're doin' it. If you want a life with me and all of this? You'll do this for us," she said while repeatedly pointing at herself from her face to her thighs.

*

Wednesday evening came, and everyone was present for the free food and alcohol. Tania was not a part of the group at this meeting or any other, as not even Slob knew about her existence.

Several people in the group of mutual friends were excluded from the murder plot out of hand for a multitude of reasons. One was the lack of need, and the other was that those people were not up to the task. The invited were present for food and alcohol, but they were also in the meeting of short straws to include or exclude themselves after hearing the stakes. If they were excluded, the expectations were that they would still provide support, ideas, and involvement if need be. After a lot of shit-talking, alcohol consumption, and pizza chewing, Shane addressed the group. He said, "Are you sick of not having enough money and workin' your ass off?"

Everyone raised their hands as if they were still in kindergarten instead of preparing to plan a murder. Shane continued, "Camille and I have a mark that has a lot of money. They got a house, cars, jewelry, tools—you know, stuff we can sell. They'll be easy to rip off since we know the layout of the house. We're talking about three hundred thousand ducats here, boys and girls."

"How do we get that money?" Slob asked after raising his hand in the air.

"If this leaks out of this room, you'll be killed. Capiche?" Shane said.

"What the Hell does capiche mean?" Eric asked.

"Understand. It means understand."

"Why didn't you just fuckin' say understand?"

"C'mon, bro, I saw it in a gangster movie, and I always wanted to say it. Now, just let me finish."

Sherry was nervous as she was no killer of men outside of sexual appeal and the attention that came with it. She asked, "How do you know these people?"

"You might know 'em—Camille's parents," Shane answered while looking Sherry over.

Sherry felt the reality of the situation strike her like molten lava poured into her lap, but since she did not really know the Deagans, nor most in the room, she didn't really care. Sherry figured that if she could play a small part in the preparation and not the actual crime, she would be good, and when it was over, she might have a few more bucks. If it went down that way, she would be glad for the money. Sherry answered, "Oh. Okay."

"Damn girl, that's some cold ass shit," Slob said softly.

Some people laughed as Camille winked at him with a smirk.

Shane interrupted again to seek ideas from the brain trust available to him. Sherry spoke up with clarity this time and said, "I'm in."

Everybody turned and looked at the new girl and then fought to jump into the fray with her.

"You know I'm down for the action and the money," Slob said.

And so it went, with the only holdout being Erin. She was just a junkie. She stole things for her habit, and her life revolved around the next fix. A large payment of money for drugs was appealing, but the route to get there was impassable. Erin's hands shook as she slowly pushed out the words, "I'm sorry, you guys. I...I hope Joe is okay with it."

Slob pulled her in and kissed her as he said, "I didn't want you involved anyway, Boo."

She hugged Slob back while leaning her head against his as she mumbled, "I need you sooo much."

"Count me in. I'm down for this, too," Eric said.

He was a petty crook at this point, but he wanted to graduate to a doctor's degree in crime, and this was his ticket. After a lot of discussion about the money and how it would be split, additional ideas were thrown about. Shane said, "Camille and I will get sixty percent of the take. That's about one hundred and eighty thousand dollars. You three will get about forty thousand dollars—each. That's easy money right there!"

Mumbles and enthusiasm were reported from the small assemblage of conspirators. After a mixture of ideas from movies and imagination, they decided that they would sneak in and kill the couple late at night. Make it look like a murder, and then wait for the Deagans' will to come through. As a short lull came in the frenzy of greed, Camille said, "When I get the money, I'll be the one giving you your cut."

The excitement then met its crescendo as materialism and bloodlust swept the room of willing participants. Since the existing brain trust was low on intellectual capital, they agreed to meet again so they could work on the details of the plan and not devolve into frivolity as to how it would be spent.

*

A few days after the meeting, Slob brought up the idea to his roommate, Jake. Even though he swore not to discuss it with anyone upon penalty of death, Slob and Shane trusted Jake, and Jake was smart, so Slob proceeded without reflection. Jake was no angel, and he knew that he lived with guys who would commit crimes if necessary, but murder was out of the question. Jake didn't think Slob would be able to remember anything he talked about or that they would really do it, so he said, "Hey, look. Don't repeat a word. Spitballin', this is what I got. The crew should be small, only two or three people. Those people should rent a car to drive to and from Mountain View. They'll need masks at the house. Oh, and gloves like they do in the movies. You need some kinda weapon. Like a gun, you know, in case shit goes south. But your main plan, you should use regular shit that's already in the house, like kitchen knives or big rocks from the yard, like that, to kill 'em with. This way, the murders will be quiet, and you won't be bringing weapons to the house or bloody things from there. Ya followin'?"

"Hold on, man, that's a lot of fucking info right there. Slow down, man!"

"Gotcha, dude. Are ya following, though?" he asked while cocking his head to the left to see if the lights were on.

"Yeah, man, just slow down."

"Okay. Put those gloves and masks in a thick plastic bag when you're done, with a couple rocks and tie it off. Then drop it off the bridge on the interstate as you come back over Benton Lake."

"Cool! That's a really good idea, man. Anything else?" Slob asked as he got out of his chair to get closer.

"Yeah, maybe you guys should take some things from the house to make it look like a burglary gone bad instead of a straight-up murder—you know?"

"Dude, have you done this shit before?"

"Nope, I watch TV and read a few books...oh, and make sure that those things that you take are in that bag when it goes over the rail for the lake bottom."

Slob was impressed with the plans and details that he just received as he reached out and clasped his friend's hand and bro-hugged him.

Camille had a new feeling at work the week after the meeting. She now knew that she would not have to work at Rusty's for the next forty years or more. She would only have to work there for another year or two after the murder as she mourned her parents' deaths and accepted the proceeds from the will. Camille's plan would have her sit on that money for at least a year before she would convince Shane to marry her, and they would move to the Bahamas and live off of her inheritance. She never had any intentions of sharing any of the money with her "friends." That money was hers to inherit and she was sacrificing her parents for it. She would only give Shane money as he needed it once they were married and out of the country. For the other participants, Camille had only two words in mind. "Fuck 'em."

Since treachery was afoot among the gang of thieves and evolving murderers, there was one other among the group that had their own plans for the money, and that was Eric Larson. He was going to force Camille and Shane to give him the majority of the money, including part of their sixty percent, or he would kill them, too. Eric did not think much about the last two possible roadblocks to the money. Those being Sherry and Slob, in his mind, neither of which possessed the capability for a premeditated murder. A killing from passion, maybe, but certainly not one where you planned, waited, and then got your hands dirty. Real dirty.

*

The next planning session was held at Shane and Slob's apartment. Jake was out bowling with Angie and was to then spend the night at her place which was beneficial for the both of them. The conniving group of five was in place and ready. The drinking had started before the arrivals and resumed to bring courage and commitment to the confab. Slob started with enthusiasm as he had ideas to share. As he stood in front of the room, he began to lay out his plan as to how the murder would take place, as he dropped into the details that Jake had given to him in their secret exchange. Everyone liked it, but Shane instantly knew that Slob had been either reading books, which he figured was impossible, or he had been talking with someone else. Shane waited until after the guests were gone before he delved further into the details of Slob's instant capabilities for thinking shit through.

Sherry agreed with the plan that the couple needed to be killed in an apparent burglary for theft. She did not care how they did it, but if they used guns, she had an idea. She said, "In the movies, the killers put the pillows on the faces of the people so they keep the brains and shit from flying all over, and it's quieter, so neighbors can't hear it. Oh, and I like the idea of using the rocks in the yard as a weapon...but—they might be hard to find. Hey Camille, do your parents have big rocks in their yard?"

Camille paused as she thought and then said, "There're softball-sized rocks in the backyard. Close to the kitchen door. Like, in the garden thing. You know what I mean, like no plants. Just rocks."

"Yep, use the rocks."

Camille said, "Hey, I have a house key. I will use the key to quietly open the door as Shane and Eric go inside and get my parents. I think I want to have them killed in their bedroom. We can shoot 'em, stab 'em, or beat 'em to death—whatever. Any of those work for me—but we need to make it look like a burglary gone wrong. If we do that, then they will have to be killed in the living room or kitchen, maybe. You know, to look like they were used to find the valuables."

The group shook their heads in the affirmative as they listened to Sherry and Camille as if they were experts in the hit game. Sherry took a few minutes to add some potential tactical detail to the desires laid out by her roommate Camille.

"Eric, are you even listening right now?" Sherry asked abruptly while glaring at him.

Eric looked up to meet Sherry's eyes and said, "Look, new girl, if you were stripping for me, I'd pay attention in order to get into your box, but on this, I'm the main hitter. You guys make the plans, and I'll fuckin execute 'em. That's all you need to know. Got it?"

"Uh, yeah, I got it," Sherry answered slowly as she realized that she had overstepped.

Once the group isolated the offerings into an overarching plan, they agreed to return one more time to work out any further ideas discussed previously and then work on the timing, participant roles, and exact execution details.

Eventually the meeting goers were off to pursue other endeavors, while Shane walked up to where Slob was still seated and said, "Hey, you going anywhere tonight?"

"I'm goin' to Erin's tonight," he said while looking up at Shane.

"I need you to stay for a few minutes."

"I only got a few minutes, man. I'm late already."

When Eric and Sherry were finally gone, Shane got back up and went and stood in front of Slob and asked, "Who in the fuck did you tell?"

"Tell what?" Slob asked with surprise as he moved back into the chair's cushion.

"You know what! Who did you talk to, and who gave you those ideas? You're way too fucking stupid to come up with that shit on your own. Who was it?" he asked as he leaned in and grabbed him by the throat.

Camille focused in with intrigue and irritation as she knew that Shane was correct. Slob grabbed Shane's hand with both of his as he started to gasp for air and writhe in pain. He started to panic as the grip tightened. Slob pulled hard with his hands as he lived off of depleted oxygen. His lips became outlined in blue upon his reddened face. He made some other sudden and frantic attempts to try and break Shane's grip in order to achieve greater success at receiving life-giving oxygen. Shane leaned in even closer as his hands relented slightly to allow Slob another chance at the gift of life and said, "I should kill you right now. Who did you talk to?"

Slob was given some more precious air by his master, and as a result, Slob bellowed out, "Jake. I talked to Jake."

"Why in the fuck would you bring Jake into this? Jake is better than us. Didn't I tell you that I would kill the person who talked?"

Slob averted his eyes and said, "We both trust Jake. I didn't think that I couldn't tell him."

"Did you see fucking Jake at the first meeting? Was he invited, you stupid bastard?" Shane quickly answered.

"No."

Shane pulled his knife and quickly flipped the blade open. He laid the knife against Slob's throat as Camille felt the excitement that she was missing in her life. He made a long, light cut with the blade tip down along Slob's neck to his clavicle. Blood began to lightly ooze out through the cut as Slob sought forgiveness.

"Dude, you put me in a bad situation, man. I got enough problems. I'm neck-deep into this shit. You can't fuck me over on this!" Shane said in a whisper into Slob's right ear.

CHAPTER 6.
FOR REAL

Inducement by alcohol has been a consistently faithful manipulation tool since its discovery. The youth learned the trade early on. It worked on friends (old and new), parents, and especially oneself. As a new day was born from the planning of the end, the vitality of the alcohol had receded. Semi-clear heads and hearts began to spin for traction in the recesses, seeking to bring forth and ascertain what had been offered from their opened mouths.

*

Sherry liked and especially needed money and seemed to be less shackled than others as to how problematic it was to obtain. Murder was excessive, but she still wanted to dip her toe in for the excitement and a potential payday. She had heard murder plots before, but mostly in jest or bravado; this one was getting real. She didn't know her roommate's parents but did know what they looked like from seeing them around town and at her school on occasion growing up in Mountain View. The impression that she got was that Camille's parents were good people, much like her own, except for one noticeable trait. The Deagans seemed like they actually cared deeply about their daughter. That is something Sherry was missing in her own life. Her parents were well-intentioned, but they really should not have had children. At least not ones that needed extra attention, which Sherry knew was the elixir that drove her into the search for attention from others. Unfortunately, the attention that she had received was topical, insincere, and fleeting. That was so in her friendships, in her relationships, and in her profession. She knew that she had some soul-searching to do, and she needed to figure it out quickly.

*

Eric Larson had no qualms. He wanted this. His family was a criminal enterprise. He needed to make his bones outside of the family business to get some respect from his line of cousins, uncles, and dad, many of whom had already seen the inside of prison walls or still resided there. He had spent a lot of time thinking about the killings. He eventually settled on the idea that since he was the main hitter, he would choose the weapon or weapons to make it final. He was going to bring his hefty camp knife. It was big, sharp, and it could put in work. He wanted quiet as he severed two souls from their mortal wrappers, and he didn't want to deal with spent shell casings from his semi-automatic pistol or have gunshot residue (GSR) anywhere on him if they were caught at the scene or stopped on the way home. Although he wasn't scared of the California Department of Corrections system, he was unwilling to help the police put him there. His main weapon would be a billy club—which was illegal to own in California in many configurations. This one was a youth-sized aluminum baseball bat that was wrapped tightly with grip tape along the handle. He chose aluminum over wood because he wanted to swing for the cheap seats and not break his bat during his precious time at the plate, seeking two homers. A shorter youth baseball bat would be easier to carry up to Mountain View and into the house. Once it was completed, he was going to use Slob's idea on how to shit-can all of the evidence by sending it over the railing and into the bottom of the lake.

*

Camille came home from a long day of work, cracked open a beer, and sat down to watch television. As soon as she sat down, she heard Sherry come down the hallway from her room.

"Hey, Sherry," she said as she still focused on the TV screen.

"Hey. How was work," Sherry said while walking into the room.

"It was the shits. Thanks for askin'."

Sherry smirked as she fell onto the couch next to Camille when she was asked, "What time are you working tonight?"

"In a couple hours. You know, I've been thinking. You can cancel this plot to steal from your mom and dad."

Camille stiffened and said, "Did you hear me explain my day? I can't do this anymore!"

"I understand. Believe me, I get it. I was supposed to be famous by now. Living in Hollywood as a singer and actor, but I'm stripping in Benton instead...It's good money though... Hey, I could get you a job there! Well, like I said, the money is good and no taxes, if you know what I mean?"

"No. What in the fuck are you talking about?"

"More money without having to kill your parents! There are two gentlemen's clubs in the area that you can work through in several years here before you have to move on. What do you think?"

"I don't know!"

"Guys dig it. It is a rush when dudes are paying you to shake your titties at them or show 'em your ass crack."

They both began to laugh as the vividness of ass crack viewing by desperate men began to play in their heads as the lonely voyeur peered into the crack while ripping off dollar bills to pay for the privilege. For both young women, it was a funny thing to behold. Camille was now smiling and then asked, "Do bigger girls still make money?"

"Hell, I don't know. Big boobs work real good. Guys like all kinds of things, so you never know. But one thing is for sure, everybody loves boobies."

Camille smiled as she wiggled her overburdened breasts inside her shirt and said, "Well, I got those for sure. Sounds kinda fun, really. You know, you're a good friend. I appreciate your concern. I might take you up on the dancing, but I need a lot of help before I could do it, you know."

"What? No way!"

"I can't dance sexy. Well, actually, I can't fucking dance at all."

They both smiled, and Sherry felt the timing and said, "I can't go through with this. I'm out. I promise I won't say anything to anyone forever, but it's too steep for me. I hope I can get paid for my help in the planning, or maybe payment to remain silent, you know, as a gift from a friend?"

"Yeah, sure. I get it. It ain't for everybody. Don't feel bad, dude."

"I'll still live here and still be your friend, but I'm just a girl trying to find her way through my current life of continuous piles of shit. I'm already running from a bad situation down in Sacramento, and I'll probably have to cut out of here in a year or so when I'm no longer the new girl at the clubs. I'm real sorry. I hope you understand."

Camille answered quickly as she nodded her head while looking into Sherry's eyes and said, "Hey, girl I understand. I really do. Sometimes, I can't believe that I'm going to do this or that I am even involved in it, but then it makes so much sense. We both have been eating shit sandwiches for far too long. It has to end. We both deserve happiness. Right?"

"Yeah, girl, we do. We certainly do."

Later, when Camille had some privacy, she called Shane and said, "Hey, guess what?"

"I fucking don't know. What?"

"Sherry just told me she's out."

"Ah, fuck."

"It's less complicated and more money for us. Right?"

"Oh yeah, she wasn't adding much anyway. Let her go."

Shane felt the disappointment of the moment. He believed that she was of little value for the job at hand, but if she was involved up to her neck, he had her. If she was dirty and looking at prison time for her involvement, he would use that leverage to nail her. He was already tied up with Camille and Tania but could not stop lusting after Sherry Burns. Camille was just a way to get money. She had a day job, and she was willing to sacrifice her own parents to provide for him. Tania was marriage material. She was the woman that he wanted to be with. She was beautiful and sexy. Other men desired her, and she was a lady. Plus, Tania told him that she needed him. No one had ever told him that before. Lastly, there was Sherry. Sherry was an outlier, a rough but soft chick. She was a stripper, and she had the face and bod to pull it off. He wanted carnal knowledge of the curves and straightaways, the hills and valleys, and most importantly, he wanted to be putting it to her in the same apartment where he was also doing the pump-n-dump with Camille. Shane chuckled as he thought of his high school teachers who told him that he had no aspirations. After Shane hung up with Camille, he realized that he needed to set a meeting of the final four in order to not let too much time pass so that he could anchor any cold feet.

That next morning, he awoke to find Slob sitting on the couch watching cartoons as he ate a little breakfast while simultaneously toking off of a water pipe. Shane asked, "Hey are you just starting on that bong or finishing?"

Slob finished his inhale, held it for about five seconds and then released it while he said, "Just getting started, bro."

"Good. I have a serious question for you. Are you really in on the plan?"

"What plan?"

"You know, the plan to get some money from Camille's parents."

"Oh yeah, that. Yeah, I think so."

"Remind me again why Erin isn't doing it?"

"Ya know, man. She's just an addict. She's not a doer like us. One of the reasons why I love her, man."

"Maybe you and Erin are a lot more alike than you think."

"Whaddya mean?"

"Dude, I love you, bro, but you're a mess. You're no killer. An addict, a thief, a liar, and a scumbag—yeah, but not a killer."

"I don't wanna let you down, bro."

"Look, dude, I ain't one either. I don't want to kill anybody. I got some financial problems that are gonna drag me in. You don't got that, man. Why don't you sit this one out? In fact, forget that you ever heard anything about it. Okay?"

Slob thought for a few moments while he took in another bong load of sativa and said, "Dude, you're right. I'm a lover, not a fighter. If you're good with it. I'll forget about it and keep on truckin'. When you're a millionaire, remember your friend Joe."

Shane started to laugh as he said, "You're such a fucking mess."

Slob smiled with a big, crooked grin as he set the water pipe back on the table in front of him and eased back into the cushions.

*

The gang of five was now down to three. Camille paid for a room at a Simple Ten Motel so that they would have some privacy if they spoke quietly in order to finalize their plans to give and receive payment for the sins of the father. The three soon-to-be assassins gathered in room twenty-seven. Camille brought burgers, fries, and a couple of milkshakes from her work so that the boys would stay on task. The meeting started as two of them sat on the bed and one on the chair at the small table. Shane cleared his mouth with a swig of milkshake and said, "Well, Eric, you got your wish."

"What wish?"

"Sherry and Slob are out. It's only gonna be the three of us."

"For real?"

"Yep," Camille answered.

"They would've gotten in the way anyway. We don't need them. I have this all planned out. Are you ready to hear it?" Eric said.

Camille and Shane nodded as Eric got up from the chair and began to pace about the small room. He said, "I'm bringing a knife as a backup weapon, with my primary being a baseball bat."

Camille interrupted and said, "Dude, that is hardcore, but why not a gun?"

"Damn, let me talk. It's too loud, okay?"

"Oh, yeah."

Looking out the window he resumed as he turned back to his small audience, "We need someone other than us to buy some disposable gloves, like from the hardware store. We need some black masks that allow us to see and breathe. You know, the ones with the holes in the face."

"I can get those!" Shane answered.

"Listen, dumbass. Listen. I said somebody else." He continued to stare directly at Shane with a hardened scowl as he said, "You can get these things though...we need a couple rocks in a garbage bag that is double bagged. The two bags have to be big, at least thirty-three gallons. Can you do that?"

"I got it."

"We'll need someone else besides us to rent a car, like a small sedan. Whoever we come up with cannot know why they are renting the car. You both get that?"

Shane interrupted again and said, "My cousin can do it for me."

Ravaged with anger, Eric said, "Damn, dude. Do you wanna get pinched? You gotta start thinkin' clearly, or you will send us all to prison. We can't have anyone related to us, living with us, or sleeping with us rent the car, dude. We need a friend of a friend. Like that. Can you understand that?"

"He's got it. Now calm the shit down," Camille said.

"Shut the fuck up, Camille! You two need to get ready. For real. This is for keeps. Got it? Look, it takes about two hours to get to Mountain View. I don't want us lingering in town there, waiting for the Deagans to go to bed, and I want a cushion, so we will do it on a weekend, arriving after midnight at the house. We'll park on the street within other cars, and approach in black clothes and masked up. Camille will take us around to the backyard."

Camille slid to the edge of the bed and said, "Ooh, that sounds good. Then we just bum rush 'em, right?"

"Wait, hold on. Let me finish. We'll leave our street clothes there. Camille will then open the kitchen door with her house key. The three of us will go into the kitchen and then head to the bedroom, where I'll break your dad's arm or leg with the bat and then bring them both into the living room. Camille, you will wait in the living room until Shane and I bring them in, and then you turn on a light. Just one fuckin' light. Got it?"

"Yes," Camille said with exasperation.

"Then, Camille, you can tell 'em whatever you fucking wanna tell 'em. Shane will hold Mrs. Deagan. What's your mom's name, Camille?"

"Lisa."

"Shane will hold Lisa while I finish off your dad. Then we kill your mom. We'll take some valuables that aren't that valuable from the house. Camille, you will relock the door with your key from the outside as we leave. We'll change out of our black clothes and put them in the garbage bag along with the stolen shit. You two take the bag to the car and put it in the trunk. Camille, you will start the car once you are both inside, and then I'll break the kitchen door open by prying it with my knife. I'll sneak back and get in the backseat of the car, and we'll be outta there."

"Dang Eric. That's the bomb," Camille said as she quickly rose up off the bed.

"I like the details, dude. That's why we need you, man. Nice," Shane said as he worked to memorize the plan.

"Hold on. Listen up. Now, remember this: NO talking outside of the house or car, and DO NOT slam or shut any doors loudly. We'll stop on one of the bridges over Lake Benton; it will be around three by then. Camille, you'll come to a stop on the side of the highway and then pop the trunk. Shane, you'll jump out from the front passenger seat, grab the bag, close the trunk, and throw it over the railing. When ya hear a splash, get your ass back into the car, and we are almost home. We all go to work or whatever the next morning like nothin', and nobody says shit about it, ever!"

"Shit, dude. That was awesome!" Shane said.

"Damn, that was super good. We'll need to keep working at our jobs for the next year or two. It'll take time for the will to be dealt with, and then when I get the money, I will put it in an offshore account. After the killings are forgotten, I'll pay out the money to just you guys."

The three conspirators looked at each other with a sense of accomplishment and excitement, mirroring that of a board of a Fortune 500 company that just reviewed their latest positive quarterly sales numbers. They needed a week or two to get bit players involved without their direct knowledge of the murder plot and pick an actual date for the trip. The wheels were in motion to the point where the trio had easily crossed the divide.

*

Slob was sitting around watching his favorite soap opera when Jake came home for lunch. As Jake was warming up some leftover chicken in the microwave, Slob said, "Hey, man, I'm not involved in that murder deal no more."

Jake paused and said, "Well, that's good. Hopefully, it was all talk."

"Nope. Shane and them are gonna kill those people in the next few weeks, I think."

"You're shitting me. That's for real? Where are Camille's parents?"

"Mountain View, man."

"When is this supposed to go down?"

"I don't know, but real soon. I think."

When Jake finished lunch and was headed back to his new job working for ABC Construction, he stopped at a payphone outside of a mini-mart. He called the operator and asked to be connected to the Mountain View Police Department. The operator asked him to deposit ninety cents. After he dumped a dollar's worth of quarters into the slot, he heard the phone ringing. Suddenly, he heard the phone get picked up, and a woman said, "Mountain View Police Department, how can I help you?"

"I want to report a murder plot."

"Okay, can I get your name and phone number?"

Jake provided his name but informed the woman that he could not give a phone number as it was too risky. She then said, "I'm going to transfer you to a detective in the homicide division. Hold for a second."

The phone line went silent, and then a voice came on and said, "This is Detective Ruffin. Am I talking to Jake Angelo?"

Just then an automated voice came over the phone and asked that Jake deposit another dollar for additional time. Since Detective Ruffin could hear it as well, he quickly asked Jake to tell him the phone number at the payphone so that he could call him right back. Jake relayed the phone number and the line disconnected. Jake had just laid the receiver back on the hook when it rang. The Detective went through the pertinents and sought some detail on the alleged crime in order to identify Jake Angelo and to see if there was any legitimacy to the call and potential crime before he took any further steps. After he heard what Jake had to say, the detective asked to meet with him in Benton the following morning at seven before Jake had to be at work. Jake agreed to the meeting and set a location on the other side of town at an out-of-the-way breakfast joint. Detective Ruffin was familiar with it and said, "I'll be there around six forty-five."

Detective Ruffin was not sure if this report was the real thing or not, but he had a duty to find out. Since the caller was in another city's jurisdiction, and no crimes had happened in Mountain View yet, Detective Ruffin called a counterpart at the Benton Police Department that he had worked with in the past. Mike Wilson had been a detective in Benton for over ten years. He started with the department as a reserve officer after obtaining a degree from California State University. He worked his way up the ladder from patrol to detective and was not stopping there. Neal asked Mike, "How've you been?"

"Oh, I'm doing pretty good."

"Your wife and kids?"

"Also, good. Thanks."

"Hey, it's rally time, isn't it? Did you go to Sturgis again this year?"

"Not this year. I have too many honey do's."

Neal then recited the story that had been relayed to him a few minutes earlier by Jake Angelo. Neal pointed out that the Benton PD may have a conspiracy at this point, but he wanted to work the case to catch the perpetrators in action. Then, they would have attempted murder charges as well.

An attempted murder conviction carried a hefty penalty in California, and if these people were threats to the public, they needed to be culled. Mike liked the proposal and was more than willing to let Mountain View and the Jefferson County DA take the case since he was swamped with his own caseload. Mike said, "I like it. I'll see you in the morning at six forty-five."

CHAPTER 7.
CONFIDENTIAL INFORMANT

Secrets are really just emphasized stories to be shared with excitement at a later date.

*

Detective Ruffin parked his government ride in the parking lot of Babe's Blue Omelet House in the old part of the northwest end of Benton at six thirty-two. He wanted to be early in order to check the place out to see if this was an officer ambush or a real story. The story seemed legitimate, but one never knew. He walked the parking lot and visually inspected the contents of each car through the window. He was really looking for a person or persons waiting in a car or truck, lying in wait for an ambush. When everything seemed normal, he saw a suspicious car pull into the small lot. He could pick out a cop and his "department-issued ride" from a long way off. He waved at the driver, who replied with his middle finger. Neal started walking toward the car as it parked in a spot near the front door of the restaurant. As the car door opened, Neal said, "That's a helluva way to greet a friend."

Mike smiled and reached out to shake Neal's hand, and said, "Hey, no offense. You know I hate the po po."

"Yeah, yeah, I hear your ilk all the time."

The men shared a laugh as they headed inside at about six forty-seven. They both had been around long enough and seen enough to know that they didn't need to express a need to watch the room; they just did it. A waitress finally looked up and then yelled out, "Sit anywhere." She worked her way over to them with her focus on finishing her scribble on the latest breakfast order. As she looked up, she said, "Oh, I'm sorry, Mike, I didn't see that was you. I'll bring coffee in a sec."

"A regular, huh," Neal asked.

"Not really."

"Wait a minute...Nooo, you two," he asked as he moved his head in the direction of the waitress while nodding sideways.

Mike looked into Neal's face with irritation.

"Not going to answer, huh?"

The frivolity quickly faded away as a young man walked in, went and sat at the front counter, and ordered without a menu. The waitress returned to the cop's table at the same time with a pot of coffee. She poured them each a cup, and as she left the pot and two menus on the table, she said, "I'll be right back," as her eyes stalled, gazing upon Mike's face.

Neal motioned to her with his index finger before she turned to walk away, asking, "Can you come closer?"

As she stepped back and leaned in, he asked, "Can you see if that man, the man who just came in, sitting at the counter, is here to meet with Neal Ruffin?"

Marilyn nodded and headed out on her errand. Neal watched as he saw her deliver the question. The man looked calm and nodded his head slightly forward and back. Neal immediately got up and went to the man and asked if he was Jake. The man confirmed that he was, and the two shook hands as he was invited over to the table where Mike was still seated. When Jake approached, Mike stood up and greeted him upon arrival. Mike then sat back down and slid around to the middle of the table in the booth, allowing Jake to take the end so that he would not feel intimidated or trapped. Neal then asked, "Are you eating breakfast this morning?"

"Go ahead, I already ate. I'm just havin' coffee."

"We're doin' the same."

Neal pulled out a tape-recording device, laid it on the table, and asked, "Hey, we need to record this so that we can make an accurate police report. Are you okay with that?"

"Yeah, sure. Why not. Hey, look, I don't have a lot of time here, so I'm going to start."

"Okay. Great. Just let me do the intro on my recorder and then hit it."

"Um, okay, I have two roommates. One is Shane Summers, and the other is Joe Jenkins. Joe and Shane grew up together, and Shane and I worked together for several years. Anyway, Shane has a girlfriend who was from Mountain View. Her parents still live there. Shane is always looking for money. He and Camille...Camille Deagan—she's the girlfriend—came up with an idea to kill her parents in Mountain View and then get their stuff and money through their will. Shane and Camille discussed this with a bunch of people, I guess. I was never there when they did, but was told about it by Joe. Anyway, Joe's not in on it now. It's Shane, Camille Deagan, and another guy named Eric Larson."

Detective Wilson interrupted as the barrage of details started to wane and asked Jake, "Do you know when this murder is going to take place.?"

"I don't know. Anytime I think."

"Do you know how they are going to do it, then?" Detective Wilson asked.

"No, I don't," Jake answered as he took a sip of coffee.

"Can you get more information for us without spooking your roommates or Camille?" Detective Ruffin asked as he slowly tapped his index finger on the table.

Jake thought about it while looking distressed and said, "I just wanted to tell you guys and then be out of it."

"And we thank you for that, but we need more information in order to stop this killing. Understand?" Detective Wilson asked while turning his head back to Jake.

Jake nodded and slowly asked, "What is it that you want me to do?"

"We need you to find out who the intended victims are, when it's going to happen, where it is going to happen, and how," Detective Wilson said.

"I don't have any direct knowledge of any of this. I'm not supposed to know. I was told by my pot-smoking roommate, who was involved for a little while. How in the heck am I gonna get this kind of information?"

"Well, you're going to get it from your roommate Joe, and then we'll have him tell us the rest," answered Detective Ruffin.

"I'll work on it." As he looked at his watch, he said, "I'm going to be late for work, so I've got to go."

"Hold on. Here is my card with my phone number, and Detective Wilson will give you his direct line. We'll need to meet again as soon as you find out when and open Joe up to the idea of talkin' with us, okay? We have to do this quick so that nobody gets killed. You understand that, right?"

"I called you. Remember? So yeah, I get it. I'll call you this evening if I find out when it's goin' down."

"I have a cellphone that you can call any time of day or night if there is cell service where I'm at. I wrote it on the back. You can also call the Mountain View Police mainline and provide a message, and then they will relay the information to me. Just to reiterate, Jake, time is of the essence and in order to save the Deagans, we need to talk again this evening, even if you don't have anything new for me," Detective Ruffin said.

"Jake, uh, we are going to treat you as a confidential informant for right now so that your name isn't on any paperwork that could be provided to the public or through a records request or things of that nature," Detective Wilson said in a lowered and calm voice.

"Oh? Hey, I appreciate that. Will I have to testify if this goes to trial?"

Detective Ruffin answered, "Well, yeah. You may have to. First things first. Let's find out when and work on the rest. Okay?"

Jake confirmed the request as he stood up. Both detectives slid out of the booth seating to shake his hand and reassure him. As Jake walked out, he was of mixed emotions. He knew that he was doing the right thing, but he felt the weight of getting involved. He was now collaborating with the police. He was a snitch, and he was going to have to spend a bunch of time and endure a lot of stress over this fucking ordeal. Jake was mad and was driving a little erratic through traffic as he cussed at a few drivers and pedestrians alike. Jake's mind was spinning with ideas on how to give the cops what they wanted, save the Deagans, and be out of this situation as soon as possible. He had realized that the police could never talk to Slob. Slob was too stupid to keep this conspiracy under wraps, like he couldn't do already, without implicating himself.

Neal paid the coffee bill as Mike hit the restroom. Neal was waiting outside of the restaurant when Mike finally walked out.

"What took so long? That prostate problem again?"

"Oh, go fuck yourself!" he replied with a grin.

"Sens-a-tive! Oh, it was a quickie with your friend, the waitress. Did you pump her for information?"

Mike had heard all of the shit-slinging in the world but still laughed.

"Okay, I'm now being serious. Back on topic, what do you think?" Neal said.

"Well, I still think you're a dick."

"I've heard that before. Maybe I should work on myself?"

"Yeh, definitely. I meant it. There're classes for that." After a short pause, he resumed, "Hey, I'll cut some paper in about an hour. I won't submit it until you send me a copy of the audio. Then, I'll run it up the chain and route a copy to you. In the meantime, I think we wait to see what this guy says tonight. If he goes squirrely, I'll meet with him again."

"Sounds good. Can your department throw any resources into this?"

"Sure. We can always sit on the perps if you lose one or need help. Have you notified the potential vics yet?"

"I didn't know who they were until now. I'll write a report too, and send you a copy of that, and the tape. I'll meet with the Assistant District Attorney in the morning to run the case by him, and then I'll call you. How does that sound?"

"Sounds good."

"Alright my friend. Good to see you, and I'll talk to you soon. Thanks for the support as always, and watch your six."

*

The following morning found Jake working a roofing project on a house that ABC was building as a spec home. It was a long, hot day in Benton. The City of Benton lay along and around the Cascade River and had an extremely large lake to the north that was great for power generation and water activities, but neither the lake nor the water that ran through the town from it did anything to slow the oppressive heat that struck the city from spring to fall. Jake used sunscreen every day but was still sunburned after roofing that day. He stopped off to get some fast food and a twelve-pack of beer and headed for home. When he got there, he found Slob and his girlfriend scarfing down a pizza and already pretty loaded off of the devil's lettuce. Although Jake was unhappy with his current predicament, he was going to complete the mission to save victims who were unknown to him. Now was as good a time as any. He unboxed his double cheeseburger and laid it on a plate. He dumped his fries onto the plate next to the main course, cracked open a beer, and then took a seat on one of the recliners in the small living room that they shared. His food-ladened plate sat precariously on the top of his thighs, while his first beer was carefully placed on his TV tray that sat to his right. Slob and Erin barely seemed to notice him. Jake then said, "Hey, Erin, how's it going?"

"It's good, man."

"Hey, Slob, is Shane home yet?"

"He was, but he went over to Camille's for the night."

"I'm so glad you two aren't involved in that idea they have to get money,"

"Yeah, me too."

"When's that going down anyway?"

"What is going down?"

Jake calmed his nerves and took a breath for patience, and said, "Killing Camille's parents."

"Oh yeah, I don't know. Soon, I think."

"I want to know because I don't want to be here when it goes down in case it ain't clean. You know, if the cops get wind of it and end up here."

"Oh, yeah. They have to rent a car and get some stuff before they do it, so it'll be a week or two."

"Look, I don't know much about this deal, but I don't want to be involved. So, I'm going to stay at Angie's the night of the job and for a few days after. Don't tell Shane. He doesn't need to worry about me. Will you keep me in the loop so I can avoid any shit that may come out of this?"

"Like what kinda shit?"

"Going to jail kinda shit."

"Oh man, that ain't gonna happen, dude."

"Well, I dunno about that. I hope not, but will you tell me what's going on anyway?"

"Yeah, sure. No problem, my friend. No problem."

Jake had gotten a little more information than expected and hung around a couple more hours before he went over to Angie's for the night. Jake liked spending the night at his girlfriend's place, but on this night, he could make the phone call to Detective Ruffin, and he could do it in confidence.

*

"Hey, baby, I gotta tell you something."

"Is it bad?"

"No. No, everything with us is fine. It's about some work shit."

"Oh. Whaddya gotta tell me?"

"I'm involved in some things, and I can't tell you now. I need to use your phone, and I can't have you in the room when I do it."

"Why can't you tell me? I think that's crap. I wanna know what you are doing. Maybe I can help."

"Don't worry, baby. You just gotta trust me. Please?"

"I've had guys pull this on me before. What's going on?"

"I'm sorry about that. I am, but you gotta trust me, okay? Just for a couple weeks."

"Alright, but if you're lying to me..."

"I'm not! This is serious shit. I'm not calling some girl or some other bullshit like that."

"Okay! Okay! I will take my shower now while you make your call," she said and turned to head to the bathroom. She looked back with reluctance to see Jake holding the phone and motioning for her to leave the room.

Jake called the cellphone number given to him, and Detective Ruffin answered.

"You have to promise me, man. You have to promise me that you won't involve Joe in any way."

"Why's that?"

"You might get him killed, that's why. I need your promise before I say anything else."

"Look, I'm not interested in Joe at this point. I promise to keep him out as long as he doesn't get involved further. You good now?"

"Yeah, I'm good."

"Did you find out anything new tonight?"

"I found out that the three of them are lookin' for someone to get them a rental car and some other stuff, so it may be a week or two. As I said, they want to kill Camille's parents, and now I am sure that they want to kill them at their house in Mountain View. I'll know more in the next few days. Trust me on this. I'll come through."

"You did good. I appreciate all that you have done for me and the Deagans so far. We should talk again tomorrow afternoon or evening."

"Alright. I'll call you."

The following morning Detective Ruffin checked in on his office to organize his thoughts, review his messages, work a couple of things on the other cases he was carrying, and then check himself out for a meeting at the DA's office. The PD was near the main street of downtown, so he needed only to go just a few blocks to the Jefferson County Courthouse, where the DA's office was housed. Detective Ruffin drove the short distance so that he had his vehicle with him in case he received an urgent call for service. He parked in police parking and made his way to the second floor to meet up with Assistant District Attorney Don Mavis.

The courthouse was a mixture of two parts and two eras of architecture. The original building was from the mid-eighteen hundreds, while the new addition was from the fifties in an art deco style. Don Mavis was expecting Neal and had asked that the DA's Chief Investigator Corwin Scott sit in for assistance, if necessary, and as a liaison between the Mountain View Police Department (MVPD) and the DA's office sworn law enforcement section.

The Investigations side of the house consisted of six investigators who were sworn police officers, and each had more than a decade's worth of law enforcement experience in other law enforcement agencies before being recruited up to the District Attorney's office. The Investigations Unit allowed for a peace officer liaison capability among law enforcement and law enforcement agencies. They also provided investigative support to local or state law enforcement agencies, the investigative capability to take over cases from those agencies, and as a police department to initiate law enforcement actions where appropriate or necessary. This specialized unit worked for the chief law enforcement officer of the county, or "Top Cop," as it was called, which was the elected District Attorney.

The front desk secretary let Detective Ruffin into the office past the ironically poor security measures. He quickly grabbed a foam cup and took advantage of all of the hot coffee he could drink for a dime. He knew where he was going as he had been there many times over the years and arrived to find the door open and Assistant District Attorney (ADA) Don Mavis seated in his big black leather chair behind his desk and on the phone, engaged in a cordial but firm discussion.

Chief Investigator Corwin Scott was seated at the front of the desk and waiting quietly like he always did. He was the boss of the Investigations Unit, but not the boss, and he kept his at-will job because he knew his place. Don Mavis waved Detective Ruffin in and said in a whispered voice as he still held the phone to his face, "Have a seat."

Neal took a seat on the prompt, and Don told the person on the other end of the phone that he had to go as he had a meeting to start and hung up. Just then, four-term District Attorney Brian DeLacey walked in and said, "We have a murder plot, huh? Well, let's hear it."

District Attorney DeLacey was well-liked in Jefferson County, as he was able to temper justice when needed and apply it harshly when necessary. Some said that Brian DeLacey was to be revered and feared. He liked to hunt and fish and work the political game. He was a former criminal defense attorney, so he knew compassion, yet he was a man who knew when to say "no" as well. His favorite saying, when he was angered, was, "Don't tug on Superman's cape; he might turn around." When that happened, even the power brokers of the secured classes in Jefferson County, such as those in business, politics, media, law enforcement, and the well-heeled, would be no match for the lightning storm to come. DeLacey was in the room to save time on hearing about his biggest general concerns: politics and optics. He did not like surprises, especially from the media, so there he sat.

"Hey guys, thanks for seeing me. We have the planning of a murder of a married couple here in Mountain View by some dirtbags in Benton."

"Cassell County?" Chief Scott said.

"Yeah. The facts and circumstances, in this case, involve potentially unreliable people, another jurisdiction, and the herculean task of getting a mutual idea brought to market as a confirmed conspiratorial agreement and then allowing that loosely tied web to move into action."

"Are you thinking about letting this proceed and catching them in the act?" DeLacey asked.

"Yes, that's where I was going. Cassell County doesn't want the conspiracy case unless we wrap it in a bow and have sworn testimony from a trial, so we let this progress to the end."

"Conspiracies are tough to make in State Court, unlike under federal law. Those guys use that and obstruction for just about everything," DeLacey said.

"More importantly, the health, safety, and welfare of David and Lisa Deagan is potentially at stake, especially this far along in the apparent planning of a murder. As a reminder, using private citizens as decoys is dangerous, and there is liability for those who put them there," Mavis said.

"We won't let anything happen," Ruffin answered.

DA DeLacey said, "No guts, no glory. You guys make sure that it doesn't go south," as he gave them the look.

They asked Detective Ruffin to keep them in the loop and offered him all the support they could provide. ADA Mavis was still concerned for the victims in the matter and said, "Neal, contact the Deagans today and set up a meeting at their house for tomorrow morning at a time of their convenience."

"I will take care of it and let you know by email and phone when the meeting is, and where," as he gave ADA Mavis and Chief Scott a copy of his initial report on the matter.

*

These pieces of paper were the beginning of what a "case" is really about—a collection of pages from a police report and its addendums containing details of the crime(s), names and addresses of witnesses and victims, volumes of legal filings, court activity notes, case memoranda, and confidential attorney work product. Deep in those papers loaded with scattered words are the witnesses who are burdened with their civic duty and what comes with it, the impacts on the lives of crime victims, the destiny of the accused hanging in the balance, and the expenditure of taxpayer funding to move this gargantuan task through the slow grind of the monolithic and yet most perfect form of crime and punishment system ever developed.

A prosecutor's foremost job is to seek the truth, not to gain convictions. Getting a conviction is relatively easy, but seeking truth in the pursuit of justice is not. A real prosecutor must know when to punish and when not to while seeking, presenting, and living in actual truth on behalf of his most important client, The People. As such, they are charged to act on their behalf in all matters allowable under the law with zeal and extreme caution. Anything else is just deadweight or a tyrant.

The report that Detective Ruffin presented contained the address of the Deagans with some physical descriptions of both David and Lisa, developed from their California driver's license records. Detective Ruffin asked if he could make a call to his counterpart in Benton to give an update. Corwin Scott rose and told Detective Ruffin to follow him as he took him to his office. Scott stepped inside his office space to the right and then turned to Detective Ruffin and said, "Make yourself at home and take as much time as you need." Neal entered the Chief's office while Corwin retreated and closed the door behind him. Detective Ruffin was only able to leave a message on Detective Wilson's phone.

"So, who are you assigning to this case?" DA DeLacey asked.

"I don't have room in my caseload since I have six trials coming up in the next several months. Some of those are estimated at two weeks of trial a piece. Who are you thinking about?" Mavis said.

This was in a jurisdiction where the presiding judge did not like to break a trial up into specific days of the week or even parts of days. She felt that it caused the prolongation of a trial event and disproportionately disrupted the lives of jurors and witnesses over the needs of the parties or the court. Therefore, it was standard practice, and more importantly, set forth in the local rules, that trials by jury were to proceed and conclude upon consecutive days, subject to holidays, emergencies, or the presiding judge's modified order.

"Does Ton have the time to handle this case," Brian DeLacey asked as he stared at Don, waiting for a confirmation.

"I think so; you know he is always pretty swamped, but this needs his touch and skill. Plus, we can have Linda Rakowski take over his arraignment and pre-trial cases, if necessary," ADA Mavis answered.

"That'll work. Remember, he's pretty picky about other people messing up his cases, so keep that in mind," DA DeLacey said and got up and headed to the door with a smile.

Just then, Detective Ruffin poked his head back into Don Mavis's office as DeLacey had just exited and said, "Thanks for the office. I'll keep you posted. Hey Don, you're taking this case, right?"

"I don't have the time, but we're assigning Ton."

"Excellent! Not that I don't want you, Don, but Ton is also very good." He then smiled and said, "When I get the meeting set up for tomorrow with the Deagans, do I just tell Ton?"

"That's fine. I'll be going too. Ton and I will ride over together and meet you there, so send us an email with the time if you would," Don answered.

"Will do."

Detective Ruffin made the short drive back to his office at MVPD and looked through the white pages of the telephone book to see if David and Lisa Deagan were listed. Like most people in a small town, the Deagans wanted to be found in the phone book. Neal called the number on the off chance that one or both of them were home. If not, he would leave a message with his name and number on their answering machine so they could call him back. Since Detective Ruffin wasn't sure as to whether or not Camille had access to the house or was currently visiting her parents, he needed a different reason for calling while seeking a return call on the answering machine since inbound calls and recorded calls were on a speaker. The phone rang, and by the third ring, the automated answering machine picked up and the voice of a man stated that it was the Deagan residence and a beep sounded.

Neal said, "This is Neal Ruffin from the Mountain View Police Department, and I'm calling you to see if you witnessed anything in the neighborhood over the last few days. A couple of items of property have been stolen, including a dog. Please give me a call back," as he slowly provided his work and cell numbers and hung up.

He then decided that he needed to try and track one of the folks down at their work as well. Neal had been in Mountain View for over a decade and knew a lot of people, but he did not know the Deagans. He asked a couple of the people in the police department who had lived there their entire lives, and by co-worker number two, he had a lead. Sheila Gorga said,

"Yeah, I know Lisa."

"Do you know her well?"

"My whole life. We went to school together. Is she in trouble? What are you calling her for?"

"No, she's not in trouble. She may have witnessed something, and I need to talk to her. Do you know where she works?"

"The Sommerset Bank."

"What does she do there?"

"She was a teller forever but has been an assistant manager for about five years."

"You're a lifesaver. Thanks!"

Back at his desk, Neal called the bank and asked to speak to Lisa Deagan. The call was transferred, and a woman's soft voice came on the line and said, "Sommerset Bank, Lisa Deagan. How can I help you?"

Neal identified himself and said, "Do you live at 725 Blumenthal Street?"

"Why yes, I do. My goodness, is something wrong?"

"I'm calling about some items that were stolen recently in your neighborhood, and I'm talking to all of the neighbors to see if they saw anything."

"Oh, that's too bad. In our neighborhood?"

"Yes, I'm looking for witnesses and desperately need to speak with you and your husband to see if either of you may have seen something."

"I don't know if we can help. I haven't seen or heard anything about stuff being stolen. We're always at work, so I don't know."

Detective Ruffin clicked his pen as he waited and then said, "I would like to meet with you both at your house before either of you go to work in the morning."

"Okay. I guess. How long will it take? Just so I can tell my boss what time I'll be in for work."

"Thirty minutes tops. Is your husband's schedule flexible as well?"

"Oh yeah, it's no problem."

"How does eight tomorrow morning sound?"

"I guess so. We don't know anything, but it will be nice to meet you. We'll see you then."

"Before you go, I have to tell you that this is an ongoing investigation and is confidential. Don't talk to anyone else other than your husband about it and please tell him to keep it confidential as well."

"Oh, uh, okay. Sure."

"Excellent. I'll see you both in the morning at eight."

Neal quickly followed up on his call with an email to Ton and Don confirming the meeting with the potential victims for the next morning at eight sharp with the address. Since email was new to the office, and was dominated by the sharing of cute animal pictures and wild stories, Neal made a follow-up phone call to Deputy District Attorney (DDA) Ton Hogan. Ton had just gotten back to his office after a long day in court and a myriad of other DDA duties that never seemed to end in a busy office. "Ton Hogan speaking."

"Hey, I sent you and Don an email with the meeting time and address a while ago, and I wanted to make sure that you remind him. I'll see you then."

"Uhm, okay. I'll print that out, and, uh, I'll remind him. See ya then."

Ton jumped up from his desk and headed down the hallways of the building to the ADA's office. As he arrived, he saw the good news. Don's door was open, and he wouldn't have to wait. He peeked in and said, "Hey, Don, got a minute?"

"Uh, yeah, sure. Everything alright?" Don said while looking up from the papers on his desk.

"No, I'm good. Hey, I just got a call and an email from Neal over at the PD, and evidently, there's a meeting at someone's house in the morning... and I'm guessing that I'm supposed to be there?"

Don laughed and said, "Yeah, perfect timing, take a seat. I

was just going to fill you in on this here shortly. We've got a murder for financial gain about to be perpetrated in the next week. The victims live here in town. There are three people involved in the plot out of Benton. Two males and a female. The female is from here. She and her two friends are planning to kill her parents in order to get their money."

"Interesting. What do you need from me?"

"I'll fill you in on the details in the morning. Meet me in the parking lot here at seven-thirty, and we can grab a java and talk about the details as we go and inform the parents that their only kid wants them dead. Should be fun."

"Oh yeah, real fun. They don't know anything about it?"

"We don't think so, but we'll find out in the morning, I guess."

"Good times. I'll be here a little early."

CHAPTER 8.

SHE'S NO ANGEL

The wisdom of evildoers is to do unto others without shame or remorse in return for what may have been done unto them.

*

Shane finally found someone who could rent a car without any close connection to him. He had a friend from high school who owed him a favor. That guy was Maurice Collins, who went by Mo.

"Hey, Mo. You got something?" Shane said after answering the phone.

"Hey, dude, I got that shit done for ya. Yeah, you'll be happy about this."

"Awesome. It ain't hot, right?"

"C'mon, man, I wouldn't do you like that."

"Why not? Everybody else does."

"Look, I got a cousin who dated a guy for a couple of years that did a lot of shady things."

"Alright."

"This guy never had nothin', but at the same time, everything. He had no job, but he was strapped with cash at all times. He would do anything for a buck, but he seemed to have a code of ethics when it came to keeping his mouth shut. Ya know—if he was financially incentivized."

"I like where you're goin'."

"He got a credit card and driver's license with a fake name, with a picture of a dude that he looks like. He's willing to rent the car for two days under his fake name and drop it off in the Kmart parking lot with the keys left under the driver's seat."

"How much?"

"A grand. Five hundred for the rental and an overhead fee of another five. Oh, in cash."

"Shit. That is some big dough, bro."

"You want it or not?"

"Nah, man, I'll take it. When do I get it?"

"Well, you gotta pay first. You know you ain't gettin' it without that."

"Yeah, I know. It's a lot of fucking money, bro, but I'll get it. What are the deets?"

"Hey, bro, you better come up with the paper, you know what I mean? This fucker don't play none."

"I will, okay! I will. Where do I get the fucking car?"

"It'll be in the Kmart parking lot. In front of Goldens' Car Stereos on the second, right after noon. It'll be a green sedan. It'll have a soda cup sittin' on the roof and the keys under the driver's seat."

"Thanks, Mo."

"Look. You gotta take it back to the same place when time runs out and leave the keys under the driver's seat where ya found 'em. Before all that, they want money, okay? Look, they'll send someone to get the cash from your girl at her restaurant. They want it in an envelope and placed in a take-out order. The person will ask for her by name. She better be there if you know what I'm sayin'."

"Thanks, man."

"Yeah, bro. We even now."

"Yep."

"Last thing, get the money ready now. When they get the money, you're up."

*

The parameters of use determined that the window of opportunity was eight days away on September 3, 1995. The only problem was the ability to come up with the thousand dollars in cash.

Camille bit the bullet and chose to push off her bills and take what she had saved and what she had at the moment to finance the ride to inevitable financial freedom and reckoning.

*

It was a busy morning in Mountain View as Don and Ton waited in line at their favorite coffee shop. As the two waited, they were quiet due to the abundance of prying ears. The pair eventually obtained their favorite drinks and were now back in their county car heading over to the Deagans' house.

"We don't want to share too much information. This is a meeting to break the news, get information, and their cooperation," Don said while looking out the passenger window.

"Understood. Who will lead, and what do you want from me?"

"Neal will lead, and I'll work on earning their trust. I want you to be subdued, but jump in when you think it's necessary. Remember, these people may be stunned, and they may not believe us. If that's the case, it'll be a longer discussion."

"I guess we'll have to improvise then, eh?" Ton said as he turned to Don.

"It all depends on how hard the news hits and where the couple are at emotionally."

"So. We are winging it?"

"No. We know what we want, although we may need to make some modifications on the fly."

"Is that not the same thing?" Ton asked as he peered slightly to his right to see the slight irritation.

"I suppose it is."

"Do you know where I'm turning next?"

"Turn on Pine, and it should be on your left a couple streets down. It's 725 Blumenthal."

After a couple of turns and straightaways, they were driving down Blumenthal and watching the house numbers to the left side of the street. As the numbers ascended, they knew they were close when Don spotted Detective Ruffin's police car sitting out front of a nice single-story house that was well-kept. It was yellow with brown trim. It had a diminutive fence along its front right side to encase the side area and backyard. Next to the house was an entry gate on a concrete path from the driveway along the side of the garage to the walk-in door. The fence gate was just past the walk-in door as the concrete walkway continued beyond the gate and on around the back of the house to the left where it ended at the kitchen door. As they slowly passed the Deagan home, they saw that Neal was still in the driver's seat waiting for their arrival as he looked at his notes.

As the prosecutors parked, Neal got out of his car and waited for them to do the same. The three huddled quickly for a short game plan, and then they headed for the front door. Neal knocked, and it suddenly opened as David Deagan stood there. Neal looked at the man's face and said, "David Deagan?" David confirmed with a nod and asked the three men into his living room. Lisa had coffee and cups ready as she asked them if they wanted one. Two of the guests declined, Ton being the exception. Most law enforcement were paranoid about having something slipped into their food or drink. It was standard operating procedure to decline out of hand, even if it came from a victim. Ton was a former sworn police officer and had years of law enforcement experience and understood the reticence, but he also did not like the appearance of paranoia as it could be taken as a display of superiority.

"Thank you. I'll take a cup, please," Ton said as he met her at the coffee table, where she filled his cup and raised it up to meet his welcoming hands.

David did not wait for his wife to finish her gesture before he asked, "So what can I do for you guys?"

Don was good with people and actually really cared for them, so he brought his voice down and said, "Thank you for entertaining our visit, and I respect your time. I'd like to have Mrs. Deagan and you take a seat if you would be so kind."

David immediately understood that he was a bit haughty and said, "I apologize for my directness, but I like to get down to brass tacks. So, I suspect this is about something more than a lost dog or something being stolen in the neighborhood. Am I right?"

"Well, yes. You're correct. Um, I'm going to be candid here. First, no one has been injured or killed, but we're here under some grave circumstances. Several days ago, we were notified of a murder plot that is to take place in the next few days in Mountain View and, since I cannot say this in a soft way... it's to take place at this house," Detective Ruffin said.

Lisa let out a little shriek and said, "Oh my! Here? Who would be killed here?"

"Let them explain."

Detective Ruffin looked at them as somber as a funeral procession and said, "I'm sorry to say it's both of you."

"Is it that dirtbag, Luke Johnson?" David asked as he looked intently at the detective.

"I know Luke and we don't believe he is involved. It's three people from the Benton area."

"Who would want to kill us from Benton?" Lisa asked.

David was silent and looked down at the floor.

Detective Ruffin's eyes caught David's realization of what could be happening, as did DDA Hogan.

"Is Camille involved in any way?" David asked.

"Unfortunately, she is," the detective answered.

"Of course, she is. And we thought she was doing so much

better," Lisa said while shaking her head.

"You're not surprised?" ADA Mavis asked.

"Our daughter has always been unhappy. She cares little about others and a lot about herself. For most of her life, she blamed us for her woes. So, no, we're not surprised," David answered.

There was a long pause as the news soaked into the fabric of the heart of the couple marked for death.

Lisa eventually broke the silence and said, "When she moved to Benton for work, we thought she would be happier. She always delighted in being amid the troubled kids and is also easily led. Do you know why she wants to kill us?"

The three law enforcement officials were not expecting the Deagans to be so undaunted, but it made it a lot easier to conduct business. Detective Ruffin provided a synopsis of what he knew as Lisa listened intently, and David got angrier.

After the plot was revealed, the intervention to stop the would-be murderers was at play. It was now time for the ask. Detective Ruffin and the two prosecutors laid out the necessity to catch their daughter and her two male accomplices in the act. That meant that they would be arrested after the trio, or a portion of the trio, entered the house to commit the murders. With hearts already soaked and a reminder of the embedded stinger long covered in scar tissue, the Deagans were all in. They had been done with the guilt and rebelliousness, and now with the plan to kill them for a little money. The ask was answered in the affirmative. They were done with their only child.

"What would happen if the three of them are arrested now?" David asked.

Don answered, "If they were arrested now, it would likely be for conspiracy to commit murder, which is going to be difficult to make at this point, and they would only be charged in Cassell County."

"Okay. So, we just sit here and wait to be killed?" David asked.

"No. But we need them to take further affirmative steps to carry out the crime in Jefferson County," Don said.

"Isn't that what I just said?"

"If I may. We'll set a trap to catch them in the act. In order to do that, we need them to come into your house to kill you. Now hold on...Let me finish. The caveat to that is you two won't be here, of course. You'll be in a hotel room in town, but we do need the use of your house to catch them. Is that something you're willing to do?" Don quickly said.

"I see this deal isn't so simple. We aren't happy about setting up our daughter, but we ain't gonna sit back and let this shit happen either. So yeah, we'll help. We'll give you the key to the house. Detective, will you be here when they come?" David then said.

"Yes, I'll be waiting with a couple of officers."

David and Lisa let that sink in for a few seconds and then said, "Okay. Do you know when this is going to take place and when we are supposed to move into the hotel?"

"We don't know the exact date and time as of yet, but it'll be in the next week. The planning is complete for the suspects, but it is contingent on a car rental. Please pack your things today so that you are ready. As soon as we find out that the car is rented, we'll contact you immediately and get you to the hotel," Neal said.

"I sure hope that no one gets injured or killed out of this stupidity," David said with his head bent down to the floor.

"I hope not, too. We'll plan for every contingency so that nothing happens to anyone, including your daughter," ADA Mavis answered.

"That's good. We don't want anyone, including Cami, to be hurt or killed," Lisa said.

"Thank you for the offer of your house key; we will need that. We'll also need you to park your cars where you usually park them when we pick you up," Detective Ruffin said.

"I can give you an extra key now," David said as he fumbled in the kitchen drawer for the spare. His hand eventually found success, and he delivered on his commitment.

"I'm going to have to tell you not to speak with nor mention this to anyone. No family, no friends, no one. Even if they don't live around here, do you both understand?"

"I understand. We won't tell a soul until after our daughter and her lowlife friends are in jail," David said.

"If Camille does this, what kind of punishment is she looking at?" Lisa asked Don while looking at David.

"Well, there are a lot of factors, but generally for attempted murder...fifteen to life," ADA Mavis answered, as his cheeks rose, lips pursed, and his eyes squinted, trying to portray compassion.

"Are we finished for the morning? I have to go to work," David asked.

"I know this has been a lot, but we need one more indulgence if you would? Can we see the layout of your house?" ADA Mavis answered.

"Sure. Go ahead. I'm going to work. You can lock up when you're done."

The government agents also wanted to see what lights were left on at night, if any, and to take a tour of the back and side yard areas to get a good grasp of ingress and egress to the house from those areas. Lisa stayed and explained their normal habits. Once the tour was complete, Lisa felt exhausted. Don, Neal, and Ton thanked her for their hospitality as they expressed their condolences for what had been and for what was about to be. Business cards were given by all three men to Lisa. They were also given an extra business card for Victim Witness Advocate Angelique Perez, who also worked under the umbrella of the District Attorney's Office.

Ton said, "Angelique will help you and David along in the process, starting with the acquisition of the hotel room, a ride over there, and any other support that you may need."

The government finally filed out of the front door, whereupon the detective and the prosecutors made the usual parting statement about keeping in touch. Don and Ton remained stern as they neared the street. Ton peered over and saw Neal looking at him askew, as a smirk arose on Neal's face only to be seen by the two prosecutors to let them know that he was pleased about how it all went.

*

Once the men were out of sight, Lisa cried as she burdened herself with the notion that she was a horrible mom. At his office, David had fought back his tender emotions for his only daughter as his mind thought of the shitbirds that his daughter seemed to collect and the self-loathing that she possessed, which always roiled out onto other lives. They both really had hopes that their Camille was going to turn things around in another town with a good job. A job with real responsibility, but alas, it now seemed that it was never meant to be.

That night the couple was able to share their emotions while they hugged for a short eternity. The joyous memories of young love, a young family, and a child that would enrich their life came thundering from their hearts while coming to full rest in their minds. The emotions melted into the confines of their thoughts and brought forth the eternal and exhausting war between emotions and logic. The parents of the lost girl pressed their foreheads together in a show of love and solidarity. As they swayed back and forth, they waited for a true path forward into peaceful waters. The continuing current was still at an imminent boil, as they felt reluctance to destroy a daughter that they still loved, but they also knew right from wrong and had the intestinal fortitude to exercise it. They would not wait to be slain by an unforgiving, spoiled, miserable girl and her vulture friends. They pronounced at once that they would prevail and that they were to blame for many things in their life, but this...this was not one of them.

CHAPTER 9.

OFFENSE DEFENSE

In any staged display, the steps and their sequence must be choreographed in order to achieve success.

*

On one of the rare nights that Shane wasn't spending the night at Tania or Camille's place, he was sipping on a beer after having just eaten dinner when the phone rang. He answered the phone to hear, "We got the money. You got the car from September second to the fourth. Do everything you've been told. If you don't, you'll be scratched off. Ya know what I'm sayin'." Then he heard a click, and the phone line went dead.

Shane pressed the hook switch and regained a dial tone as he dialed Camille's phone number. She picked up immediately, and Shane said, "It's set. We've got all the stuff and the car."

"For Saturday?"

"Yep. Saturday at noon. We've only got three days until we're meeting with your parents for the last time. We'll talk more tomorrow with Eric."

"Yeah. Okay. Hey, honey bunny, are you coming over tonight? I'm horny...."

"No. I wish I could, but I'm really tired and sore from work today. Maybe tomorrow night, okay?"

"Ooh, okay. Tomorrow. I'll give you some special luvin' before Sunday."

"Okay. Okay. I gotta go."

"I love you, baby."

Shane paused as the man of general appeasement felt conflict on par with his grave undertaking and was compelled to answer, "Me too."

When that call was over, he saw his two roommates sitting in the kitchen having ice cream. Thinking nothing of it, he dialed the next number. Tania answered the phone, and he said, "Hey, I'm on my way over."

"Oh, good. I can't wait to see you. Bring some KFC for dinner."

"I just ate, but I could eat a little more, I guess. For just me and you?"

"For everyone, you dumbass. If KFC is super busy, get some Chinese. You know that Angel likes those shrimps in that sauce. That spicy sauce. Get that, then."

Shane hung up and grabbed his things as he told his boys to have a good night and he would see them later. Jake was working over a bowl of chocolate ice cream as Shane walked out. After he finished and rinsed his bowl and spoon, he said, "I'm going over to Angie's to get my dick wet. I'll see you tomorrow."

Slob was still eating his rocky road ice cream with portions of it running down his shirt as he waved goodbye to Jake and then resumed his carefree ways.

*

Shane knocked on Tania's front door. The door opened as Tania's mom said, "It's about time. What took so damn long?"

Shane ignored her as he sidestepped her to get inside and share the news. Tania raced up to him and gave him a kiss and said, "You got dinner, right? I hope so, 'cause the kids are really hungry, and mom is being such a bitch."

"Yeah. I got the Chinese."

"Let me feed the kids and mom, then tell me what's going on."

As the pair sat down to eat with Grandma and the kids, she asked, "Is it finally happening?"

"We're on. We get the car and do the deed on the third and will be in the clear once we are back here. I think the money will come a lot faster than Camille thinks it will. When it does, I'll get it from her, and we're out of here!"

Tania smiled and said, "Finally. I'll be glad when you're not porking that skank anymore. Who knows what kind of VD you can get from that."

"Hey, the things I do for you! It's pretty gross, and I throw up in my mouth after every fucking job I have to do with her. Thank goodness I've got some good cooter to wash it down with."

Tania rolled her eyes toward her mom and answered, "Yeah, you do, and don't forget it. Hey, Mom, did you hear that?"

"What? You've found the one guy that's got the beaver fever and likes your pussy? You seem to collect 'em."

"No. Well, yeah, that too, but that we're about to get the money."

"Well, looky there. That cooter, as he calls it, is worth something after all."

*

Jake knocked on Angie's door as he made the porch landing. She quickly let him in, and he headed for her phone. He immediately dialed Detective Ruffin on his cell. Once again, he caught Neal in his house in bed, working his way toward a restful break from his daily activities. "Detective Ruffin" was spoken into the phone after he was able to get the large flip phone open and the "Call" button pressed. As Neal heard Jake's voice, he said, "Okay, slow down. Slow down. Do you have a solid date?"

"Yep. They pick up the car on Saturday the second. They'll be heading your way sometime the next day."

"Are you sure?"

"As sure as I can be. That's what I know."

"Who told you?"

"I overheard Shane telling Camille over the phone. The best you're gonna get. Right?"

"You did great! Nice job. Okay, now you have to go about your business. I'll be coming down to Benton to talk with some people, and we may need to meet again."

"Really? What for now? I just did what you asked. I'm done."

"Yeah, almost. There are a couple more things I need your help on. You've done a great job so far, and I'm grateful. But don't get weak-kneed on me now. Get some rest, and I'll talk with you soon. The hard part is done, Jake. The hard part is done."

"Alright. Alright. I gotcha, man. I'm just caught in a shit sandwich, and my nerves are shot."

*

At eight a.m. Ton Hogan's desk phone rang as he came back from getting a cup of coffee down the hall. He answered the phone, and Neal said, "Hey, we have a date for the car pickup in the Deagan matter."

"We do? Great. When is it?"

"My CI called last night and told me he overheard Shane on the phone. Pickup of the car is for the second, and the hit is confirmed for the next afternoon or night. That's Sunday the third."

"Good job! I have some court appearances this morning, but I want to go over to the house at noon to see your plan and the placement of everybody. Do you mind?"

"Noon...yeah, I can do it if we're in and out."

"Yeah, quick on the details and placements. Just want to make sure I have a visual on the plan."

DDA Hogan knew that even when you think the matter is shut tight as far as making the beyond-a-reasonable-doubt standard for conviction, the wildest arguments can be made by skilled and even unskilled defense attorneys. The results could make for a hung jury or, alternatively, a full acquittal with a unanimous "not guilty" verdict.

Neal was sure that his work in public safety had value. He was the tip of the spear, but he only did the initial dirty work—the heavy lifting took place after it was handed to the District Attorney's office. He also knew that most cops thought the Deputy DAs were picayune and lazy, and some were, but cases needed to proceed to court and to juries with no rough edges. A police officer's reputation, the public trust, and the justice system's participants deserved no less.

Ton had his morning pre-trial calendar at eight-thirty. Most of the defense attorneys in the courtroom were public defenders who also worked for the County of Jefferson. Same employer, sometimes friends with the prosecutors on a personal level, sometimes bitter enemies, but almost always fierce advocates for their clients. The Public Defenders represented individuals who were found to be "indigent" based on income and assets. Sometimes, that standard fluctuated, but it was typically not an issue since most people didn't have access to the amount of money needed to pay for attorney representation. Most importantly, the Sixth Amendment to the US Constitution requires it. Most of the hardworking people in the Public Defender's office believed in the Constitution, while a small group were just gullible cartoons who never understood that they were drenched in bias and not fact. The job eats lawyers, especially those in the group who just do not get that people can and do evil things. Even though they are typically overworked, rarely win a trial, and exist as county employees who don't quite fit in since they work for the man and then fight the same man every day, they are serious people who possess extraordinary stamina.

On this morning, Public Defenders Lori Swain, Joe Tan, and Ting Bellows were in the courtroom that reeked of fear, body odor, and resentment, with a trace of history and a tinge of justice. They were representing the majority of the accused on the calendar. Ting Bellows and Ton Hogan worked a lot of the same cases. Both were believers in their cause and were workaholics. There were several private criminal defense attorneys present who worked the trial court systems as well. Ting had a lot of respect for Ton, as did Ton for Ting. In fact, Ton was well-liked by the defense bar and other attorneys in the county, so much so that they eventually made him the president of the local bar association.

The election for president had occurred while Ton missed the meeting and election, and therefore, the chance to agree or disagree to be placed on the ballot, while he and Neal worked the plan to capture three assassins at 725 Blumenthal Street in two days.

Detective Ruffin had called David Deagan earlier in the day and asked if he would be home for lunch and, if not, whether they could let themselves into his house at that time. David quickly agreed and said that he would meet them there at the noon hour. When they met him at the front door, Neal said, "Hello, David, thanks for letting us in. We have a date. We'll need you to move to the hotel anytime tomorrow or Sunday by noon."

"You've got a date, huh? She's going through with it then," as he shook his head in disappointment.

"I'm sorry, but it looks like they are. You should be back in your home by Monday afternoon."

"What do you mean should?"

"It depends on how it all progresses. We may need the house a little longer," Neal carefully said while looking about the living room.

David could read between the lines, knowing that if someone was injured or killed, there would be a delay in getting back into their house and more guilt to bear. Neal then said, "We don't want to take up more of your time during lunch, but can you give us some privacy? We have a couple of quick things to go over, and you shouldn't be a witness to the discussion in order to retain integrity and confidentiality."

"Yeah, sure. Do what you gotta do. I'll be on the back patio."

David walked out through the kitchen door into the backyard and took a seat on the bench.

"We'll set up around one on Sunday. We'll have some lights and the television on during the day," Neal said. He then winked and added, "And no, we won't be watching football!"

"Yeah, sure. Well, it's better than staring at each other! Right?" Ton said while he looked over the floorplan of the living room and kitchen.

"We'll have the shades slightly cracked open to provide an appearance that the Deagans are home. We will have our unmarked police cars parked down the street. The captain has stepped up patrols for the evening and night. We'll have uniformed officers waiting in the wings to provide quick assistance from the patrols in the vicinity."

"Sounds good. Now, I'm not trying to be an asshole, but this is what I want so that we have no loose ends at trial. I want the primary participants all the way inside the house. Let 'em come down the hall and into the bedroom. I don't want to hear a whiny defense that they were just visiting and were heading to Camille's bedroom for the night."

"You don't want much, do ya?"

"Yeah, I know, it's easy for me to say...Okay, I want video rolling of them coming into the house and down the hallway right there. If you have a red light on that video camera, you know to make sure to put a piece of tape over it so they can't see it."

"Yep. We're on the same page."

"I also think that we should dummy up the bed and get them attacking the human shapes lying in the bed. Take advantage of the situation and especially the shock of being caught and get their statements on tape here at the house and back at the department."

"Your list is getting longer. We'll get their statements here if they make 'em, but we won't interview anyone here. Just so you know."

"Yep. Just the statement. Hey, I don't want the rental car to get away if a driver stays with it. Once you confirm their arrival, you're gonna have your patrol guys seal off the neighborhood without spooking the perpetrators, I suppose. Are we on the same page?"

"I think so. Nothing goes to plan, but we'll do our best."

"Nice. Once we get that car, see if you get consent to search on video. If not, we'll sit on it until we get a search warrant to go through it. We could conjure something up, I suppose, for an inventory search if parked in the driveway or whatever, but I want little wiggle room on this one. Okay, I'm done preaching. Thank you for enduring that. Do you have anything to add or anything you want to talk about?"

"Nope. We'll take care of it."

"I know you will. You're the best," Ton said while he gently patted the back of Neal's shoulder.

*

Shane was nervous, and fear was taking root. He had nothing to do that Saturday except pick up the car and then fixate on the job that he had waiting the following evening. He was up around ten in the morning and Camille already had his breakfast waiting for him in the microwave. Shane sat down on the stool next to a small table that was near the apartment's kitchen. Camille and Sherry had a nicely decorated, feminine, comfortable apartment. It wasn't the stark and messy place that he lived in with his boys nearby. The girls even had stacks of fresh towels in the bathroom instead of the one towel that he used over and over again at his place. As he ate his recently warmed frozen breakfast sandwich, he drank some orange juice with vodka. The liquid spirits and instant breakfast met in a flourish, giving him strength and nerve. He got up, left the dirty plate and single utensil sitting at the table, and turned on the television. He looked through the channels to watch any sporting event that he could find in order to try and hold the fixation and fear at bay.

Camille came and sat down with him on the couch as the drone of commentators dithered on about a once-storied football program that had seen its better days. Camille said, "Hey, baby. Nervous?"

"No. What makes you say that?"

"Well, the vodka, I guess. Were there any changes on the car pick up?"

"No. I think that I'll have you drop me off half a block away. You know, so I can check things as I walk in. Then you go and wait at my apartment. I'll take it to my dad's place and leave it there like we planned. Then I'll just walk up that steep ass hill back to the apartment."

"I still think that's a stupid ass idea. Leavin' it at your crazy-ass dad's? He'll fuck this up somehow."

"Would ya stop worrying? Rein it in, man...Remember, we're killing your pops, not mine!"

"Sorry, babe. I shouldn't have said that."

"I'll park it in the tall grass on the side of the house with all them other cars you can't see. Besides, even if I put it by the front door, he still probably wouldn't even fucking notice it."

Shane's dad participated in the meth program, not as a counselor but as a manufacturer and dealer. His dad rarely used it, but he didn't use a lot of protection in the manufacture of it either, which affected a mind that was already neither that astute nor profound. A contributing factor may have also been the breadth of his reckless life and departure from any educational structure except for basic chemistry with store-bought materials.

Camille said, "What about all them cops that watch that place?"

"Fuck! Just listen and stop askin' me shit! I don't want the car at my apartment! I don't want it stored anywhere near me in case the cops show up. Besides, it could get towed here if I don't tell the apartment manager it'll be here overnight. Now that'd be fuckin stupid if it was here, right? So quit bugging the shit out of me."

"Okay, I fucking get it. Never mind."

"You need to listen and then do. Not fucking ask questions!"

*

After a couple of hours of waiting and anxious boredom, Camille asked, "Are you ready to pick up the car?"

"Yeah. Let's go."

As Camille drove toward acquiring one of two classic getaway cars: borrowed or stolen, Shane said, "I've decided you're driving to Mountain View and back."

"Why's that?"

"Well, uh, you're a woman. Insurance companies say women are safer drivers, so cops don't spend a lot of time looking their way. Plus, you know, chicks literally get away with murder. No cop is gonna stop you goin' up or comin' back. If they do, you deny everything...act stupid and tell 'em you're sorry. You do that, you're getting a pass."

"That's cool. Girl power, baby!"

As she finished her diet cola, they were nearing the location of the sedan. The potential killers turned the corner and immediately spotted a lone car where they were told it would be. A large and colorful soda cup was lying on the blacktop, gently changing directions with the light breeze. "Oh, hey, there it is!" Shane said.

Camille giggled with glee as she was told, "Stop right here. I'll go from here."

"Okay. Right here?"

"YEAH, HERE!"

"Shit, dude, stop yelling at me! Who needs to calm the shit down now?"

As he leaned back into the Accord's open door, he said, "Go. And don't fucking speed!"

He walked up to the sedan and looked it over to make sure it was good. He inspected the tires as he walked around the car. When he got to the driver's door, he opened it and sat down inside. He left the door open as he reached under the seat and fished for the keys with his fingers. He finally felt what he thought might be a key ring and reeled it in. He inserted the ignition key and brought the car back to life. The air conditioning was already blasting away as he closed the door and then turned down the fan so that he could look for cameras or audio devices. He was not sure what he was really looking for, but he looked anyway. After going through the car for about a minute, he felt satisfied, and then he relaxed. He sat back in the driver's seat and put his seatbelt on. He put the car in gear and pulled away from the parking spot as he fidgeted with the radio to get his favorite local station. He wanted to move it out of there before any chance of suspicion fell upon the stationary car or on him. What he didn't know was that he had been surveilled for the past two days by a couple of undercover police from the BPD.

The surveillance team was made up of a couple of officers from vice and one from the traffic division. Officer Leona Ramsey watched the acquisition of the car and took several digital photographs of the vehicle, the plate, Camille dropping him off, and Shane behind the wheel. Shane had no idea that he had been followed as he was heading down the road to financial freedom. As he settled into the new ride, he turned the air conditioner fan back up to meet the usual heat of a Benton summer. As he drove, he waited for the insufficient air conditioning unit to work hard enough to beat back the cruel temperatures inside his mid-sized rental.

He made his way across parts of Benton and out to his dad's place, where he pulled onto the property and then around back. His dad's house sat below the road abutting a tall weed patch that surrounded the place similar to New York City around Central Park. The house itself was enveloped in scaley whitewash paint, overburdened by time and the treacherous heat, with broken-down cars sprinkled about the front, back, and side.

Shane parked the sedan around the side, seemingly out of view from curious eyes above, when he suddenly realized that putting a car in a drug dealer's yard was actually a dumb fucking idea. He then concluded that paranoia had gotten the better of him in his planning and its application. Shane then calmed down and decided to leave the car there after all. He realized that such a move could potentially set up his dad, who was just off of parole, rather than himself. If the car was actually stolen or if, after the murders, the vehicle was connected to his dad, it would be his dad's problem and not his. Shane made the short walk up the steep road through the residual heat back to his apartment complex. Constant surveillance was actually very difficult for the police trailing him since the apartment complex was at the rise of a hill, with little tree cover in the area and no other buildings to mask their presence. Since Officer Ramsey would be in an exposed position if she moved into or immediately around the apartment complex, she decided to prolong her positioning between the apartment and the house as she frantically looked for an inconspicuous place to park. She found one in a vacant, run-down old grocery store parking lot on an adjacent hill. From there, she watched the goings-on through binoculars while the vehicle that she sat in worked to capacity to try and churn out a full fan's speed of conditioned air for hours on end.

As Shane walked into his apartment complex parking lot, now drenched in sweat from the walk, he saw Camille's car. His thoughts raced as he could not wait for this scam to be over. It had been a long one as he sat between one woman needing more money than he could provide and the other who would provide it. He arrived at his apartment door and opened it to find Camille eating his ice cream and sitting at his table. Shane snapped under the pressure and increased disdain for Camille and said, "You shouldn't eat that now! You'll have the shits all the way to Mountain View and back!"

He grabbed a beer out of the refrigerator and then sat on the couch to calm his nerves. Camille met him there with ice cream melting in her mouth as she tried to be sexy, seeking some sack time to take the edge off.

*

Later in the day, Shane called Eric and said, "We got the car, and everything's ready to go."

Eric was silent, and Shane asked, "Did you hear what I said?"

"I heard, man. Good to go. That's enough over the phone. Come by after dark."

Shane heard a click and then hung up the phone, too. "Damn! That dude is one crazy-ass paranoid schizo!"

As Shane heard his own words, he again realized the depth of the endeavor and that he was a bit careless. At that moment, Shane thought, "I need to be more professional and quit acting like an amateur. I'm about to be part of a real murder." As sweat beaded onto his forehead, he added, "Get with it, Shane, you might have to do this again for Tania after we move away...."

Rising tension and heat forced Shane to take a needed break from Camille after getting the car, so he told her to go home. He hung out with Slob and Erin while the young couple smoked pot until they ran out of their little stash. Another college football game commenced, and they watched and ate junk food for the rest of the afternoon. Shane planned on spending that night at Tania's place since he needed her support, and if something happened to him, he would have spent his last erotic, compassionate, and sentimental time with the woman he loved, and not the trick he had strung along for a couple of years. He knew that he still would be with Camille in proximity if the end came the following day, but that was business and not devoted adherence.

Camille called him later that evening, just before he had left for Tania's. She said, "Hey, Honey Bear, I don't want to be alone. I'm a little scared, and I need my brave man to snuggle and hold me."

"I can't."

"Why not?"

"I, I need to focus. We want to do this right. Right?"

"Yeah. I guess. Tomorrow night, when we get back, I'm spending the night with you."

"Fine. Fine. I'll give it to you good."

"You promise?"

"Sure. It'll be worth the wait. I have to go. Look, I gotta go."

Camille agreed as she really didn't care that much since she wouldn't need to expend the energy of manipulation that night. Shane had told her long ago to never stop by his apartment without calling first and to not call him after bedtime. Even more specifically, if she did call before then, and he didn't answer, then he was already asleep or getting ready for bed and to leave a message. Camille was fine with those arrangements since she really had little emotion for Shane beyond the sex and the spells that she used to finesse him into doing her bidding. She had known about Tania for quite some time, having followed him on numerous occasions to keep her tool and his secrets useful. She felt that his wandering eye and lack of faithfulness was good, and Tania? Well, she was indifferent about it.

*

Camille stayed up late watching movies on television. Her roommate sat with her for about an hour after she got home around two in the morning. Sherry asked, "Hey, you okay? You look pretty tense. You going through with it?"

"Yeah, a little tense, I guess. I feel good for once. I'm a bit stressed about making sure the plan works. All the way to the payout. I don't want it to fail and set us back, and I don't want them boys getting arrested."

"You're not worried about yourself?"

"No! But if them boys get arrested, they'll rat me out. Then I got a problem. Otherwise, nobody is gonna do anything to me. They'll see that my parents were monsters and feel bad for me. This is totally justifiable. You know that, right?"

Camille was now staring at Sherry, not to seek fake approval, but to see that Sherry was loyal and that she really understood. Sherry was in the stripper game. She could read people and act accordingly. Sherry looked Camille straight in the face and said, "Hey, girl, I do. I don't know how you were able to be so successful when you were treated so fucking poorly by your parents. Everybody knows that. If something happens, they'll see it too. For sure."

"Bitch, I knew you were my girl and understood the complexity of this shit. You were there with me when all of this shit went down," she said as a smile came back to her face while she eased back into the sofa cushions.

Eric was already fast asleep in his apartment while the other two were trying to make sense of their present, as they tried to wring out the last bits of happiness from life before they were to be neck deep in the shit. Eric had kept his mouth shut around family and friends about his potential high-level criminal activity. He would share if it worked, but until then, he was mum on the subject.

Shane was seeking financial independence and a fresh start in life with Tania and other men's children. While Eric was seeking status in his lifelong surroundings of hard criminals who could pull a 187, if necessary, and Camille, well, she was seeking revenge for a lifetime of abuse that was really just self-inflicted.

*

The day had finally arrived. It was September 3, 1995. Camille was ready to get it started and she didn't want to be alone in her own head, as she reached for the telephone. Shane had been back for only about an hour when the phone rang.

"Hey, it's me. When can I come over?"

"Now, I guess. It'll be a long day, though. What are you gonna do for all that time?"

"I can't be by myself. I'll be quiet. I promise."

"I need to concentrate, so you better keep it on the down low, or you won't come back from Jefferson County."

Camille quickly hung up and left her apartment. Sherry was still asleep in her room or pretending to be so, as Camille closed the apartment door and locked the bolt.

She arrived at Shane's in about thirty minutes after getting some caffeine on the way. She was already intense, and the coffee didn't help as she drove through the city like a lunatic.

She walked in with attitude and her mouth flapping. She proceeded to inform her boyfriend about her drive over as she said, "Because I didn't get any last night, and I'm out of my mind right now, I need some stress relief! I'll make it worth your while, Babe. I really will."

"Didn't you just tell me you were going to be quiet here

and not a pain in my ass? This isn't the time. Today is about risky business, not frisky business! You need to get your priorities straight," he quickly said while he sat on the couch and stared at the TV.

He resumed working his way to the calm before the storm as he drank a few beers to shed the immediate tension.

"Hey, I want a beer!"

"Then get one. Only one, though! You gotta drive and stay awake the whole damned time. We don't need to have all of this work go down the shitter because you caught a DUI on the way to Mountain View or fell asleep and killed us all."

Camille knew he was right and tried to wait out the time, watching the usual cartoons or sports that played endlessly on the guy's television set while she sipped her beer and another two that she snuck.

*

As the sun set on the city of Benton, Shane got the bag out of his room that had everybody's clothing for the job inside. They had called an audible and would be riding up in the black outfits, which would make for only one change of clothes in the Deagans' yard. Soon, they would be changing into those clothes and riding off into the dark of night. Since they were not to stop anywhere, their black outfits would not draw attention as they traveled up the interstate to the Deagans' home.

At around nine that night, the pair left the apartment and walked down to pick up the rental car at his dad's. Once there, they changed into their black clothing in the tall, dry grass next to the car under the cloak of darkness. Then, they loaded up their bag with the street clothes and headed over to Eric's place to pick him up. Camille was really chatty after they got the car. It annoyed Shane, and he hoped that Eric would shut her up once they picked him up. She was rambling on about nothing out of nervousness as the deadly trip began. Shane was trying to ignore the diarrhea of words that flowed from her annoying mouth, as he caught the sentence, "...and we'll take all the money...."

He smirked and then said, "Try to calm down! Hey, don't talk about any of this once we get Eric."

Camille nodded her head in agreement and murmured, "I won't. I'm not stupid, ya know."

Eric was waiting on the almost insignificant-sized deck of his apartment. He waved like a politician walking off an airplane into a crowd when he suddenly went back inside and grabbed a piss bottle, a couple of sodas, and a stick of jerky for the road. He then picked up his knife and the small baseball bat near the door where he had set them earlier and walked out. As he approached the car, Camille and Shane had already switched seats, and Camille had popped the trunk open. Eric dropped his stuff in the trunk, except for his snacks. He then grabbed the last pair of all-black clothing from the bag and went back up to his apartment on a jog so that he could change into his killer outfit. Soon, he was on his way back down and entered the dingy yellow illumination, which barely penetrated the immediate dark of night from the old overhead lights around the complex. He placed his street clothes in the trunk along with his good tennis shoes and then found his way to the open backseat for the ride.

CHAPTER 10.

DEMONS OF DARKNESS

In any era of human existence, people first seek survival and then glory—the glory of baubles and things, experiences, sex, love, and purpose. As the circular routine repeats itself among the ages, those who dream have lived, and those who execute live on.

*

Detective Ruffin had been at the Deagan house since one that afternoon. Two DA Investigators, John Suarez and Greg Kemp, accompanied him. The switch to DA Investigators was made in the eleventh hour as Detective Ruffin was told by MVPD command that since they were a small police department, they needed more uniform cops on the street for public safety and to ensure that the suspects in this caper didn't get away.

The California Highway Patrol had been briefed a couple of days prior to set up a series of rolling surveillance vehicles manned by State Traffic Officers (STO) from Benton to Mountain View. The STOs in the Mountain View area were to be on alert for the suspects when they arrived in town. They had been given strict orders to not engage the suspects whatsoever en route from Benton to the house on Blumenthal Street. The STOs were further instructed that once the murder attempt was executed, they would be notified to cover all of the onramps to the interstate from the surface streets in

Mountain View in the event that a suspect or suspects had escaped the scene and were on the run.

John Suarez had worked as a local law enforcement officer for twenty years in the big city. He was tired of the overwhelming crime but still needed to increase his time in service for retirement's sake while generally working a Monday through Friday gig in a District Attorney's office. He had grown up in Northern California and wanted to return to his roots. He was a solid cop, investigator, and person. He did not get excited over the small stuff. He was eager enough to do the work yet laid back enough not to be a hard-ass jerk.

The third peace officer to sit in the baited trap was Greg Kemp. Greg was past retirement age but was thrice divorced and had a strained relationship with all of his children. For the past four generations the men in his family were cops. They took jobs in various law enforcement agencies, doing various duties, and the DNA seemed to like it. Greg couldn't leave law enforcement as it was all he had left. If he were to ever leave, he would be all alone in the world. He needed an understanding social network, and deep down he knew that when the day of separation came, he would go home to his empty little house and eat his gun. On the job, he could be trusted and was very thorough. He, too, was a transplant from distances south. He had come from the fake landscapes of California where water was delivered on high in copious amounts only to be wasted by arrogance in a vast desert of illusion. He had grown tired of being awash in the folderol and self-centeredness that made up large swaths of his life, with the remainder being its opposite, consisting of bloodthirsty criminals that seemed to never end. Mostly, he desperately needed a break from the ball-busting of his ex-wives, their lawyers, their shared children, and all of the anger that came with it.

He was working way past retirement for camaraderie but also money. He had been soaked by the family law system in California, as he failed in his search for lasting love. He had made a series of commitments to it, with payment to the government for the privilege to do so, while eagerly reciting vows, ending with a determined "I do." Then, he was divorced every time by the woman who swore to stay through thick and thin, while each declared that their departure was his fault. He knew he had a bad picker and that he was an acquired taste for those with a discerning palate. He couldn't afford another foray into the game of commitment, so he had a couple of barren women on the side who enjoyed his company and paid for it with entry into their infertile mantraps every so often.

Greg had been a beat cop, a field training officer, a detective, a SWAT member, and a sergeant at his southern California agency. He had even had time on a couple of multi-agency task force projects, one with the DEA and another with the California Department of Justice's Bureau of Investigations. For the past five years, he specialized in homicide cases and sex-based crimes with Ton Hogan in Jefferson County.

On this night, he and Neal had brought manikin heads and wigs and set up a scene in the bed of Lisa and David. When they were done, it was as realistic as a Hollywood movie tableau. Since Greg was more experienced with the ways of mankind, he brought a department-issued Remington 870 twelve-gauge pump action shotgun along with his old-school service handgun, a Colt 1911 in .45 ACP.

Neal had only his trusty service weapon in his duty holster, while John had gotten an MP-5 from the sheriff's armory on loan in case they needed some automatic fire. Since it was a nine-millimeter, it had less chance of over-penetrating a wall and killing a neighbor.

The house was now dark. John and Neal were going to be hiding in the living room near each other so that they could shoot if necessary and could easily move into the area of the front door or kitchen to stop vermin from exiting. The cameras were already rolling in the locations requested, and small bits of electrical tape covered the aggravating red light on each unit. Greg was in Camille's room across the hall from the master bedroom with the door open. He was seated in a chair while twisting his grey handlebar mustache tips with his fingers, while his shotgun laid across his lap. He could lean over to the window shade and see out to the front of the house as he routinely checked for the coming infiltration as the night moved ever so slowly.

*

Camille was driving the sixty-five-mile-an-hour speed limit northbound on the interstate toward the Oregon border. Eric was calm and focused while sitting in the back seat. Camille erupted, "Would you stop messing with the fucking radio," as she turned her head and stared at Shane.

"Hey, watch the road! I'm just tryin' to get a station that I can listen to. I need some music to take my mind off things."

"Try concentrating on what you have to do instead of making me mad as Hell!"

"Okay, okay. Damn," he said as he turned it off.

Just a few miles into the journey, they were about to cross one of the numerous high bridges that suspended the freeway over Benton Lake. The bridges were high for two reasons. First, the water laid into a series of deep canyons that comprised the body of the lake, so the roads crossed the hillsides and ridges as they made their way north and south. Secondarily, the water in the lake fluctuated greatly depending on the season, as room was needed to meet the dictates of Mother Nature, electricity customers, cities, farmers, and wildlife.

Shane could see lights hovering above the water down below the freeway from the large houseboats sitting in the darkness. He asked, "Hey, Camille, what's the best bridge to throw our shit off of on the way back?"

"I think it's this one. It has a long approach, so you can get off on the side—well, kinda. They can see you on the way onto the bridge, but they still gotta make the turn, so they can't focus on what the fuck we're doin'."

"Wouldn't that be the shits if we dropped our stuff over the rail and one of those houseboats was going under, and our shit landed on the boat?" Shane said with a smile.

"Let's put bigger rocks in it then," Eric said with a cold smile from the darkness of the backseat.

"As funny as that is, it would be really fucked-up. We gotta make sure that doesn't happen. We don't need all our stuff landing on a boat instead of the bottom of the lake, that's for sure," Shane said.

As the bridges over Benton Lake ceased to be of discussion, the occupants in the car were silent as they penetrated the thick forests near the edge of Cassell County. About that time, the rental car approached a sign with illuminated lettering that read "Jefferson County" as Camille spotted a California Highway Patrol car heading southbound on the interstate. As she commented, Shane quickly caught sight of the police car and said, "Oh yeah, I see that bastard," as he watched it continue out of sight on the southbound curvatures of Interstate 1.

"He's just cruisin', man," Shane then said.

The STO in that CHP car notified his dispatcher of the visual on the sedan as it crossed into Jefferson County. Neal Ruffin received the news about thirty seconds later. Since Neal now had a recent confirmation of location, they could stand up and relax a bit. For a few minutes, they could drink some coffee, take a leak, and work out the kinks in old bones. The guys did the aforementioned and looked around the house one more time and took turns peeking out the window when another sighting was relayed from a CHP unit at the commercial truck weigh station just inside Jefferson County on the downhill, southbound side. Neal said, "They just passed the weigh station. It'll be another forty minutes or so. Relax for the next twenty-five. No lights on unless you have to piss. I don't want a mess to clean up, so aim straight!"

"You know Greg, he has to take a piss every ten minutes, and he is half blind," John said with his head lifted up in the air.

Neal and John instantly heard a "Fuck you!" come out of the darkness of the back bedroom. After a short pause, it was followed by, "You'd better edit that shit out of the video!"

The men at the Deagans' house felt the pressure and excitement build as the clock showed the time, moving them forward into confrontation. CHP reported over the radio, "We are dark at the Hawk Road overpass, and the suspects just entered the city limits."

Camille hadn't seen either of the last two highway patrol units who reported their location, but she did see the Mountain View city limits sign on the right side of the freeway. She quickly looked at both passengers and said, "Get ready. We're close."

Shane immediately felt like he was going to throw up as Eric prepared for war. In four more minutes, Camille was approaching the offramp to her parents' house. She followed the rules of the road as if she had a DMV employee onboard while she worked her way to her parents' last night with the living. She maneuvered her way through the city streets to her childhood home. In her mind, she replayed the fear and remorse that her parents would show her in the next few minutes as they begged for their lives.

*

David and Lisa were in bed watching a little television to ease the nerves. The hotel was only a few minutes away from the treachery and violence that was closing in on their home. Although they would not be struck by the horrors of seeing their only child standing over them as they were about to be beaten to death, they still felt the fear and remorse that

Camille wanted from them, only she would never see it. As timepieces moved numbers forward in succession, nervousness turned to anxiety and then distress as they waited for word on whether their daughter was dead or alive in the aftermath.

*

Suddenly, Eric looked up from his dull gaze upon the floor of the car as Camille said in a whisper as if she thought her parents could hear, "Here we come."

She crept along the street and then by the house, made a U-turn, and eased back to park on the street adjacent to her parents' yard and just before their driveway. The car stopped, went into park, and the engine ceased to run. As the soon-to-be assassins exited the car, the dome light came on and illuminated their presence to anyone who bothered to see. The three killers clad in all black closed the car doors quickly but softly with only a demure "clunk." The trunk was then opened in order to pull out their bag of tricks. Eric had taken his aluminum bat from the trunk first as it dispelled its accouterments of mayhem and murder. Eric had left Benton with his knife already strapped to his waist, and he was now ready to go.

The men inside had earpieces readied in an ear to keep the radio noise from being heard by the cautious or fervent intruders. Greg spotted the trio from Camille's bedroom window and broadcast over the radio, "The suspects have exited the vehicle and are headed around back. Stand by."

Camille guided them up to the right side of the house, next to the garage. She was hunched down as she turned and told the men, "Stay close," and then continued on the sidewalk to the entry gate into the backyard. Camille was in front, Eric was immediately behind her, and Shane fluttered after them. Freshly cut grass could be smelled as it lay horizontal among the vertical near the sidewalk. Eric noticed that the next house on the block to the right was about thirty yards away. Those neighbors' lights were still on, and he could hear the slight noise of late-night television. The three stalkers in the night eased through the gate as they left it ajar and entered the darkness of the backyard.

There were no lights on inside the Deagan house. The only illumination came from the yellow din overhead from the small town surrounding them and the sporadic porch lights that were lit to ironically welcome friends and warn strangers with the same message. Those, coupled with some escaping rays through gaps in window blinds from neighboring homes, provided the only aid. As Camille led the men to the back door, she reached for her house key and said, "Sure could've used a fucking flashlight."

It was a single key, something easier to lose or misplace without its numerous companions sharing a ring, but alone, it was quiet in use. It made its way into the firm grip of her thumb and index finger. Even though it was likely that Camille would fail on this trip, so far, she was on point. She turned the key, and the bolt slid back into the door from the frame. She reached down with her gloved hands and turned the knob. The door eased open as she put the key back in her pocket. She slowly stepped inside as Eric waited impatiently. He then said, "Move in. Move in!" as he pushed her the rest of the way inside as Shane followed them. They waited in the kitchen for their eyes to adjust to the various night lights around the kitchen and living room. Camille knew the layout by heart and touched them both to gain their attention, and then pointed toward the hallway that led to the bedrooms.

Camille smiled as she took a quick look to see if anything was amiss. She missed the tripod and camera near the kitchen table as she became confident that they were on the verge of the ultimate vengeance. She pointed down the darkened hallway once again and said, "Go past the bathroom on the right... Go!"

Eric choked up on his bat as he held it with two hands and moved swiftly down the hallway, past the bathroom, and made a right through the doorway. Camille was trailing right behind him and then came Shane. Eric saw the Deagans in bed just like they planned and went to work. He struck the legs of the body whom he believed to be David Deagan. Hearing no cry of pain, Camille yelled, "Fuck you, David and Lisa. Beat them, Eric! Kill them!"

Eric was now swinging the bat repeatedly onto both figures with speed as Shane stood there in a blank stare of disbelief. Camille then screamed, "How does that feel, Daddy? I bet that hurts, huh? It's me, Camille! You two can kiss my ass goodbye!"

As Eric ran out of breath from the deadly exercise, he still was able to produce enough air to laugh triumphantly.

Camille climbed onto the bed and started clawing at her mom and dad. Then suddenly, the lights came on as Eric looked into a shotgun barrel opening, and Camille turned to meet Detective Ruffin's handgun pointed at her face. Neal said, "Police. Don't make a fucking move."

The two seasoned law enforcement officers immediately noticed that Shane was not in the room. He had turned and ran like Hell after the vicious and repeated blows began raining down on the Deagans. Shane passed Investigator Suarez just as he was about to enter the room from the left side of the door. Suarez was struck in the shoulder by a speeding young white male coming full tilt out of the small gap in the doorway to his right as he blew by, heading down the hallway looking for a different reality.

Investigator Suarez notified the troops by radio, "We've got a runner. One WMA on foot, headed to the suspect's vehicle on Blumenthal."

Shane had made it out of the back door and through the yard. He didn't see any cops as he reached the green sedan, steadily waiting for the metamorphosis of young fools turned into hardened killers. The keys were left inside in the ignition in case the plan went awry. According to Shane, it was fully awry as he got in and started the car. He threw it into drive and sped down the street in front of him as he repeatedly said, "Oh shit!"

He passed two MVPD police cars with decals on the doors, sitting on the next four-way stop intersection. Their positioning was blocking both right and left turns which forced Shane to continue straight away as he felt his stomach drop and the greatest of fears overwhelm him. He accelerated as he approached the next intersection with little distance left before he was on the interstate heading home to Tania. Just then, he struck a pair of spike strips laid out on the road before him. His tires opened from the spikes as the previously confined air was released back into the wild. He continued driving as fast as he could. It was a bumpy and sloppy ride as he spotted more MVPD and Highway Patrol tactically set to the left and to the right in front of him. He worked the engine and the folded rubber as hard as he could, limping along as the police waited for the ending. Shane neared the interstate with little traction as his tires began to peel. As he entered the onramp to the two-lane interstate, he veered into the number two lane as the entry lane slowly melted into the wide-open road ahead. Shane instantly felt freedom as he believed he could escape in a bout of pigeonholed delusion. At that precise moment, a Highway Patrol Ford Expedition struck his driver's side rear quarter panel from out of nowhere in a PIT maneuver. The blow was intentionally hard, and the force sent Shane's foot down violently onto the gas pedal as he absorbed the blast. The combination caused the sedan to rapidly move sharply to the right and away from the number two lane. Now out of control, he began to drop down and away from the freeway above and then over the embankment as the sedan rolled a couple of times to find itself landing on its wheels down below on a flat grassy surface. Police officers began to run from their vehicles in synchronous chaos in order to catch their attempted murder suspect before he could run any further.

Shane had been slightly injured in the rollover and was subdued easily as they extracted him from the sedan. Shane was handcuffed as an ambulance arrived to provide any necessary first aid. Shane was fine, but for some head trauma that was bandaged by an EMT. Officers patted him for weapons, and after finding none, they put him in a patrol car and took him to the hospital to get him cleared before they could take him to an interview room at the Jefferson County Jail.

*

Eric was winded from the animation and vigor that was just on full display as he tried to kill Lisa and David Deagan. He was now staring at a shotgun barrel with an old man on the other side who was presenting one helluva scowl and gravitas. Eric lamented the lack of a gun in his preparation during that split second as he started to make a move.

"Don't lose your head, boy," suddenly came from a gravelly voice underneath the handlebar mustache of the grey-haired man with the gun pointed at Eric's head.

Greg watched the tension on the young man's body start to simmer as Eric focused on fighting another day. Eric wanted freedom, but he was good either way. If he went to prison on this caper, he would be a big man in the family business when he came out of the joint and would finally have the credibility that he had been waiting for. As Eric appeared to comply, he was told, "Drop the bat on the floor. Drop it. Good, now turn slowly and put your face on that bed!" Eric could now feel the cold steel of the shotgun barrel pressing on his face and dropped the bat immediately. Now face-down, John cuffed him up.

Camille feigned tears and hysteria as she said, "Thank God you're here! These guys kidnapped me! They kidnapped me in Benton and forced me to help them. They wanted money. They wanted my mom and dad dead to get their money."

Camille was able to shed even more tears after that fabrication was fully pronounced. Holding a pistol pointed at her head, Neal pushed her face down onto the floor while telling her to put her hands behind her back as he re-holstered his weapon and reached for his handcuffs. As he hit each wrist with the handcuff, the force caused the ratchets to click and secure. When Neal snugged them down, the crying increased to wailing. Camille said, "You can't do this to me! I was forced into this. What the fuck! I'm the victim!"

As the handcuffs were punch-locked into position by Detective Ruffin, he helped her up off the floor. He then turned her quickly away from the "murder scene," and he walked her out of the house through the front door. Once outside of the house, he patted her for weapons with the back of his hands and in the view of other police officers. He walked her over to a waiting MVPD patrol car. Neal opened the back passenger door of the car, sat her in the back seat, and closed the door. Detective Ruffin turned and said, "Thank you, Officer Burrows, I appreciate it. Do me a favor and record her statements on the way to the station. Put her in interview room four. Have a good night, and thanks again."

Just then, Investigator Kemp walked out with Eric Larson. They walked to a waiting Highway Patrol car for transport to the county jail to await interviewing.

Detective Ruffin and the two District Attorney Investigators were glad to have the three suspects in custody. Neal and John went back inside to take photographs of the crime scene and quickly checked the video recordings to see if they got what they needed. After a very quick review, they both smiled at having visual evidence if this case went to trial.

Greg had disappeared into the covert darkness as he made the walk of about a hundred yards to their unmarked police car and drove it back to the Deagans' house. John saw him from the window and went outside and said, "Thanks for getting the car. The video appears to be good. I'm going to grab our handheld unit and video where the vehicle was parked and their mode of access to the house."

Greg went back inside the house and waited for the filming to be completed so that they could start processing the crime scene. A few minutes later, Evidence Technician Sam Blades walked into the Deagans' home carrying his basic crime scene kit and was all smiles. "Nice job, guys. What do we have, and what do you want us to focus on?"

"We've got a search warrant on the green sedan sitting with the CHP out on the interstate. Can you photograph that thing on-site and then have it towed to your place for follow-up and holding?" Neal asked.

"Sure thing," Sam said when he turned and headed back out of the door for the rental car waiting in the grass.

CHAPTER 11.

THE POINT

When a criminal acts alone, they can assert guilt or innocence. When criminals act in unison, they have three options for having worked with those who cannot refuse the opportunity to talk. Innocence, guilt, or the ever-intriguing assignment of guilt.

*

As one of two detectives at MVPD, Detective Ruffin had his hands full already before this case. He needed the two District Attorney Investigators to stay on and work it through with him. Neal's department had limited resources, and none of the seasoned guys on the force at MVPD had interview skills that fit this scenario. The guys from the DA's office did.

"Hey, you guys ready to do the interviews?" Neal asked.

"I am," Greg answered.

"I'll be ready in about five minutes. I just gotta put my stuff in the car," John answered.

"Who do you want on what perps?" Greg asked.

"Why don't you take the guy you collared? John can take the runner. They're both at the jail. Camille's at the PD, so I'll interview her. Does that work?"

"That works," Greg said as he grabbed a couple of pieces of John's equipment and headed for the car.

Just before he walked out the front door, Detective Ruffin

said, "Make sure and tell the staff at the jail that we want these three kept apart for interviews and in housing."

"You got it," answered Greg.

"Oh, and they need to be separated everywhere else. Like medical, transport, chow, or for court. They move separately or separated."

"I appreciate the reminder. We'll take care of it," Greg answered.

*

Greg Kemp and John Suarez drove up to the prisoner entry gate at the Jefferson County Jail. Greg pressed the button to roll down his window as he approached the squawk box. As they stopped at the box, jail staff identified them through the security camera. The squawk box came to life as a voice said, "Who are you?"

"Donut delivery. Now open the fucking gate," Greg answered.

"Donuts? You need more than stinking donuts to get in here, boys. We like favors or cash," the voice on the intercom blared into the car once more after a short pause.

Greg was pissed and was about to respond when the gate started to open.

"I think they gotcha again," John said while looking at Greg.

"Son of a bitch!" Greg said as he shook his head from side to side.

Greg drove in and parked in one of the spaces assigned to allied law enforcement agencies. He and John unholstered their pistols and put them in the onboard lockbox in the center console of the car.

As Greg and John were buzzed into the sally port, they waited for the door behind them to close before the control center staff electronically unlocked the second entry door. At the final buzzing sound, Greg and John walked in when Greg said, "Hey ladies and pricks, I might do you a favor someday, but I sure in the Hell ain't giving you any damned money!" He kept walking past the control center and headed to the towering coffee production system that kept the operation moving. As he sipped his coffee, he walked up to the main security operations desk and said, "Hey, Shelly. How's it goin'?"

"Oh, you know. Another day in paradise. I love my job. Just had a raging drunk come through. We had vomit and piss everywhere," she said as she smiled while rolling her eyes.

"I thought the smell of disinfectant was stronger than usual. Man or a woman?"

"It was a guy. CHP got him on Interstate 1, south of town. I guess he was going fifteen miles an hour and couldn't stay on the road."

"Yeah, well, it's a good thing they picked him up before anyone got killed. Hey, I have two guys who were brought in earlier on an attempted murder. Did they get papered yet?"

"No, we had the officers bag the gloves they were wearing and take them out with them. They printed them, too. They said that they would cut paper back at the station. We decided not to do anything with them until you got here. They're in separate holding cells."

"Great. We're ready to see them separately. This is Ruffin's case, and he wants you to tag them with a no-contact so they are housed, showered, and shit in separate places. He doesn't even want them moved next to each other."

"I will note that and add the code. Who's taking who right now?"

"I'm interviewing Shane Summers," Suarez said.

"You're in interview room two. Head on down, and I'll have him there in about five."

As John headed off to meet up with the weak link in the triad of suspects, Greg continued to lean on the counter as he sipped his coffee. Once Shane Summers had moved and was in room two with Investigator Suarez, Shelly said, "Alright, good talkin' with you, Greg. Your guy is in seven."

Greg casually refilled his coffee and said, "Thanks. See ya next time," as he headed off to interview the strongest of the three.

Shane was escorted into room two by a correctional officer. His face had some butterfly dressing in a couple of places, but otherwise, he was in good shape. John already had his video recorder running when he asked Shane to sit at the opposite side of the table. Shane did as he asked when John said, "Shane, my name is John Suarez. I'm an investigator with the Jefferson County District Attorney's Office, and I'm here, um, to get your side of the story regarding what happened tonight."

"Oh, good. I need to go home," Shane answered.

"Well, that'll have to wait. Do you have any questions so far?"

"I don't, but I got mixed up in something that I didn't wanna do."

John then told Shane that he was under arrest and was to be interviewed as they investigated the attempted murder of Lisa and David Deagan. He stopped Shane as Shane began to try to explain his version of events and read him the Miranda Warning from his department-issued card to ensure that it was said exactly as the attorneys wanted it every time.

Shane eased back into his seat and softly felt the butterfly bandages on his face with his fingertips. John then asked, "After hearing those rights, do you understand them?"

"Yeah, I do."

"Do you have any questions about your rights as I have given them to you?"

"No."

"After hearing and understanding your rights as explained, are you willing to talk with me?"

"YES! I'll tell you everything. They set me up. They set me up, man! Eric is a criminal, and he wanted to commit these murders. He's the killer here. He told me that if I didn't do this, he'd kill me too."

"Is that right? Why would he do that?"

"I don't know. Camille and Eric are crazy."

"What's your relationship with Camille?"

"We were, just, um, friends with benefits, but not boyfriend-girlfriend. You know what I mean? Oh, man, she lured me into this with sex!"

"Sure. I see how that can happen. It is the thing that makes the world turn, eh?"

"Huh?"

"Yeah, okay. Why would she do that? Do that to her own parents, I mean."

"She hated 'em. I mean, she really hated 'em!"

"Have you ever been to the Deagans' before last night—or this morning, I guess?"

"Okay, I was in the Deagans' house before to visit, but this time, I was threatened by Eric to go on the trip and to go into the house!"

"How were you threatened?"

"They told me they would kill me, man. You saw me at the house running away the first chance I got."

"Why were you dressed in all black?"

"I dunno. They made me change into the black clothes to be like them. They made me."

"If you were running from them, why didn't you ask us, the police, for help as soon as we turned on the lights?"

"I didn't know who you guys were. I didn't hear you say you were the police, and I didn't see no badges. I just started running."

Shane added more details as they were asked and then admitted that he drove past at least six police cars and did not ask any of them for help. Shane's head tilted downward, and he quietly said, "I didn't do anything. I was forced to come here by Eric and Camille." He started to cry and asked,

"What's going to happen next?"

"Well, we're going to keep on talking until, um, until your story makes sense."

Shane sat in silence for about three minutes as John waited for him to regain his composure. Shane then asked, "Am I goin' to go to jail?"

"I got news for you. This place that you're at is called jail."

"They told me I was just goin' to holding."

"Yep! And how much time you do depends on what you tell me today. You tell the truth, and I will talk to the District Attorney on your behalf. If you don't, you're looking at life in prison."

John could see the fear wash over Shane as he turned a pale white sequined with sweat beads. Shane suddenly thought of never seeing Tania again, and he broke down—again. John left the room and stood outside giving Shane time to break himself down even further. He waited about fifteen minutes before he came back inside with some tissues and a bottle of water. Shane looked up at John as though he had been half beaten to death. He then solemnly spoke about the parts that Camille and Eric played in the planning and execution of the attempt to kill Mr. and Mrs. Deagan. Even with the delivery of detail, he continued to blame the whole sequence of events on the other two.

At the conclusion of a lengthy interview, Shane was escorted to the booking area, where the jail paperwork was completed. A mugshot was taken, and he was escorted to a room and told to disrobe. All of his clothing was put into an evidence bag and sealed. He was then directed through a series of positions to expose his body folds front and back as well as the heels of his feet and the bottom of his testicles. He was then told to turn, squat, and cough to see if he had drugs or a weapon stashed in his anus. The last directive he received required Shane to run his fingers through his hair and then allow his new master to look into his mouth and under his tongue for any drugs or any other thing hidden in there as well. At the end of the standard and necessary humiliation exercise, he was then sent into the shower room to shower quickly and return.

He returned within a minute, still bathed in fear and loathing, as he was handed a roll of clothes wrapped in a towel. He was told to dry himself off and put his new yet old county-issued clothing on before he would be escorted to a housing unit and a cell that would be his new home.

*

In the meantime, Eric Larson had been seated down the hallway with new nemesis Greg Kemp. Investigator Kemp gave Eric his Miranda Warning and said, "I understand the predicament that you are in right now. Do you?"

Eric did not respond and looked unmoved in his resolve. Investigator Kemp looked him in the face and said, "Look. We know Shane is the ringleader. He was interviewed earlier and said that it was all his idea and that he was going to take all the money after Camille got it."

"Really, how was he gonna do that?"

"Well, what he said was that he was going to kill her and take it all. When we asked about you, he told us that you were just the driver and were doing it for two hundred bucks, you know, since you were down-n-out and had, well, let me see my notes…Oh yeah, he said, um, and I quote, 'He's got no balls.'"

Eric looked at Greg's face with steely eyes, and his jaw clenched. He then told Eric, "We ran you in the system. You have a little bit of a record, mostly petty crimes, but your dad! Your dad is a real player in the game. It must be hard living in a hardcore family that does time like it's nothing, and here you were just a two-bit chauffeur—who got caught."

After a few seconds, he continued, "The way it's going, it looks like Camille and Shane will go down for first-degree murder, and you, Eric, my boy, you will only be a petty accessory. You know, like a bracelet on a centerfold."

"Those pathetic fucks didn't do shit, and if you call me boy one more time, I'll show you gangster, motherfucker. I'm straight up Wood, and I ain't no boy," Eric said while leaning into the table and staring at Greg.

Greg feigned alarm as if he was nervous and regretted his offense. He then brought his voice down and said, "Well, what was your part in this?"

"This was all Camille's idea. She's a sick bitch. That girl is one big bummer. She has a job as a manager of a fast-food place makin' money and still complains. She talked about this for years, man. Shane's a shit-talker and a pussy. But as you said, I was just riding along as a whaddya call that, an, a tourist. Yeah. You know, I was just ridin'."

Greg then reminded the sightseer that he had been filmed and watched while he killed Lisa and David Deagan.

"Oh, that, well, those two fags were all talk and no show, so I was showing them how to do it. By the way, I know them Deagans weren't in that bed. Didn't feel like hitting a real body, ya know? And you guys didn't do nuthin' after I hit 'em. Plus, I didn't see no ambulance, so yeah, that was me ridin' and takin' a little batting practice. That's all."

"Well, boy, since they are still alive, you are only looking at fifteen to life instead of twenty-five to life. You saved yourself ten years by fucking up and listening to stupid."

"How about this, pig? I'm going to fucking kill you. I'm gonna kill you for your lack of fucking respect and for being in my way. Those two pieces of shit needed me. Why? Cuz I'm a fucking hitman," Eric aggressively said while leaning in toward Greg once again.

"Really? Ya got no record to speak of."

"My record is short because I don't get cases put on me. I beat ass, ya know what I'm sayin'? I'd have a hundred 245s

(*California assault with a deadly weapon statute*) if I'd been caught on half of 'em."

"Looking at your short rap sheet, I see that you're really just a wannabe. You've never done anything hardcore in your whole pathetic life," Greg said after looking through some paperwork in a file folder.

"Okay, bitch. I'm glad I went to kill those fuckin old people. I'll shiv Shane in this fucking jail, and I'll contact my family in Benton, and you'll have a contract on your ass!"

"Oh great, I'll add it to my list of lowlifes that want to kill me. It'll be on the fuckin' bottom. Well, boy, it looks like we are done here. You are under arrest for two counts of attempted murder and one count of burglary of a dwelling."

"That's more like it," Eric answered quietly.

*

Detective Ruffin was tired when the sun had moved from the easternmost skies, and the streets that had swollen in the morning hours to the commute traffic had since subsided. He called Lisa and David Deagan individually at their offices to tell them that they were cleared to go back home, as the authorities had their daughter and her two accomplices in custody. The parents were individually saddened by the finality of the news but were happy that their lost Camille had not been killed. Neal made another quick call on that Monday morning, and that was to Detective Mike Wilson down in Benton. He said, "Hey, we got those three dirtbags in custody."

"Nice job, my friend. Anybody hurt?"

"Nope. It went down easy. I have an interview, and then I need some sleep. After I get caught up, I'm hoping you could assist me in interviews with the perps' roommates in your town?"

"Of course. Of course. Get some rest—and good job."

*

Camille received a more intimate search upon her arrival at MVPD by a female officer who found just one thing: a key. It was bagged as a piece of evidence and noted for Detective Ruffin.

Camille had been in interview room four at the Mountain View Police Department for hours. She was given a sack lunch breakfast a few hours back and had slept a little since then. She came to from drifting off when she heard a knock on the door and then saw Detective Ruffin, through her groggy eyes, come in with a woman. She had calmed some since her arrival as she had gone in and out of a series of short catnaps from emotional exhaustion. "Did you get some food?" Neal asked.

"No. They gave me a bag of garbage and said it was food. A crusty muffin, powdered eggs, and milk? Yuck. If you were a restaurant, you'd go out of business in a week. You know, you look a little skinny though—want it?"

"Well, I'm sorry that you didn't like it. I'll make sure the next one is better. This is Officer Jaime Longtree. She's going to sit with us while we talk."

Camille waved her hand that was free at the introduction. The other hand was cuffed to the bar on the edge of the table since MVPD didn't have enough staff to watch everybody at all times.

"I know it's been a long night, but how are you doing?" asked Officer Longtree.

"Hey, since you finally asked, not fucking great. I was threatened and kidnapped, and I'm in jail! How was your breakfast this morning? I bet it was better than mine. Look, I'm the victim here! Is this how you treat crime victims?"

"That's what we need to talk about to see if we can straighten this out."

"Finally!"

"Can I get you anything?"

"Yeah, let me out and drive me to work."

"That's not going to happen right now, so anything that I can get?"

"An orange juice, and I would love a smoke."

"Well, is orange soda okay? We don't have the budget for orange juice. I'll take you on a smoke break after we talk a bit. Does that work?"

"Yeah, I'll take the orange soda, and I promise to tell the whole truth if I can just get a cigarette."

"See if you can get a smoke from Rodger," Neal said, looking over at Jaime.

Camille perked up and smiled at her captors as Jaime walked out of the room.

"I'm going to uncuff your wrist, but if you do anything, I'll have to handcuff both hands to the table," Neal said.

"Thank you. Remember, I'm on your side here, handsome."

The handcuffs were removed, and Camille began to rub her formerly shackled wrist with her free hand to subdue the pain and numbness that came with the wearing of police-issue bracelets.

Smoking had been banned statewide in California. It was illegal to smoke indoors in a facility open to the public. For Jefferson County, no one had gotten the memo, and if they did, many could have cared less.

When Officer Longtree came back with an orange soda and a smoke, Camille eagerly took both as Jaime lit her cigarette so that she could smoke in custody and not in a back alley as a flight risk. This minor gesture was not aimed at soothing a monster but to build rapport. Camille took her first drag and let it linger in her lungs before she sent it into the vacancy of the stark white room. Camille then said, "Must be nice to be cops and smoke at work."

"We don't. We're making an exception for you only. We want to make sure you're comfortable," Neal quickly answered.

"Hmm. I don't smoke usually. Nasty little habit, but I need

to calm my nerves from my terrible ordeal. You know what I mean?" Camille said as she held dearly to her little cigarette in between her index and middle finger.

After a few more minutes of getting to know each other in a trust-building exercise, Neal read Camille her Miranda Warning and asked if she wanted to proceed with talking with them. She took another drag and was now calm as a cucumber and expecting to baffle the cops with her wit, wisdom, and bullshitting capabilities. Camille then said, "Yeah, I wanna get this straightened out."

"You're willing to talk with us, and you waive your rights as given?" Neal shot back.

"Yeah."

"You understand your rights as I have read them to you and you're waiving those rights and are willing to speak with us?" Neal again asked while he was recording this session in the only room where they had a camera in the wall and a two-way mirror for others to witness.

As Camille started to answer with another ambiguous response, Neal said, "Answer yes or no."

Camille stopped and saw that she was trapped in her attempt to gain a possible argument to a way out in the future, so she affirmed and proceeded.

"Are my parents dead?" Camille asked.

"Your dad is deceased, and your mom is in the ICU," Neal answered.

Camille paused in confusion. She then said, "I pray that my mom makes it through. Can I see her?"

"Maybe, but not right now."

"Shane forced me into this mess," she said while looking down at the table in front of her and then paused and tapped the tabletop with her finger. "I've been working since I was a teenager and am the manager of the Rusty's on Hilltop—I make good money. I don't have a, um, motive to get more money—Shane does, though!" She looked into the eyes of the two cops with a smile and said, "I have money. Why would I need to be involved with murder for money?"

"What do you make a month at Rusty's?" Neal asked.

Camille told them what her income was per month. Detective Ruffin replied, "Impressive. Do you like it there?"

"Oh yeah."

"What are your future plans? Do you see yourself working there for thirty-five, forty years?"

"That would be horrible." As her eyes looked down and her facial expression froze, she said, "Oh, I'm just kidding. I like it there, ya know. I really do."

"Why would you say that this was a murder for money?"

"Wasn't it? I thought you knew."

"How would we know? This is the first we've heard about it."

"Really? Kinda slow, huh?"

"How were you going to get money if your parents were dead?"

"Look, Shane wanted them dead so I could get money from the will. I figured that you figured that out already. Yeah, not a great plan, but I had nothing to do with it!"

"If you don't need the money, why did you do it?"

"Damn, dude. Like I said, I was forced to. You know what? You are a hot-lookin' guy for a cop and an old guy—did you know that? When you find out I didn't do anything, let's have dinner and maybe more," as she winked.

"Um, thank you. What a compliment. You know, unfortunately, I'm married, and I prefer mature over 'old.' So, tell us, how were you forced into doing this?"

"Your loss, Neal. Oh, the things we could do together—hmm. Hey, look. I loved my parents, even though they neglected me. They never gave me anything I needed. They worked all the time. I was like a latchkey kid, you know. They told me I was fat and worthless—all the time. They kept me from my friends. Like that."

"Wow. That sounds terrible, but what does that have to do

with Shane forcing you into killing your dad and maybe your mom?"

"Oh yeah. Because he saw the way they treated me, and he wanted to protect me. He said that they should pay for that. I told him to forget it, but he wouldn't stop. I love him, you know. I didn't want to lose him. He can be scary when he is mad, too. I call it 'scary mad.'"

"Clever. How did you meet Shane? Tell us about him."

"Okay. At work, you know. He was so fine. When I first met him, he was fun and mysterious. After dating for quite a while, I decided to introduce him to my mom and dad. When I asked Shane if he wanted to go to Mountain View one weekend to visit, he seemed excited. The visit was great, but on the way back to Happy Valley, he started talking about all the money that my parents had and them having a nice house. He said he wanted to kill them for abusing me and take their money."

"What did you think of that?"

"I told him that they didn't have a lot of money, and he argued with me and said that he wanted some of it. That scared me.... When we got back to Benton, I separated myself from him for a while."

"So, you broke up?"

"Yeah. For a while, then he apologized, and I took him back. My parents told me that they didn't like him. They never liked anybody that I did. I had to keep them apart, so I didn't see or talk to my mom and dad much during that time."

"Did Shane ever talk about it again?"

"He let it go for a long time but then brought it up again. When I told him that I didn't want him to talk about it anymore, he told me that he wanted their money and the house and that I would help him get it. I argued with him, and he got scary mad. Then he grabbed my throat with his hands and squeezed. He said he would kill me if I didn't help him. I was so scared. I was crying, and I didn't know what to do, so I said, okay."

"What did Eric have to do with this thing?"

"I'm terrified of that dude."

"How so?"

She looked away and rubbed her eyes until tears ran down her face. "He comes from violence. His family is hardcore. Once I was forced into the car, I couldn't escape, you know," she said while making her voice crackle.

"Why didn't you try to alert one of the Highway Patrol Officers that you saw on the way up to Mountain View?" Detective Ruffin asked while handing her a box of tissues.

"They weren't close enough," she quickly replied.

Camille suddenly realized that the police may have been watching them in Jefferson County on their way to Mountain View. She stopped and took some tissues from the box. She then looked at the table as her hands came together, and she shifted in the chair away from Neal. The detective could see the hamster wheel spinning in her evil head.

"Why were you wearing black from Benton to the house if you were just the driver?" he then asked.

"You mean you watched the whole time and didn't save me? I got a fat lawsuit over you for sure."

"We did. And nothing happened to you, so good luck with your lawsuit!"

"I was forced to. How many times do I have to say it? Shane and Eric wanted me involved. You know, all of us wearing black. They had me drive so that they could be able to kill me if they wanted to. I couldn't do anything. If I tried, they would've killed me for sure. Right?"

"Why do you think they were wearing black clothing and gloves?"

"To not leave fingerprints and uh, um, to not be seen in the dark?" as she slowed her response.

"Hey, I'm asking you! Is that your answer?"

"Yeah."

"By now, you can tell we knew of this plan long before you

drove to your parents' house. We watched you before you left and on your way here. So, we were aware of the planning and the impending commission of the crimes long before you got here. Why do you think we were waiting in the house?"

Camille stopped talking and then asked, "Can I have another smoke?"

This time, she was told that she could not have one. Camille felt the rope tightening. Detective Ruffin then said, "Look, I need to make a call, so we'll take a break for a few minutes."

Officer Longtree handcuffed Camille's right wrist back to the bar under the table. As the two cops walked out, Detective Ruffin said, "Oh yeah. Both your parents are very much alive and well," as the door closed behind them.

The pair of interviewers got some coffee and then went to a broom-closet-sized room and closed the door. In front of them was the other side of the two-way mirror that looked into the room along the length of the table centered in the middle of it. It wasn't much, and it wasn't fancy, but it worked. They stood in the darkness of the room and sipped their coffee as they watched Camille squirm about. It was easy to tell that she was nervous and confused. The pair waited another ten minutes before re-entering the interview room. Camille was unrestrained once more and given another orange soda.

"How about that smoke break now?" she asked.

"When I told you that your parents were alive, you didn't say anything. Not a word. You didn't ask how they were or even say thank goodness! Why's that?"

"If you knew what they did to me as a child, you would have them in this room and not me."

"Well, tell me! I'm all ears."

"My dad molested me! Are you satisfied now? My mom let it happen. She knew all about it and didn't lift a finger to help me!"

"Why's this the first time that we've heard about this?" Neal asked while staring into her eyes intently.

"It's not! Everybody knows about it."

"You know, I thought you might say that, and I went through our records going back to when you were a kid. Nothing. Nothing from you. Nothing about this from a relative or a neighbor, and nothing was reported to Child Protective Services, a school nurse, or your private physician. So now what? Why don't you just tell the truth?"

"I am, dammit!"

"Early admission to a crime is a positive factor for a lighter sentence. You could save yourself time in prison right now."

"Prison? Oh no, I'm not going to prison. I'm going home to Benton when I get bail, and then when the jury sees the abuse that I got from my parents and from Shane and Eric... I want an attorney."

Detective Ruffin then said, "You had a key on you when we got you here. That key shape is the same as your mom and dad's house key. I will go over there today and see if it works in the lock. When it does, it'll prove to everyone that you are a liar. How? Because you brought that key to let you and your accomplices into the house to kill your parents."

"It didn't happen that way. Can't you hear?"

"You. You are the ringleader in this ordeal."

"Ah, fuck you. I want a lawyer."

"You'll need one. Get up. We're taking you to the jail to book you on attempted murder charges."

CHAPTER 12.

PRELIMINARY HEARINGS

It has often been said that the wheels of justice grind slow. Even in the lowly bogs of highly contested traffic court, legal matters come to fruition and conclusion at a snail's pace.

*

The three suspects were eventually booked in the morning hours of Monday, September 4, 1995. The clock had now started, and all three needed to be formally charged within forty-eight hours, or they would be set free. Ton Hogan did not want these three released from custody, and he never failed to meet the timeframe unless it was a tactical move.

Detective Ruffin worked hard on getting his report precise, complete, and submitted before the time expired. It was something that he was used to doing, and this would be no exception. The addendum reports from the STOs, other MVPD officers, Benton PD, and the DA Investigators would trickle in thereafter. It was important for those reports to be completed, but the most important one, for now, came from the typing fingers of Neal Ruffin. He was low on sleep and was pushing himself to get his work completed so that he could finally get home and rest. Eventually, he could not proceed any further with clarity of mind and headed home. When he pulled into his driveway, he put the car in park, and about fifteen minutes later, he found himself gripping the steering wheel tightly with his hands while he gasped for air in shock and pressed down as hard as he could on the brake pedal. He made a few unusual noises as he realized that he wasn't moving but was looking at the garage door in his driveway. He slowly brought his eyes to the dashboard above his steering column and saw that he was in park, but the engine was still running. Neal breathed a sigh of relief and turned off the engine. He then released his seatbelt and got out of the car and headed for the front door. While the jitters of exhaustion consumed him, he went to the sink and got himself a glass of water. He then took his belt and holster off as he stumbled for the center of the living room where he dropped onto the couch. With a couple of adjustments to comfort, he was captured by the Sandman.

*

Ton Hogan continued on with his daily caseload without spending any thought about when the reports would arrive, since he had other work to do. Those reports from law enforcement laid the groundwork to show the conduct of the bad actor or actors through a writing technique typically used by law enforcement. That technique was taught in middle school and at the law enforcement academies. It was the "Who, What, When, Where, Why, and How" method. It was not sophisticated, but it was easy to remember, and it worked. Since most police officers are laymen with no legal training, their submitted requests for specific charges were not always on point, but they helped the DDA figure out the tenor of the case and the desires of the referring officer beyond the slim facts captured in the report. In the end, the DDA was the responsible charging agent for felonies and most misdemeanors.

Ton Hogan's experience included previous DDA work in one of the most populated counties in California before his arrival in the land of extreme beauty and extreme indifference. That prior experience included massive amounts of cases to deal with day in and day out where a DDA just tries to keep their head above water and not drown. There was not much time to spend on each matter and snap judgments were the rule and not the rare occasion. In Jefferson County, Ton got the best of both worlds. He had a volume that was at the edge of manageable, but with that, he could take some time, if needed, on a case or cases for further investigation, time with witnesses, or was able to hear more than a "pitch" from a criminal defense attorney in order to reach the most just result possible.

*

Neal got about two hours of sleep and was then back at the station to finish his report, which, by then, was almost complete. By the late afternoon of Tuesday, the fifth, that document was being reviewed by DDA Hogan as he penned out the charges for each defendant, which were as follows:

Shane Summers: Charged with:

Count One: Attempted Murder in the First Degree of Lisa Deagan, a felony, on or about September 3, 1995, in the County of Jefferson.

Count Two: Attempted Murder in the First Degree of David Deagan, a felony, on or about September 3, 1995, in the County of Jefferson.

Count Three: Burglary of a Residence, a felony, on or about September 3, 1995, in the County of Jefferson.

Count Four: Assault with a Deadly Weapon upon Lisa and David Deagan, to wit: a bat and/or billy, a felony, on or about September 3, 1995, in the County of Jefferson.

Count Five: Evading a Peace Officer, a misdemeanor, on or about September 3, 1995, in the County of Jefferson.

Count Six: Reckless Driving, a misdemeanor, on or about September 3, 1995, in the County of Jefferson.

Eric Larson: Charged with:

Count One: Attempted Murder in the First Degree of Lisa Deagan, a felony, on or about September 3, 1995, in the County of Jefferson.

Count Two: Attempted Murder in the First Degree of David Deagan, a felony, on or about September 3, 1995, in the County of Jefferson.

Count Three: Burglary of a Residence, a felony, on or about September 3, 1995, in the County of Jefferson.

Count Four: Assault with a Deadly Weapon upon Lisa and David Deagan, to wit: a bat and/or billy, a felony, on or about September 3, 1995, in the County of Jefferson.

Camille Deagan: Charged with:

Count One: Attempted Murder in the First Degree of Lisa Deagan, a felony, on or about September 3, 1995, in the County of Jefferson.

Count Two: Attempted Murder in the First Degree of David Deagan, a felony, on or about September 3, 1995, in the County of Jefferson.

Count Three: Burglary of a Residence, a felony, on or about September 3, 1995, in the County of Jefferson.

Count Four: Assault with a Deadly Weapon upon Lisa and David Deagan, to wit: a bat and/or billy, a felony, on or about September 3, 1995, in the County of Jefferson.

They would be charged together in one complaint as accomplices and co-defendants, with the specificity of premeditation and/or in the commission of a felony.

Once the criminal complaint was completed and signed by DDA Hogan, the clerical staff of the DA's office filed the documents with the Jefferson County Municipal Court, where the official legal proceedings were now set to begin.

*

The in-custody felony arraignment calendar was already full for that late afternoon as the inmates filed in through the back of the dimly lit courtroom with shackles clinking and faces askew as they took a seat in the jury box. They were all in their easily distinguishable county-issued orange clothing and slip-on shoes. The slip-on shoes prevented access to laces, which could be used as a government-issued instrument for strangulation. Additionally, they aided in slowing escapees down for those who got an opportunity to run and took it. The inmates were mostly males of varying ages, but not exclusively. The women had to have a lengthy record, failed to appear in court, were on probation or parole, or had severely hurt someone before the justice system paid close attention to them due to the stereotypes and sexism that cut their way.

The air in the courtroom reeked of desperation, hopes of leniency, and, most of all, the desire for release that afternoon. All of the faces, but one, contained their best presentation, while the holdout was a career criminal, and he knew the ropes. He was ready to make a different presentation. That presentation was to show defiance and disdain for the operations before him that continued to take his freedom in the amorphous name of public safety.

As the arraignments proceeded in the Jefferson County Municipal Courtroom that afternoon, the three defendants, as they would now be called thereinafter, got ready for chow in their cells as the jail staff worked on how the movement of their three guests from the City of Benton would transpire.

*

On the next afternoon, DDA Linda Rakowski was assigned to the felony arraignment calendar for the day, and she headed to Department Five of the Municipal Court. As DDA Rakowski sat down, she began to organize herself for the fast and furious work ahead. She laid out the document depicting the listing and information for each defendant to be arraigned and the order they would be called. These included notes marking off five defendants who were looking at drug charges and three others for attempted murder. Her files were already organized to match the sequenced call of cases. She placed her trusty pen atop her yellow legal-sized notepad for additional notes and reminders as she began to quickly review the cases regarding arguments on bail or release on a person's own recognizance (OR).

Just then, Deputy DA Ben Cox casually strolled through the door and sat down in the front row of seating behind the counsel's desk. He was the DDA that oversaw drug cases that arose out of the countywide agency drug task force. He was there to represent The People versus five defendants swept up in the raid of a meth lab operation out in the county two days before. Soon, the door opened again as Ton Hogan came through and into the courtroom. Hogan walked up to DDA Rakowski and whispered in her ear, "I'm here for the *Summers et al.* matters."

She kept her eyes on the open file in front of her as she continued reading and shook her head in the affirmative. Hogan caught a look from DDA Cox, who was sitting nearby as he surreptitiously nodded at his coworker and friend. Suddenly, a couple of the correctional officers from the jail walked into the side of the courtroom tailed by the sounds of chattering shackles as they began to point to seating for the inmates as they arrived ready for arraignment. Interspersed in the line were Hogan's three defendants. As they sat down in the jury chairs, they began to look curiously at each other when a correctional officer loudly said, "Keep your eyes forward!" just as the Court Bailiff stood and drew all eyes toward him. The bailiff said, "All rise, the Honorable Carol Barrington of the Jefferson County Municipal Court presiding."

Everyone stood, and a door began to open from the opposite side of the courtroom from where the defendants had just arrived. A man in a black robe entered the old, stiff courtroom with purpose and a cocked smile. The defendants looked at the man to size him up while also wanting to look compliant as they awaited news of their release on OR, or so they hoped.

Judge Barrington ignored the attendees as he took his seat and began to review his arraignment list to refresh his memory and make sure all was in order. DDA Rakowski used that moment in time and looked upon the waiting defendants standing across from her as if she were sizing up her opponent for a fight. Judge Barrington finally looked about the room with wandering eyes and without any movement of his head when he finally said, "Yes. You may be seated."

All of the captives began to take their seats, except for the defendants beyond the number fourteen. The jury seating had twelve seats and two additional for the alternates. As those seats were filled, the rest of the inmates had to stand against the wall and wait.

Several cases were called and disposed of with efficient skill. Defense attorneys waited in the wings to step forward to waive the notice and reading of the charges on behalf of their paying clients, as they then sought their release from the confines of jail with failure or success. Of those defendants being represented by private counsel, five of them were in on drug charges stemming from the meth lab raid over the weekend. DDA Cox was firm in his argument as the defense attorneys used their best tactics. Those five had bail set for each. Some of the five would make bail, while others would have to stay put in the county hotel.

As things continued, some arguments for OR were successful, and some were not, as DDA Rakowski worked her way down the calendar. Once the private bar was finished, the court proceeded with the defendants who had not been able to retain counsel as of this moment. Judge Barrington was running out of time and wanted to proceed quickly as the public defenders were readying for assignment. Inevitably, there would be conflict cases, and if the private defense attorneys lingered long enough, they could catch one or two and get a paid case by the county. Indigent defendant cases paid less than the standard rate charged by private counsel, but they paid.

As the case was called, Shane Summers was already standing as the other two followed suit and rose from their chairs. The Court asked each of them if they had an attorney. They all shook their heads in the negative. The judge then assigned Public Defender Ting Bellows to Camille Deagan, subject to a financial review to meet the low standard of indigence. Ting quickly said, "My client enters a plea of not guilty; we waive further reading of the complaint and ask that the matter be set for the pre-trial conference and a preliminary examination. My client does not waive time."

Judge Barrington replied, "Very good," as the court clerk gave the next date and time for appearance.

Eric was assigned to a private defense attorney from Mountain View named Che Lopez. Ms. Lopez was dressed impeccably and presented a fierce look. She was a tough and semi-principled attorney who needed lots of money for her lifestyle. Because of that, she handled matters in other areas of law besides just criminal. She was known to have a tendency to plead her clients fairly early in the process due to her large caseload and need for cash flow. It was one of two ways to go. Have lots of clients and get them over with quickly, or have fewer clients and milk them out of all their money over time. The latter practice required more work, and Che Lopez didn't have time for that. Che recited similar words to what had just been spoken by Ting Bellows, with less accuracy but a lot more pizazz as she commanded the attention of the courtroom.

Finally, it was Shane Summers' turn. He needed counsel, too, as the remaining attorneys in the room declined the assignment due to their caseload size or due to a conflict. The clerk of the court looked down the list of conflict attorneys and said, "Judge, it looks like Dean D'Pare from Benton is next on the list for appointment."

"Benton? Well, the travel will be expensive. Anyone else available?"

"No, Judge."

"Okay, Dean D'Pare is appointed as counsel for Mr. Shane Summers in the matter, subject to his refusal due to conflict upon receipt of notification from this court," said the deep-voiced, robed man on high.

The court began to read the charges to Shane when Ting Bellows and Che Lopez parted from talking among themselves quietly, as Che said, "Your Honor, I will special for Mr. D'Pare for this proceeding and defer entry of plea and waive reading for Mr. D'Pare's client and ask that the matter be set for pretrial and a date for preliminary examination. Mr. D'Pare's client does not waive time."

The judge answered, "Okay, Ms. Lopez. Very well. Madam Clerk, can you provide the complaint to Miss Lopez for Mr. D'Pare?"

"Yes, Your Honor."

Just then, Ting Bellows addressed the court and said, "After conferring with my client, I would like to be heard on bail, Your Honor."

Just as he finished, Che Lopez said, "As would I, Your Honor."

Judge Barrington turned to the next defendant to be arraigned as he said, "Okay, we will come back to you both."

And so it went through the remainder of the calendar until the end was reached. At that point, Judge Barrington returned to those cases that were passed in order to hear arguments on bail.

It started with DDA Hogan giving the court the facts and circumstances of the case in brief while arguing, "All three defendants are a flight risk. Defendant Summers attempted to flee at the scene of the crime, which resulted in a chase and him crashing the car he was driving. Your Honor, all three are also a danger to the community and to the victims who survived the attempt to kill them. The People are asking that bail be set for the defendants in the amount of five hundred thousand dollars bond, apiece."

That was cash money or a bail bond from assets that could not typically be produced in the northern California county in that amount by almost anyone.

Defense counsel began their arguments as Ting said, "My client is the manager at a restaurant in Benton and needs to work to pay her bills and keep that business running. It's the second in a chain of stores that Rusty's hopes to be successful."

The judge could tell that the defendants couldn't make bail in the amount of even fifty thousand based on the previous inquiry regarding their ability to obtain private counsel. Judge Barrington ordered, "I have heard the party's arguments and see that the defendants are a flight risk and a danger to the community. Bail is set forth as requested by The People for Ms. Deagan in the amount of five hundred thousand dollars.

Would you still like to be heard, Ms. Lopez?"

"Yes. My client is also employed full-time in Benton and needs to work to pay his rent and take care of his commitments. We're asking that the court reduce the amount of bond to fifty thousand, Your Honor."

"Sorry, Counselor, your request is denied. Bail is set for Mr. Larson and Mr. Summers in the same amount. Anything else? Hearing none, court is adjourned."

The Public Defenders worked through the arraignment calendar on their feet as they accepted representation and the initial paperwork to make their file while trying to work out as much client counsel time as they could in the courtroom before the orange line of shackled alleged outlaws returned to the jail. This amount of communication was usually not nearly enough, and so they generally stopped by the jail on the way back to their office or scheduled an early morning visit for the next day.

On this calendar, Ting understood that he needed to get on top of this matter quickly due to the time exposure for his new client. He organized his files while the correctional officers proceeded with the roundup and movement of the prisoners back to the jail, carefully keeping the three co-defendants apart.

Che wanted to get a leg up on her representation before she went home as well. Her caseload was too large to be able to dally, so she had already packed her things and had beat the crowd to the industrial-looking, well-used jail interview rooms. As she waited, she read through her files and made her case note entries from the arraignment. She would bill both of her cases for her time in court and for her time at the jail making notes about it. Lastly, she would be paid for her meeting time with her new client, Eric, as well.

Eventually, the inmates arrived back at the jail and were sent in different routes throughout the concourses of the jail, depending on where that inmate was expected. Some went to chow, while others went back to their units. Three were singled out for attorney visits. Two of those three were Camille and Eric.

Camille met with Ting Bellows in an attorney-client interview room. She was glad to have a lawyer and was ready to tell him to get her out of jail. As she was sent into the room, Ting said, "I'm Ting Bellows, and I have practiced criminal defense law for the past twenty-five years."

"Ting? What kind of weird-ass name is that?"

"That's of no import. What is important here is that we use our limited time wisely."

"Okay, Mr. Experience. Whadda we do now?"

"Well, first, you're now protected by attorney-client privilege, and I need you to tell me what happened. Everything. Do you understand?"

"What do you wanna know?"

"Well, I want to know the truth so that I can defend you the best I can."

"Okay, Ting. Let's do it. Hmm, do you want to hear the dirty stuff, too? Ooh, I can see by your eyes that you do."

"Look, you damned fool; this ain't no game! Your freedom is on the line, so pull your head outta your ass."

With that, the pair briskly worked through the history and sequence of things that brought Camille into court that afternoon. The exchanges between the client and her attorney lasted an hour.

*

Nearby, Che was working her charm and wit on Eric Larson. She quickly interviewed him to see what kind of defenses Eric may be able to assert. She was able to wrap up the meeting in thirty minutes, telling Eric, "I'll see you again in a couple days. Keep your mouth shut until then. That means do not talk to any cops, guards, or other inmates. And do not talk about this crime in letters or on telephone calls. Any questions?"

"Yeah, I got it."

He was then escorted out of the interview area by a single correctional officer who said, "You're about to get a sack lunch for dinner since you missed hot chow."

"Are you fucking kidding me? That's some shit right there. You fucked me screw."

"No, your lawyer did, and you didn't even get to nut. Now start walking," he said as he laughed at Eric shuffling down the hallway in front of him.

*

The next morning, attorney Dean D'Pare walked into his office just after eight to be handed his messages from his secretary, one of which was a notification that he had been appointed to a felony case up in Mountain View.

Dean D'Pare had plans. He wanted to build a law practice that would span multiple counties and employ more than twenty attorneys. To do this, he needed to make contacts in the surrounding counties and to do so meant taking cases in them. For now, he was satisfied even though that meant long hours traveling and handling cases over a large geographical area, in a network of courts, with different local rules. When it came to Jefferson County, he knew a couple of defense attorneys that he had worked with in Mountain View, and some of its other municipalities that held court. He had also met one or two attorneys from Jefferson County who took cases on occasion in his home court in Cassell County. One of those people was Che Lopez. Dean sipped his espresso while he made some phone calls and read a couple of emails. His last task, before client meetings commenced, was a call to Che.

Che took the call and quickly filled him in on the preliminary details. She only took the call and gave Dean her time because she was able to bill the government for it, and she wanted to ride on the coattails of Dean D'Pare's skillset during the course of legal events in case she couldn't plead her client out. As Dean concluded his telephone call, he asked, "Did you or the other attorney get the charging documents at the arraignment?"

"No. You gotta get that from the DA in a discovery request."

*

As the time allowed for other ventures in justice, the four attorneys worked their other cases. That meant that the defense attorneys had other client interviews, court hearings, trials, and lots of reading and paperwork to fill their time.

Ton Hogan had matters to decline, cases to move forward, and those to dispose of in other creative ways while juggling court appearances. On that cluttered plate, he also had the continuous interviews of law enforcement, witnesses, and victims. These various meetings took place at his office, over the phone, or at a place that was more convenient to the unfortunate participants.

The three defense attorneys had contacted Ton a day or two before the next hearing in order to seek or proffer a resolution. Some district attorneys only accept offers for disposition, as they do not like to bargain against their position of strength, while others have no problem offering a lighter plea agreement in order to dispose of matters at an early stage in the proceedings. In the latter, though, strength must be consistent as sentences begin to stiffen the closer that a trial by court or by jury is to appear on the horizon.

Ton believed that early acceptance of guilt was good for the soul and was preferred since it was a factor for a lighter sentence under state law. He also believed that if he had to prepare for a series of court hearings and for a trial by jury, he wasn't going to accept less than his last offer. Each offer made ratcheted up the stakes. Routinely accepting less would eventually sink one into a reputation where they lacked credibility.

If that were to occur, it would dramatically increase the workload as the defense attorneys rode all of their cases to the end, waiting for the best deal from the feckless.

In this instance, he wanted a plea of guilty to attempted murder for each co-defendant, and it was their choice as to which victim they pled to attempting to murder, as long as the three co-defendants covered both victims. In exchange for that plea, each defendant would be sentenced to fifteen years to life.

As the case of *The People vs. Summers, Larson, and Deagan*, was called on the pre-trial calendar, Ton lifted his head from staring down at the counsel's table to see if any of the defendants were going to accept the plea deal. Ting Bellows spoke on behalf of the other two attorneys. "Your Honor, we have all received a plea offer from the DA. We have individually discussed it with our respective clients, and they are not willing to accept The People's offer. We're ready to proceed to the preliminary examination as set."

"Okay. Thank you, Counselor. The case is continued to the preliminary hearing as set," said Judge Barrington.

"Typical," was muttered quietly by Ton Hogan as he started to scribble notes in his case files. Ton then stood and nodded at the three defense counsels while he packed up his things and headed for the exit.

CHAPTER 13.

THE TWO-FACED SLOB

Obfuscation and falsity are the friends of the fork-tongued—techniques used daily by sinners and saints alike. In the trenches of the legal system, it is at the core of the chess match between grandmasters in the pursuit of justice.

*

The preliminary hearing set in the *Summers et al.* matter was going to come up fast since none of the defendants waived time. Ton had received all of the police reports by then, and they had been provided to the defense in discovery, but he needed the follow-up with Joe Jenkins and Sherry Burns to finish his due diligence. Ton picked up the phone and called Detective Ruffin.

"Hey, Ton, I was just gonna call you!"

"Perfect timing, I guess. Hey, I wanted to let you know that we are proceeding to prelim, and I made a fifteen-to-life offer at the first hearing."

"Ha, you don't say. I wonder what they think they've got. That sounds like a steal."

"They've got nothing. As you know, they're just stalling for time. So, where are we on the interviews of Sherry Burns and Joe Jenkins?"

"That's why I was gonna call you. I've got a meeting with both of them down in Benton."

"Oh, thanks. That's good," Ton said while glancing at his list of calls to make.

"You know I'm working with Mike Wilson at BPD. We're going to meet with each one of the witnesses tomorrow at the department."

"You know they say that great minds work alike. I knew you were on it. Appreciate it, Neal. Let me know what you find out."

"Will do."

The next morning found Detective Ruffin on the road again. He carefully sipped on his energy lifeline in order to not scald his tongue as he drove the serpentine road down the mountains to the valley floor. He arrived at the Benton Police Department earlier than expected and found a good parking spot for allied agency parking near the front of the building. He had not been in the BPD for a few years as he looked up at the pigeon droppings dried onto the large sign overhead that read, "Benton Police Department." He said out loud, "Well, that shit would drive me crazy. Don't they have a maintenance department or even a fucking hose? So unprofessional."

He walked inside and was met with a hardened glass window with a speaker hole in two places in the window. The bullet-resistant glass was centered in the wall and was encompassed by a small room that was painted powder blue. The room had one other door in it to the left of the bullet-resistant glass reception window, and it was unmarked. A woman suddenly appeared inside the glass as she rolled in from the left side of the window on her office chair and came to a stop with her hands grabbing the window ledge. As she looked up, her face displayed her hatred of her job, and the arrogance and contempt for the public that came with it from a decade of grooming by the modern police officer and their command staff. The woman didn't say anything as the awkward silence forced Neal to offer, "Um, I'm here to meet with Mike Wilson."

The woman pushed a piece of paper through the slot in

the window and said, "Fill this out."

Neal put his name down, the person's name who he was there to meet, his agency, and the reason for the visit and slid it back through.

The woman looked at it and then picked up the phone. Neal could hear her say, "Hey, there's a guy here named Ruffin...yeah, Neal Ruffin." She listened, and she then said, "Okay," and hung up the phone. The woman left the room that was to provide protection but instead built superiority, and within ten seconds, the door to the left was pushed open as the woman appeared next to it. Without saying a word, she waved at Neal to come with her as she walked him to Detective Wilson's Office.

As Neal stopped at Mike's door, Mike looked up and said, "Come on in, my friend."

Just before Neal made a step forward to enter, he turned to the receptionist to say "thanks" when he saw that she wasn't there but some fifteen feet away going back up front. Neal entered the office and said, "What in the fuck, man! What is wrong with that woman? Wait, did you do her, too? Now, it makes sense."

"Man, you think I'm some sorta gigolo or somethin'? I'm startin' to believe you've got some sorta Freudian latent homosexuality thing goin' on. Does your wife know?"

"You wish. That market is a dead end. Back to your lady friend there—I could see the fire and hatred in her eyes. Hell, I even saw it in her walk."

"That's just Kate. A dedicated member of the force."

"I mean, really, what's her fucking problem?"

"What do ya mean? What isn't wrong with her?"

"Whew, that one is a real delight!"

"Yep, thirty years of worthless. The last ten were dripping with bile, vile, and discontent. I gotta warn ya, she's mean. Really, really mean."

"Ridiculous," Neal said, shaking his head left to right

while looking at the floor.

"I guess you don't have that problem in your office, huh?"

"We do, but not like that! It's ridiculous, considering what is condoned in the workplace. Especially government work. To make it worse, they get placed in a spot where they are the first face that the public sees when engaging the bureaucracy and the barricades to service."

"Yeah, it is, but them dirtbags deserve it."

"That's the problem. I know everyone thinks they know who's who, but it gets mixed up. Just treat everyone well. If they're assholes, it's on them."

"Well, we can't solve everything. I ain't the boss, but I'd put her in the file room."

"Better yet, the unemployment line. Hey, are the witnesses here yet?"

"They aren't. We'll be notified when they get here, and then they'll be taken to separate interview rooms."

"Do they have to go through the Wolverine up front too?"

"Heck no! That is our new parolee and sex offender registration center. They're coming in a different way."

"That's good...Hey, wait. Oh, damn, that was a good one! Now, who's really mean?"

As Mike laughed hard at the results, he said, "That was pretty good. Right?"

"Yep, real funny. Ya got me back for sure. Hat's off. So, who do you want to interview?"

"Sherry. Even though it could get me into having to testify in your case."

"I can interview both and keep you out of that."

"It's okay. I want to find out if we have a crime in Cassell County, and if we do, you'll be coming back here as well."

"Wait, you want to interview Sherry? The stripper? I should've known. She probably knows you from being a regular, huh? Walk in with your dollar bills, and I'm sure she'll recognize your cheap ass."

The phone rang, and Mike picked up after reading the name of the caller on the telephone screen. Mike was informed that both of the people were there to meet with him and that they were ready and waiting in the interview rooms. Mike stood up and said, "They're here and waiting. Ready?"

Neal nodded his head as he stepped back and let Mike walk out of his office. Mike turned left, and Neal followed. The walk was long and convoluted as they eventually made their way to the interview rooms. Mike looked through the glass in each room until he saw a young man seated in one and a woman in the next. Mike then said, "That's your room back there," as he entered interview room nine and closed the door behind him.

Mike introduced himself and thanked her for coming down to speak with him. Sherry answered in her sweetest voice, "You're welcome. How long is this gonna take?"

"It'll take about an hour or so, I would guess. You are not under arrest, and you could leave at any time."

"I can leave at any time? Can I leave now?"

"Yes, but I wish you would stay."

"I hear that a lot, ya know."

Detective Wilson broke a smile and then said, "I want to know about your roommate, Camille Deagan."

"Why do you want to talk about her? I haven't seen her in a week or more."

"Camille has been arrested. I think you already knew that, though."

"For what?"

"Attempted murder."

"Ooh, that sounds serious, now, doesn't it?"

"It does. How do you know her besides being her roommate?"

Sherry walked him through her high school experience and that she had known Camille since they were little.

"Did you know her parents?"

"Yeah, I knew of them. I mean, it's a small town."

Sherry saw where this was headed and proceeded to tell Detective Wilson about stopping in at Rusty's and seeing Camille working there and that they struck up a conversation. She explained how it ended with her getting a place to live as Camille's roommate.

As the struggle for information and truth proceeded onward, Sherry asked, "Can we take a break? I need to get a soda and make a call."

"Sure. Make your call, take a bathroom break or whatever you need. I can get you a soda. What would you like?"

"I'll take a diet cola."

After Mike left, Sherry called a local attorney named Darnell Howard. Darnell had been an attorney for about a decade, and he handled criminal defense and tort cases in Cassell County. He was on contract with Prancers as a perk for the talent and the bouncers. People in the type of entertainment that went on at Prancers tended to live around the fringes of criminality, and Darnell was there to fix things and get them back to work as soon as possible if problems arose.

The receptionist for Darnell's law office said, "Honey, you stop talking to the police right now. Nothing else, you hear. Darnell will be over in a few minutes."

Mike walked back into the room with a coffee in a Styrofoam cup and a bottle of soda and sat them on the table. "Everything okay?" he asked.

"I thought Camille was into some sorta shit. I may or may not have anything to tell you, but my attorney is on the way, and I'm not saying another fucking word until he walks into this room."

Detective Wilson knew that he got swindled, but he also saw it as a sign that Sherry may have something that he wanted beyond the obvious. After some small talk about Prancers and what it is like to have people throw money at you for your sexuality and their experience, there was a knock on the door, and then Darnell Howard walked in. He was in an expensive suit and tie, with dress shoes that cost over a grand. He was bigger than life, and he quickly introduced himself and said, "If you can give me some time alone with my client, I would appreciate it."

"Sure," Detective Wilson said as he walked out and closed the door.

Darnell cautioned Sherry to only whisper in his ear as the police were recording the room. As they whispered back and forth, Darnell soon got the gist of what was happening and had a plan as to how he would protect his client and get her away from this quagmire. Darnell suspected that Detective Wilson was watching and listening, but proceeded professionally as if Mike Wilson had ethics and went and opened the door to invite him back inside the room. Much to his chagrin, Mike Wilson was nowhere near a place to lurk about the two-way mirror.

Detective Wilson walked back into the room when he cut to the chase and said, "Listen, we know that you were involved in the planning of a murder along with Camille Deagan, Eric Larson, and Shane Summers. What I want from you are details about that planning and any evidence that you may have regarding the plot to kill Lisa and David Deagan."

"Hold on now. My client may know something, but she will need full immunity from the District Attorney of Cassell County before she says a word."

"I understand. Please excuse me while I make a quick phone call to the DA's office. I'll be right back."

Mike Wilson headed for his office with glee as he made the phone call to an available DDA just down the street from the police department. He was soon talking with Lena Lawson as he laid out the facts as quickly as he could. She asked, "Do we have enough for a conspiracy in Cassell County?"

"You know those are hard to make. I doubt we have one that we can prove. If we give immunity on this, then the

Jefferson County DA can say that they did not grant, nor had any involvement in the grant of immunity for this witness."

"Nice chess match. Sounds like we would only offer qualified transactional immunity to only cover her on conspiracy and in this county. I think Darnell will take that," said DDA Lawson.

"Yeah, let's do it. When can you get it to me?"

"Ten minutes?"

"Perfect. Thanks."

Detective Wilson walked back into the room fifteen minutes later and said, "Here's qualified transactional immunity for your client for the crime of conspiracy," as he handed the stapled papers to Darnell. Darnell read through them quickly and was amazed that they got what they asked for, at least relatively, but more importantly, it showed that they were not interested in going after his client at all.

"My client and I will sign it right now. I have another meeting to attend, and I'll leave my client here to fulfill her part of the bargain."

Darnell Howard was true to his word, and as the ink dried, Sherry detailed all that she knew, with the exception of the parts about her giving any advice, comments of encouragement, or her desire for payment, helping to seal the fate of her old frenemy and two new acquaintances.

*

In interview room five, Joe Jenkins was semi-alert after having smoked a bowl that morning to prepare himself for the meeting. Detective Ruffin entered the room and was hit by the pungent smell of marijuana. He introduced himself to Slob and then took a seat. He then said, "Now, Joe, I want to thank you for being here this morning. You are not under arrest and are free to leave at any time. Do you understand?"

Joe looked up and said, "Yeah, man, I get that, but why am

I here? I didn't do anything, ya know?"

"We need to ask you some questions about a man named Shane Summers. Do you know him?"

"I do know that dude. He's my best friend," Joe quickly answered with a smile.

"I can tell that you smoked some marijuana this morning. How often do you use it?"

"Marijuana? No, man, I don't touch the stuff. I like a clear mind. Drugs are bad for ya, ya know?"

"You can stop with that. I can smell it on you right now. You reek, dude."

"That's my girlfriend, bro. She smoked a joint while she drove me here. I didn't take a toke off that. No sir."

"Joe—Joe, listen. I don't care if you smoked weed this morning, okay? I just need to make sure that you have a clear mind. Clear enough for us to talk. That's it."

"Oh, okay. Look, I smoked a little joint before I got here to calm me down. I was kinda scared, ya know? Hey, I can smoke a lot of weed and be good. This is how I am, man," Joe said, sitting there and looking at the door.

Detective Ruffin knew that Joe was possibly untrustworthy due to his mental state and that there was a high likelihood that this interview was going to go down the toilet, and as such, it couldn't be used at trial. What he did like was that Joe was willing to talk to him, and this interview could lead him to someone else or, at least, fill in some context.

"You said that you and Shane were best friends. How did you two become best friends?"

"We've known each other since we was little. I've known him my whole life. I don't have any family, but Shane's my family. He's all I got. That's my bro."

With that, the face of Detective Ruffin tilted in defeat, thinking that the interview was now over. To be sure, he then asked Joe to talk about Shane and his relationship with Camille. Joe started talking about how close the two were and that he and his girlfriend Erin were tight with them and went on dates with them a lot.

"Did Camille and Shane ever discuss getting married?" Ruffin then asked.

"I don't think they are getting married. Dude, I don't really know, but she talks about it, and he doesn't. Ya know what I mean?"

"Do you know if Camille or Shane have any money?"

"Oh, man, money is tight for all of us dudes, but we're making it."

"You're doing great, Joe. Do you know if Shane or Camille had come up with any ideas to make extra money recently?"

"No. No, I don't think so. They did talk about money from Camille's parents after they died, though," he said with eagerness.

"How were they going to do that?" asked Detective Ruffin as he leaned in toward Joe.

"I think that Shane, and Camille, and this dude named Eric were going to kill them and get the money. They asked me to help, and Sherry, too. We tried, but they didn't need us, so they were going to do it without us. Kind of a bummer 'cause I need some money."

"Sure. We all do, right? When was that?"

"They got a car from a dude, and they left for Mountain View a couple weeks ago," he said as he stared at the lights overhead.

"Have you talked to him since he left?"

"No man, he's been gone."

"I meant, has Shane called you on the phone since he left?"

"No, I don't think so. I haven't seen him either. He's probably at Camille's celebrating, ya know?"

"He and the other two are locked up in the Jefferson County Jail in Mountain View," Ruffin said while looking directly into Joe's eyes.

Joe paused as if the power that ran his brain failed in a catastrophic outage. "Shane's in jail? For what?"

"For trying to kill Camille's parents...."

Joe then softly said, "I'm so glad I didn't go. That sucks, man. What a bummer."

Detective Ruffin tried to keep Joe focused as he poked and prodded to get as much information as he could. Joe eventually described the first meeting and then the second, and then how the final three went about getting a car and why they wanted the money as well as how they were going to get it. In the end, the audio, video, and information were good, but the witness was problematic.

When the interview was finished, Joe smiled, got up, and walked out as if nothing happened. He had, in some ways, anchored his best friend to the bottom of the ocean, all while implicating himself in the planning. As Neal escorted Joe to the front exit, he really noticed how disheveled Joe was and that he may have had a week's worth of weed smoke embedded in the fibers of his clothes. Neal thanked him, gave him his business card, and watched Slob walk out into the sunshine. The light struck him hard, and Joe immediately turned away from the rays of life and squinted like a vampire at dawn.

Neal headed back to Mike's office to wait for him and compare notes. When he got to Mike's office, he saw a chance for some more coffee and indulged. He waited over an hour in Mike's office while employees passed by in the hallway and the shadows outside got smaller as the sun centered itself in the sky. He finally heard Mike's familiar voice talking with someone outside of his office door. Neal stood up as Mike walked in, and they both smiled at each other. Neal said, "Before you share, get squared away, and then let's have lunch. My treat, and we can talk about the interviews."

Mike jumped at the chance for food and a change in scenery. They ended up at a sandwich shop within walking distance and ordered lunch. When they got their food, they stopped for a soda from a self-service fountain machine and took their trays to a corner table where they began to dish.

Mike laid out the results of his interview and the need for an immunity agreement while getting very credible details about the planning and preparation of the crimes, along with the motive.

As they shared details and tidbits about the results of their interviews, Neal asked, "By the way, how's the family doing?"

Mike's face shifted from jubilance to angst as he said, "Michelle left me."

"Oh no, I'm so sorry. How are the kids? How are you?"

"It was tough, but I'm better emotionally. I think the kids are finally better, too. We have shared custody. By shared custody, I mean that Michelle has the kids seventy percent of the time!"

"That figures! Well, at least you get them some of the time, right? Where are you livin' at now?"

"I'm still at the house."

"Really? How in the Hell did you get that lucky?"

"Well, Michelle moved out with a guy friend 'who listens' to her."

"How long's it been?"

"Nine months since the divorce papers were filed. The final divorce is currently about fifty thousand dollars away."

Neal felt bad and said, "Hey, you know, if you need anything, just call someone else... I mean, just call me." As the two laughed, Neal clarified, "Seriously, call me for anything, and I'll be there."

"Thanks, my friend. I appreciate that. I'm about to lose a lot in the divorce, and I'll have to work at least another decade longer than I wanted now."

Neal shook his head in repudiation when it was decided that they should head back to the office.

On the walk back, Neal meekly said, "Hey, I'm sorry about all the shit I've been throwing, you know, about you sleeping with other women. Sorry, my friend."

Mike chuckled and turned his head and said, "Thanks. I

appreciate that. I have to admit that I did sleep with the waitress at Babe's Blue Omelet a couple of times, though. And I might do it again...."

Neal started to laugh so hard that he howled. He then said, "Oh man, that's the guy I know. I felt so bad after hearing the news of your pending divorce, but you're still dipping your willy at your age, so good for you!"

CHAPTER 14.

MOTIONS AND EMOTIONS

The Defense Counsel's representation of the accused is heralded. The lies told to support the defense are accepted without question. The struggles of these lowly few stir the heights of emotion as they chase the rarity of the game.

*

The plea deals provided at the last court hearing were still on the table until the start of the preliminary hearing scheduled for the next morning at ten.

As Ton Hogan prepared for the preliminary hearing, he saw a group of people turning on each other in a delightful twist of events. Ting, Che, and Dean saw a conflict arising out of that very same betrayal and also some wiggle room developing from it. At this point, defense counsel would work the angle for each one of their clients. Their position was that their client was unwillingly forced into the conduct by the other two. As each of the three accused the other two, they believed that they might be able to insert reasonable doubt as they tried to work their own client out of some or all of the criminal liability.

The three defense attorneys had a conference call the afternoon before the prelim. "So, Ting, what's the play for the prelim?" Dean asked.

"I like to let it run and see the evidence and hope for a

mistake. Doesn't happen often."

"Since the cop just recites his report, I don't see the need. Why don't we just waive the prelim?" asked Che.

"I think we should proceed like Ting wants to do. I need to see some cracks so I can start thinking about any challenges to the DA's case. Maybe tease out some statements from our clients' interviews that help them for a motion," Dean answered.

"Okay. I'm in. Might as well. Play it by ear?" Che said.

"We can be the steel curtain defense later. For this, we just make 'em do their job," Ting said.

*

Several matters were set for the preliminary hearing on the calendar that morning. Due to the severity of the charges, the co-defendant murder case would be last on the docket. The preliminary hearing calendar commenced, and Ton Hogan prosecuted two other matters while Ting Bellows defended two clients and pled another in a plea deal.

The courtroom finally emptied. Most of the attorneys, defendants, their family members, and police officers were now gone. The *Summers* co-defendant case was finally called. Che Lopez moved up to the counsel's table as she said, "Che Lopez for Eric Larson, Your Honor," followed by Ting Bellows and Dean D'Pare. Judge Tompkins' eyes moved to look at Ton, who finished out the perfunctory introductions.

"Are all parties ready to proceed?" said Judge Tompkins.

As the attorneys affirmed that they were, Ton began by calling Detective Ruffin to the stand.

Neal headed for the witness chair to deliver his testimony. After Detective Ruffin was sworn in, Ton began his line of questioning. Due to the volume of evidence, the testimony took almost forty-five minutes with few objections from the defense. When Ton was satisfied, he completed his last question and the defense was then allowed to question the witness.

Dean D'Pare was the lead, as the defense team tried to build in or find issues that they could challenge before the trial, as they had previously discussed. D'Pare asked for all of the statements made by his client where his client claimed coercion. Those questions were easily answered as the exact quotes were read into the record. D'Pare then resumed questioning as he tried to challenge the evidence that the three defendants went to the house with murder in mind. He was trying to defeat the assertion that there was premeditation and that the use of the key to open the door proved that it was a friendly visit to try to defeat the burglary charge.

"If there was agency through Ms. Deagan, then Eric Larson and Shane Summers were also guests and there should be no holding order as to the burglary charge for my client. In addition, my client was forced to participate and cannot be responsible for the acts of the other two. With that, I ask that you not hold my client to answer on the attempted murder counts and other charges," Dean said while standing next to his chair.

Che Lopez and Ting Bellows tried to fortify the points made by attorney Dean D'Pare while Ton Hogan argued the existing law and the facts, seeking to make the finding of probable cause on each charge.

Judge Tompkins issued a holding order on all charges for all three defendants.

The three defendants were seated at counsel table with their attorneys for the entirety of the hearing. Animation and emotion were seen for those few left in attendance who carefully watched; otherwise, they adhered to the conduct outlined in their attorney's coaching and were initially subdued and mature. As the holding order was issued and the defense attorneys reminded their clients what that meant, Eric had a strong bout of anger as he stood and began to yell.

"That DA is a fucking liar! This is bullshit! You're in deep shit motherfucker, just like that pig next to you!"

As he stiffened, he was met by the bailiff and a correctional officer who had advanced quickly to restrain him and physically remove him from the courtroom. On the way out, Eric screamed, "Fuck all of you!" while he fiercely resisted by pushing and trying to bite. He was forced out and into the courthouse hallway by the correctional officers.

In the hallway, he had his head covered with a spit mask made out of pantyhose as he started to spit saliva at anyone and anything. He was placed into a further control hold and taken to the elevator and back down to the first floor for removal to the jail. He became more compliant on his way back as his face was compacted by the constriction of the nylon around his mouth that had darkened from the saliva blockade.

As Ton started to gather his files and notes, Ting Bellows stepped over and said, "We'll talk," as he continued walking past. Ton shook his head to affirm what he heard while Ting peered back, looking for subtle acknowledgment on his way out of the courtroom.

Ton started heading to the exit as well when Che said, "I'll call you about my client."

"Yep."

As he neared the door, he had not received any word from Dean D'Pare and suddenly knew that this guy was going to fight all the way to the trial date, at the least, or all the way to his client's departure to state prison at the most.

Detective Ruffin had left the witness stand before the attorneys commenced argument on the holding order and was waiting outside of the courtroom. As Ton walked out, Neal joined him in the short walk down the hallway to the gates of the District Attorney's office, which was also within the walls of the courthouse. As the pair entered, Ton asked quietly, "Well, how're you feeling?"

"I think it went well." His eyebrows raised above his brown eyes.

Once inside the tight and bare confines of Ton's assigned office space, they both relaxed as they dropped their files and notebooks on Ton's desk, covered in mounds of existing file folders and paper and then took a seat to comment on the proceeding. "Hey, you missed all the commotion," Ton said.

"Oh, yeah? That dumbass Eric Larson?" Neal said.

"He is a dumbass. I liked that presentation. Pretty sweet."

"I heard that and then saw the guys drag him out. That was pretty sweet!"

"I know that Che, like a lot of attorneys, can't handle a client like that. And because of it, she'll want out."

"That poor bastard is going down hard now after that little show. What's next?"

"Oh, these three attorneys are going to try and obfuscate and blame each other to cause reasonable doubt."

"I totally agree. I think that with the video and physical evidence, confessions, and witness statements, they have to seek a plea deal. Don't ya think?"

"Oh, they'll file a bunch of motions to milk some money out and to look like they were effective counsel. They could go to trial, but that seems unlikely. It's pretty overwhelming."

"What do you think the Benton attorney will do?"

"I think he's goin' to drag it along the same way. Provide the appearance of a vigorous defense and squeeze it as hard as possible for county checks," Ton said, leaning back in his chair and gripping the armrests tightly.

*

It had been about an hour and a half after Detective Ruffin had left Ton's office when Ton got a call from the front desk of the DA's office saying, "Che Lopez is here and wants to see you if you are available—are you?"

"I'll be right there," he said while he arose and then laid the handset onto the telephone body. He then continued out of his office and headed for the main entrance.

"Hey, Che, what's up?" Ton said as he met her in the hallway.

"Can we talk in your office?"

"Yeah, sure. Follow me."

Once they arrived in the spartan office with the cluttered desk, Ton said, "Take a seat. What's on your agenda?"

"Well, what's the best deal I can get for my client?" She said after getting comfortable in an open chair.

"How about a plea to both attempted first-degree charges—count one and count two? The term would be the statutory fifteen to life, and the time would run concurrently."

"Dang! That's not much of a deal. I could plead him to the sheet with the judge and get that. How about one attempted murder charge as to the dad and the burglary charge to run concurrently? You still get your fifteen to life, but he gets a burg instead of two murder attempts. What do ya say?"

"Well, your guy is cooked. If anyone gets out of this, I'll be shocked, but with that said, that person definitely won't be your client. He was the main guy. I'll tell you this: I would take the attempted murder as to David for the fifteen to life and the burg to run concurrently and that he testify truthfully at trial."

"Yeah, you saw that behavior in court earlier. He has some pressure and some anger issues. His family is statutorily challenged, if you know what I mean. I'm pretty sure he won't want to testify. I'll take him that offer, but I'm not guaranteeing anything."

"Oh, and he has to enter a guilty plea." Ton eased off on the pressure and asked, "How's business these days?"

"Good. I've got client meetings...."

"Yep, well, thanks for stopping by. Let me know."

Che grabbed her purse, and as she walked out, she said, "We'll talk."

*

Che followed up a few days later with her co-counsel in the *Summers* matter through a three-person conference call. Dean D'Pare said, "Hey, Che may know this, but I am not sure if you do, Ting, but my specialty is law and motion practice. I did that exclusively for a couple of years in the Cook County Public Defender's Office."

"Nope. Didn't know that. Where are you going with this? You have some ideas for some challenges?" Ting asked.

"I do. I'll share the work with you, and then we can have them filed after the arraignment in Superior Court."

Che and Ting liked the idea and said that they could discuss it when Dean was up in Mountain View for the arraignment. Silence came when Dean said, "Che, I can't make that appearance. Can you specially appear for me in court again?"

"Sure, why not."

"Thank you. I owe you big time. I'm going to start work on the motions, and as I said, I'll share my work with you both."

"Great. Hey, I have to go. Talk with you both soon," Ting said.

"I have to go, too. I'll appear for you, then let you know what happened," Che added.

*

Che wanted to wait to see how the motions were laid out and to get a court ruling on them before she had any serious plea discussions with her client. To test her client's potential, she proceeded to the jail that afternoon to meet with Eric and a couple of other clients to discuss new offers. She met with her other clients first since she knew that Eric would be a challenge, and she did not want to burn herself out by starting with him. As she worked her way through her frank discussions, she finally was ready to meet Eric.

"Hey, how's my favorite client doing?"

"Whaddya got for me?"

Che explained the predicament that Eric was in and that she had a new offer from the district attorney. She first laid out the offer made for fifteen to life on both attempted murder counts with a guilty plea. She then said, "Here is his last offer. You plead guilty to the attempted murder of David Deagan in count two and burglary in count three, to run concurrently, but you must promise to testify at trial against Camille and Shane, and it has to be truthful testimony." She saw her client lean back on two chair legs and then come aggressively forward onto all four legs. He was tense, and Che could see the anger building.

"You got it all wrong bitch. I'm not gonna testify! There's no fuckin way! I would be a snitch in prison. And I ain't goin' to help those corrupt bastards convict anyone. That's a Hell-ta-the-fuckin-no, right there."

Che tried to calm him, but it got worse. Eric then said, "You think I give a shit about the time? I don't. I'm going down like a made man, and that's it. What else you got?"

Che tried to compose herself, since she was usually in charge in these meetings, when she said, "We're preparing some motions to knock the case out of court," while glowing in prowess.

"That sounds good. Let's see how that goes. I need a lawyer, not a dump truck. Understand?"

*

Camille Deagan had already informed her attorney that she wasn't pleading to shit and wanted to walk out the door at trial. Ting laughed and said, "I like to win. I'll do everything I can for you, but I don't think you're looking at a full acquittal here."

"You don't understand my abilities to persuade people. I

will testify at trial, and you'll see."

"I don't want you to testify, at least not at this point. The government has to make their case, and I don't like helping them. Do you at least understand that?"

"Oh yeah, I understand. I understand that you're lazy as shit, and even though you're worn out, you still like to fuck as many people as you can. How'd I do?"

Ting held his tongue as Camille then said, "I want you to assert the coercion under force and fear as my defense. Do you at least understand that? The jury will be sympathetic. If you can at least do that, you'll see."

"Look, I have been doing this a long time, and I run the case, not my client. I appreciate your assistance, but you, skating on this case before a jury in Jefferson County, is a pipe dream."

Ting then played the video of Camille and her co-defendants entering the house up until they were stopped and arrested.

Camille watched patiently, but when it was over, she said, "That doesn't mean shit. I did that but against my will. Do you get it?"

"Look, I get it. That'll be our defense on the charges or what is left of the charges after we file a few motions. We're done for now. I'll see you at the arraignment."

*

Ton was not expecting a plea at the arraignment on the information, and he figured the defense would throw a few motions at him before trial, and then they would tire and plead the trio to some charges with feigned remorse. They would then be sentenced, and it would be over. Ton was acutely aware of the poker hand that he had in this case since he rarely possessed this volume of incriminating evidence.

Shane finally got a second visit with his attorney, Dean D'Pare. Dean said, "Alright, Shane you are now going to be arraigned, which means told of the charges against you, but this charging document is called an information instead of a complaint."

"Okay."

"Since you were held to answer on the charges in municipal court, this charging document will have the same charges as before."

"Why are you telling me all this stupid shit? When do I get out?"

"Look at me, Shane. I'm working on that. Things take time. We are going to assert that there was no premeditation to support the first-degree murder charge. Okay?"

"Sure, I guess."

"As I said, it's a process. We will get some dates for pre-trial motions on the law and motion calendar to try and defeat some of these charges before you get to trial."

"Has that ever worked before?"

"Yeah. Yeah, it has worked more often than you think. It's the process. Let me ask you a couple more things. You were going to visit the Deagans and didn't tell them since Camille wanted to surprise them with the visit, but then you arrived late. You guys didn't want to wake her parents, and since Camille had a key, you believed that it was okay to be let in by her. Right?" Dean asked as he wrote notes on his yellow pad of lined paper.

"Yeah, that's what I thought."

"Right. So I'm going to also assert that by her having a house key, she was a co-owner or an invitee and could not, therefore, 'break' to enter the dwelling and try and get the burglary charge dismissed."

"Really? That would be awesome. Can that happen?" Shane

asked as he came alive after hearing the last word.

"It can. I'm pretty good at this. Have some faith. Lastly, I'm going to assert that assuming arguendo, if you and the other two defendants were there to inflict harm, they could not achieve said harm since the parents were completely safe someplace else out of harm's way. So, the three of you could not have killed them. Therefore, you could not have attempted to kill them either."

"I don't know what you just said, but it sounded good. What are my chances?"

"Pretty good."

"Like in percentages, man. Like ninety percent?"

"Probably like forty percent—maybe."

"Shit! That's not very good. Oh, man, I'm screwed!"

"No. No. Don't think like that, okay? The other two attorneys and I are also talking about possible bifurcation of the trial."

"What in the Hell does that mean?"

"It's where each of you would be tried separately and not together. Each of you would have a better chance alone unless we are sure that the defense of coercion and fear asserted three ways supplies the best ability for mass confusion with the jury—when they aren't sure who to believe."

Shane felt hope based on the words that rained down from the smooth-talking lawyer. Dean said, "Alright, my friend. Take it easy. Don't worry. By the way, I have to be in another court instead of at your arraignment. Ms. Lopez will stand in for me and help you while I'm helping another client."

As Dean left the Jefferson County Jail, he knew that he may have overstepped since he had not done any research on the case law to support his claims yet, but he also knew that he needed to represent his client zealously and with that, he would bring any argument, no matter how silly, as long as it wasn't unethical.

All of the co-defendants, two of their attorneys, and Ton Hogan were reunited again in court for their second arraignment on the same charges, this time in Superior Court, where they could proceed to law and motion and eventually to a trial by jury. As the case was called by the Jefferson County Superior Court Judge Teri Alexandria Porter, the defendants stood from their separate seats in the bowels of the large courtroom that they had not yet seen before. As Judge Porter stared at the well, Ton did not even lift his head to announce himself. The two defense attorneys were now standing within inches of their individual clients, almost as if they were drapes on a window frame. Che added the soft touch of laying her right hand on Eric's left shoulder to provide persuasion through intimacy and trust. The attorneys began their roles as actors in a live play in the round, where all in attendance could see every calculated move. The attorneys waived reading of the charges against their clients, waived time for trial and sought a spot on the pre-trial calendar with success.

Their clients still wondered what the fuck was going on as they listened to their harsh destiny from the mouths of their lawyers, with little sprinkles of hope. They were still separated within the jail, but they had people by now who moved among the facility and shared information when they could get away with it. These traders of information were invariably self-appointed purveyors of legal advice as well, as they worked to explain the process and the nomenclature to the frightened mice caught in a trap awaiting rescue. Jailhouse lawyers use their gift of gab to obtain payment of all kinds in exchange for common terms and made-up conclusions. This was rarely helpful as it generally deepened the divide between their real lawyer and the bamboozled layman.

*

The trio were weeks into their stay at the county lockup and wondering when they could leave. Each one had reached out to what friends and family they had through letters and attempts to get someone to answer a jail call where the toll charges and add-on fees were shifted to the recipient of the call. The response was a quick view of what was to come.

Eric had gotten a hold of his dad, who refused to discuss anything over a jail phone line based on previous personal experience. Sherry Burns accepted one call initially from Camille, but when she came under the microscope, she bailed.

Sherry did write letters to Camille seeking reimbursement for Camille's portion of the rent that Sherry had already paid and got no response.

Shane was certain that Tania would come to see him. She did not. She didn't even call, nor did she accept a call from her now-former sugar daddy. They were getting iced out, and they knew it.

They had not even been convicted yet, and they were alone. Shane was devastated and heartbroken when the abandonment came from his true love. He was emotional and became withdrawn in jail and in his meetings with his attorney. As Shane's physical and emotional state declined, Dean became concerned that his client may try to hurt himself, and he started to feel as though Shane was nearing the brink where he would be unable to assist in the preparation of his defense. He decided that he was going to seek a psychological evaluation through a motion to the court.

*

Angelique Perez had been working with the Deagans since before the move to the hotel on the night to remember. They were stoic and kept their emotions and confidential business just that, private. They were generally interested in the legal process and its outcomes as well as the progress of the prosecution against their daughter and, to a lesser extent, the other two. They were glad to be past the preliminary stages of Municipal Court and knew that the place they found themselves in would grind their emotions to near breakdown. It would be a long one. They refused to visit their daughter even though they received numerous letters from her, trying to build her defense with their support and assistance.

Lisa and David were good people who liked to give the benefit of the doubt to others, especially family, but in this instance, they refused—until one evening when the telephone rang, and Lisa answered. It was a call from the jail. A call from their very own daughter. Lisa looked around and saw that her husband was engrossed in the newspaper as she accepted the charges for the call. As the line brought Camille into the dialogue, Camille said, "Hello?"

"Yes?"

"Don't hang up, Mom! I want to know how you and Dad are doing."

"We're just fine, and you?"

"Mom, I'm so sorry. I have learned a lot while I've been locked up in this place. I see what a terrible person I was when I lived with you. You have to know that I didn't plan this. I was forced into it. That's the truth. You gotta believe me!"

"Uh huh, sure didn't look that way to us."

David was now tuned in to the call when he got up and asked, "Is that Cami? Hang up. Hang up."

Lisa tried to ignore him when he asked for the phone. As she relented, she handed it to him while her hands shook, and her facial expression portrayed exhaustion and heartbreak.

David got on the line and said, "We did everything we could for you. We gave you all we had, and you repay us with this shit? You're on your own. The only thing we will help you with is making sure that you get punished for what you've done. You tried to kill us! You understand that, right? Leave us alone and stop with the letters!"

David pushed the phone back onto its base after he pressed the call button to disconnect. Tears began to rise and fall as the two felt the remorse come back like a hurricane, as it mixed with the betrayal of wanting to be killed by their very own child.

Camille heard the line go dead. Before she hung up the phone, she said, "Ahh! Fuck you both."

*

Dean D'Pare was back in Mountain View, this time with a legal motion for a psychological examination for his client. The motion was coupled with an order shortening time in order to get it on the calendar quickly since he felt that time was of the essence. The order shortening time was signed by the court, and a hearing was set for that afternoon. Ton received the documents and appeared in court to hear the results. The time waiting was spent on some extra work that he had brought with him.

*

"Your Honor, my client has had some mental health setbacks and is in severe decline. Therefore, I'm seeking an order for a psychological evaluation."

"Alright, Mr. D'Pare, come on back, and we can discuss it in private," Judge Porter answered.

"My client is withdrawing from his defense counsel. He's depressed—and I think bordering on suicide or at least contemplating self-harm. Judge, I need an order to make sure my client gets the medical attention he deserves and that I'm covered ethically and morally," Dean said once he sat down in the judge's office.

"I understand. It sounds like your client is suffering. I'm going to grant your request, and we'll see how he is and where we are at. Okay?"

"Thank you. I'm definitely worried about him."

"I can see that. It's a good thing he has you. Anything else, Dean?"

"Can I choose the shrink?"

"Sure. If you want to pay for it. If not, we have a list of two. Our primary is Dr. Ray Mier here in town. Any objections?"

"I guess not."

Dean walked back into the courtroom where Ton Hogan believed that Dean had just either obtained a possible defense for the crimes or used the issue as a way to further postpone the trial. Ton was notified of the court's order for the psych evaluation and knew that he could only wait.

D'Pare had a lot of work to do, and the more time that he was given to prepare for trial provided a greater possibility that the prosecutor would become bored and lose their zeal. Especially if a newly publicized matter arose to excitement, and the previous case of the month degraded to the back folds of the local newspaper. It could also be advantageous for either side to let a matter simmer on the back of the stove, allowing for boredom and a burgeoning caseload to dislodge an acceptable resolution.

*

Shane was evaluated by Dr. Mier, who, after an interview and the application of a series of tests, submitted his findings.

DR. RAYMOND MIER, PSYCHIATRIC MEDICINE
104 S. MAIN STREET, MOUNTAIN VIEW

The Superior Court of Jefferson County
The Honorable Judge Porter:

Court Ordered Psychological Evaluation, Findings and Report. Patient: Shane Summers

Shane Summers was found to have some post-traumatic stress disorder from his childhood. His parents separated when he was five years of age, and his mother was murdered by his uncle when he was ten years old. The patient's father has been in and out of jail or prison his whole life. He is needful of a caring relationship and human interactions. He needs to fill the void of losing his mother with other women and will do anything to please them in order to avoid abandonment.

In addition, Shane was found to have a learning disability that has affected him greatly since he was young. He has never been treated for this disability, only finding ways to utilize coping mechanisms to meet the progressions in the various stages of life.

As a side note, Shane is currently exhibiting acute trauma from his recent break-up with a woman he intended on marrying. He has had no contact with the woman or her children since his arrest. Although this heartbreak could be considered normal, it could certainly also be a triggering factor for the patient, causing ideations for self-harm or suicide.

I do find that Mr. Summers is currently able to assist in his own defense and understands the charges and gravity of the situation that he is in.

It is recommended that the patient takes the medication that is prescribed and that Mr. Summers be considered a suicide risk until the medication is administered for at least a month, and at that time, further examination should be conducted by a licensed psychiatrist.

Ray Mier   M.D./Psychiatry

Dean noticed that Dr. Mier did not make any comments about whether Shane Summers was clear of mind when he committed the crimes, but that was a stream too deep and one that Dean did not seek to cross at his own request, especially now. What D'Pare and Shane had now was a possible defense and a factor or two that could possibly lessen his sentence if convicted.

*

Angelique was now checking in with and monitoring all of the witnesses that could be called at trial, as well as the two victims. She had her hands full with Slob since he varied in his responses and capability hour by hour, but he was always cordial and happy to help. As time moved on, she found that Jake Angelo was less interested in his duties as a citizen. He was having trouble in his relationship with Angie. He had also been labeled a rat by some mutual friends that he shared with Shane. He felt like he was getting shit on for doing the right thing, and he did not like it.

*

At the first pre-trial conference in the Jefferson County Superior Court, all of the defense attorneys were present, as was Ton Hogan. When Judge Porter called the case, she asked, "So, is there any chance of resolution in this matter?"

"Indeed, there is. Not only is there a chance, it should've happened already. I've never had a case as solid as this one, except one where the jury was out for two-and-a-half minutes. The evidence here is overwhelming. We're now to modified offers since the earlier ones were rejected," answered Ton while he looked into the eyes of Judge Porter.

"I don't like that characterization, Your Honor. My client has a right to proceed without the scorn of a scarlet letter! We filed a series of motions this morning in the Clerk's Office. They're set to be heard on the next law and motion calendar," Dean answered after getting up from his chair to address the court.

"We want to be heard on the same motions, Your Honor," Che Lopez said without pause.

"As do we," Ting Bellows said.

"I would like to meet with the attorneys in my chambers to discuss the issues and the possibility of resolution, short of further court proceedings. So, come on back," Judge Porter said as she stood and then turned and started to walk off the bench.

The attorneys seeking her pleasure grabbed their things and scurried along to catch her. They entered her office and closed the door, while two of the attorneys tried to act comfortable as they eased-in looking for seating, while the DA and the PD accelerated to their favorite chairs in their favorite power position in the room.

"Ton, why don't you give me the facts briefly from The People's perspective and all offers made," Judge Porter asked, from her desk.

Ton tried to be brief but needed to be thorough in order to show the greed and level of planning, sophistication, and violence that was perpetrated in the attempted murder.

"I have a motion to dismiss counts one through five for my client. This motion has to do with the fact that the Deagans were not even in the house. They were at a swanky hotel across town. Therefore, they could not have been assaulted with a deadly weapon nor murdered. So, counts one, two and four should be dismissed," Dean said, once Ton had finished.

"I see. What about the rest of the charges?" Judge Porter asked.

"Yes, so on count three, Camille used her house key to gain access to the Deagan home. The home that she grew up in. A home that she visited many times since she moved to Benton after turning eighteen. This is a house where her parents had given her the key to come home whenever she wanted! This makes her a permanent invitee. Someone who can come and go as she pleases, any day and at any time. So, there is no breaking to meet the burglary statute. Lastly, my client has post-traumatic stress disorder from trauma in his formative years."

"Oh, here we go! I knew this was coming. C'mon, Dean, really?" Ton said while looking at the judge.

"Please don't interrupt! This affects—this affects his ability to function in stressful situations. In this case, he was carried away by the other two people involved as he couldn't deal with the stress and coercion. His disorder caused him to be forced into this trip to meet with Camille Deagan's parents, and so when he finally saw a way out while the other two were focused on what they thought were the alleged victims, he turned and ran from the house and left. He got in the car that they drove to the Deagans' house. One that was loaned to him from an acquaintance of his. He left the Deagans' house and drove past the police. He drove past since he didn't think that he had done anything wrong. He kept driving after the spike strip was deployed since he was scared that they would kill him."

"Uh-huh. That's quite the story, counsel. I can't wait to read your motion and your case law. What do The People say in response?" Judge Porter said.

"As you know, Your Honor, the breaking doesn't mean breaking of material. Breaking under the current case law means breaking the horizontal plane of the dwelling itself. In this case, walking through the threshold of the open door was a breaking. Next, assault with a deadly weapon is applicable since an assault is an attempt at a battery. And as you know, a battery is the unlawful touching of another person against their will. Their intention was to kill both Mr. and Mrs. Deagan, and they took action to do so. Therefore, they did, in fact, commit an assault."

"What about the fact that your victims were not present?" Judge Porter asked as she looked through her notes.

"Well, we couldn't have left the Deagans in their bed to

prove an assault and attempted murder and get them injured or killed. That would be absurd. We have the intent to kill with planning, preparation, and travel, and it took place in the commission of a burglary, which then circles back to one of the theories on making the burglary—specifically, that they were breaking and entering to commit a felony. The 245(a) assault and/or the 187 murder. The striking of the bed where the defendants believed that the victims were lying meets the case law and the statutory requirements for an attempted murder. By the way, Your Honor, as I mentioned earlier, we have it all on video! Camille Deagan actually jumped onto the outline of the bodies and tried to inflict further damage with her hands as she yelled for her two compatriots to kill her parents."

"I see. What was Mr. Summers doing at that point?"

"Well, the police were in marked patrol cars and attempted to stop him through a series of roadblocks. After his tires hit the spikes, he continued driving and made it onto Interstate 1. At that point, he was away from residents and local traffic. He was physically knocked from the road by the Highway Patrol, and he was finally arrested at the bottom of the embankment, where he could no longer flee from the police. Lastly, I would say that whether Mr. Summers has mental health issues or not is immaterial since there was no professional opinion given as to his state of mind at the time of the crimes."

"Hmm, you do have a tough uphill battle, Mr. D'Pare. What do the other two counsel say?" Judge Porter said.

"We have joined in the motion as presented," Che answered.

"I disagree that my client was an instigator, as she, too, was forced into this activity. My client had the house key and was welcome at any time, day or night, and had been welcome since she moved out at eighteen," Ting said while looking down at his legal pad and then at the judge while displaying a face that carried no emotion.

"I know the answer, but is there any chance for a disposition today?" Judge Porter asked with a smile.

"No, Your Honor," the three defense attorneys answered in unison.

"Just so defense counsel knows, from what I've heard today, your chances are very slim. You can cut your losses now and I'm sure The People would offer a kind resolution for your clients."

"Thank you, but we are proceeding," answered D'Pare.

"Very well. We'll go back out and put it on the record and continue the matter to the law and motion calendar already scheduled for defense counsel motions."

*

After the hearing, Ton walked back into his office from the courtroom as he understood the bluster but disliked the extra work it caused—especially when Dean's motion had almost no chance of survival. As Ton settled into his chair to work on other pending matters, he had a knock on his door and was told that Che Lopez was there to see him. Ton was a bit agitated as he had finally made it back to his office and Che did not try to catch him earlier in the courtroom or in the hallway. He also knew that Ms. Lopez's request for a meeting was a solitary endeavor. She was taking action in the matter all on her own and only for her client, out of sight of the other attorneys.

Ton walked out of his office and headed back to the courthouse hallway outside the DA's office, whereupon he met her standing in the hallway. "Hey, can't leave, huh?" Ton said as he walked up to her.

"I'm working on it. Believe me," Che answered with a big smile.

Ton walked her back to his office and said, "Take a seat. Oh wait, let me move a couple of things out of your way here. Yeah, sorry, I probably said this to you before, but those two little chairs are all they gave me. So—what can I do for you?"

Ton had nothing on the walls and no pictures of anything to tie back to his personal life. Nothing like what is usually found in a person's office, such as a nod to a hobby, their subtle or direct position that reveals their political sway, or any other of life's diversions usually on display within an office space.

"Still depressing as Hell in here. Damn, Ton, get a picture of your dog or something," Che said after sitting down and crossing her legs.

"I don't have a dog," Ton said with a smile.

"Of course you don't, you unfeeling bastard.... Hey, look, what can I get for my client if our motions fail?"

"That was a very politically correct segue there. Let's see—how about the death penalty?" he said with a laugh.

"You are such an asshole. You're lucky that I like you. So, what are we looking at? Really."

"Well, after law and motion, he can plead guilty to the sheet, counts one through four. He'll get fifteen to life on count one, concurrent time for the remaining counts, and I still want him to testify truthfully."

"Really? Okay, first, he's not going to testify. He's adamant that he won't do that. Please trust me on that one," she said with revealed anxiety on her face and in her voice.

"Just that one, huh?"

"It's a figure of speech, you ass. Listen, I could plead him to the sheet before Judge Porter and get what you're offering."

"Maybe, or maybe more. It looks like your client wants to be done and to go and do his time. If after the motions fail, he can plead no contest to the four counts and get thirty to life. What do you think?"

"Okay, I get it. He's a bad guy, but if we fail, he's still pleading early in the process. He should get something for that. He's just exercising his rights, you know."

"Not really. What do you want?"

"Look, I'll prep him for a loss on the motion and see what

he can live with and call you or talk with you after the motion. Okay?"

"That's fine. We'll work it out," Ton said while grinning from the stiff banter.

Che got up, and as she opened his office door to leave, she said, "How about I plead him to everything, and you get some fucking pictures and maybe a piece of art or something in this depressing ass office," as she winked and disappeared.

After work that evening, Ton drove to the local Walmart and looked for a couple of pictures for his office. He found a nice eight-by-ten picture frame holding an image of a man, a woman and presumably their dog. He scooped it up since it was only five dollars. He also selected a cheap landscape art piece that he could hang somewhere for about fifteen bucks. As he carried them to the register, he mumbled, "Hopefully, this will keep these people off my ass."

*

Ton lived in a rental house just outside of town with his wife. They were newlyweds of a sort. They had been married a couple of years but were already in trouble. His wife Sandra was a city girl and didn't really fit into their new environment. She was also battling some emotional and psychological trauma of her own. Her parents were incredibly involved in her life, which was overwhelming. They demanded time from her every day, if not in person, then by telephone. They were not close in proximity anymore, so the demands for her to travel to see them were constant and expensive. Ultimately, because of her parent's manipulation that was entrenched into her mind and the effect it had on her body, she would fall away in a vacuum of angry devotion to her enslaving mom and dad while adding it as another factor that would eventually destroy her marriage.

Sandra also could not fathom a professional work life.

When a salaried position demands time, it must be given. She could not understand why Ton was working long hours for the same income since that income was never enough to meet her needs, and she expended almost no effort to assist in the endeavor for additional money—with the only exception that she never missed an opportunity to bitch at Ton by telling him to get a better job, or a substantial raise, on a continuous basis.

Sandra was a gold digger and a tool. Those characteristics were exhausting for Ton to deal with on top of his workload and the expectations from the District Attorney, the judges, his co-workers, law enforcement, witnesses, and most importantly, the victims of crime. Sandra was not pictured in his office because the office was where Ton got away from her. He did not need to be haunted there, as well.

After he left the Walmart and headed home, he pulled off of the freeway at his exit and came to a stop on the side of the road. He was tired and needed a break from work, yet he needed a break from home as well. More specifically, a break from the constant repression from his wife. He turned off the engine as he stared out of the windshield toward the hills beyond his car hood.

An occasional tear fell away as he felt trapped with no way out. He could file for divorce, but then he would be a failure—something that he rarely experienced in life in the endeavors that he took on with verve and pointed direction. Plus, he did not have the time to deal with such an undertaking, nor the money. As he cried out his existing emotions, he was able to eventually come to calm after forty minutes on the side of the road. He started his car and slowly headed to the house for the last battles of the day.

*

The next morning, Ton grabbed his hammer and a nail with a wire hanger attachment from his garage and headed back to his office. He carried his hard-sided file suitcase by the handle along with his art piece and the picture from his fantasy life to his office, trying carefully not to display the objects inside the frames. Legal Secretary Jennifer Solomon heard the hammer in his office making a racket and walked in to see what he was putting on the wall. As Ton saw Jennifer enter, he heard her say, "A picture. Nice! Walmart?"

"Yep."

Jennifer watched as he finished and then turned to leave as she spotted the fake family photo and said, "Nice touch. That ought to get 'em off your back. What are you gonna do when your wife sees it?"

"She's never even been here, so I guess it won't be a problem."

CHAPTER 15.

EVERYONE FOR THEMSELVES!

The appearance of nobility in the ignoble is a quandary. The guilty accepting guilt with praise and generally lesser conditions to avoid the wrath of their peers is American jurisprudence.

*

The Law and Motion Calendar was called in the courtroom with Judge Porter at the helm. It was a small calendar, and with that came fewer attorneys and more time to spend on each matter. The *People v. Summers, Larson and Deagan* was called first. All of the respective attorneys were present. Judge Porter asked, "Are counsel ready?"

"Oh yes, the defense is more than ready!" Dean answered while he stood and stared at Ton.

"Okay. Well then, how about The People?"

"The People are ready to watch the grasping at straws, Your Honor."

Dean had conducted his legal research and found that most of the case law was against him, so he had to be creative. He had found a couple of cases where the attorney had made similar arguments, so he used the dicta and the minority opinions of those cases to see if he could get the Judge to go out on a limb and risk a reversal on appeal or to make new case law.

D'Pare said, "'One could not assault the air and have the reverberations reach another nearby.' I am quoting the California Appellate Court case from 1952 in *James v. California*. This case may be in the minority, but it is still solid case law. Therefore, there has to be some proximity for an assault, or it could be used in the most absurd circumstances, as it is here in the case against the defendants."

Ton stood and surreptitiously winked at Dean and said, "Your Honor, the 1952 case of *James v. California* is an absolute outlier. It's not followed by any court. The cases of *The People v. Kingston* (1977) and *Bellamy v. Kingsly* (1983) are both solid case law and refute the ridiculous assertion by the defense."

Dean also had a potentially convincing argument for the access to the house by Camille Deagan in his points and authorities that was argued by Ting Bellows, who said, "The burglary charge should be dismissed in this matter against all three defendants. My client, Camille Deagan, was clearly a permanent invitee who could come and go as she pleased with the key that her own parents gave to her."

"Your Honor, the real question here is whether that invitation would cease if or when that person who held the key was entering to do harm. And secondarily, as to whether the possession of a key that was not returned or forgotten as loaned provided carte blanche access thereafter...The People assert that it would cease and that access on a loaned or forgotten key does not provide access in perpetuity," Ton said.

Eventually, after the heated exchange, Judge Porter had her ruling.

She recited the strong points of each argument asserted by the defense but then carefully and completely dismantled each based upon the argument by The People and the current case law that supported it. Ultimately, she said, "Therefore, the motions by all are denied in their entirety."

Shane was distraught and sobbing as the other two defendants seemed prepared for the loss. Dean dropped his head in apparent disappointment as an act to show his client that he was emotionally hurting as well when deep down he already knew it would be a failure.

Dean had to spend a little time with his inconsolable client at counsel's table. Eventually, Shane was removed from the courtroom and taken back to jail. Dean followed him over to resume talking with his client in order to keep him from hurting himself and to provide another ray of hope for the future. Dean had another card up his sleeve and he was about to share that with his client.

Ting told Camille, "This was a long shot. I have other tactics to use along the way through the trial. We've got to keep asserting defenses to get one to stick. Spaghetti on the wall, girl. Spaghetti on the wall."

"Don't worry, old man. I know that this shit is a charade. I ain't walkin' out of here because of what you did or your fuckin mystical spaghetti. I'm walkin' outta here because I'm gonna get the jury. Those people will believe me. You watch and see how it's done, old man. You'll see. When it happens, they'll wanna make a movie about me."

With that, she shuffled off in leg restraints and handcuffs, with her captors herding her back to the jail.

Che had asked the jail staff if she could keep Eric Larson in the courtroom after the hearing for negotiations, to which they obliged. Che told Ton, "Will you wait until the other defendants and counsel are gone so we can negotiate a resolution for Eric?"

"Yeah. But I'll only wait if you think it'll be fruitful."

"I do, or I wouldn't have said it."

"You've got client control? I've got too much to do to waste time getting jerked around."

"Hey, just do your fucking job, and I'll do mine. Okay?"

As the other two defendants were separately taken back to the jail, the courtroom finally emptied, and Eric was moved down to the counselor's table once again to have a seat next to his attorney. Judge Porter was in her chambers and the two attorneys had the courtroom almost to themselves. The two counsel tables faced the judge's bench. Ton sat at the long table to the left and Che to the right. Eric, who was still in leg irons but without handcuffs so that he could write and make notes, was seated to her right side, with a corrections officer sitting directly behind. Che talked with her client for a few minutes in a whisper as Ton got up and walked to the back of the courtroom to provide some privacy for the sacred attorney-client communications.

Eventually he had spotted Che Lopez look back at him and nod. As he got back to his seat, Che turned to him and said, "Okay. I think we're good here. My client will plead no contest to counts one and two for a fifteen to life term on each count consecutive, with a dismissal of the remaining charges against him, no testimony, and that he can leave for the Department of Corrections forthwith to commence his sentence. How does that sound for client control you, caveman?"

"I don't know how you did that, but done! Do you want me to get the judge, and we can put it on the record now?" Ton said while leaning in close to Che's left ear.

Che quickly turned to talk with her client, and after about forty seconds of whispers, she turned back and said, "Yes."

Ton got up from his chair and walked up to where the bailiff was seated reading the newspaper and informed him that they needed the judge, the clerk, and the court reporter back in the courtroom for a resolution in the Larson matter. The bailiff looked at Ton with irritation as he folded his newspaper back in an orderly fashion and got up. It took about fifteen minutes to round up the players, and eventually, Eric was standing with his attorney, ready for a plea. He had already completed the acknowledgment and waiver of his rights, as the court reporter had her machine ready and fingers in place as she nodded to Judge Porter. The Judge then asked, "I hear that there may be a disposition in this matter. Ms. Lopez, are you ready to proceed?"

"Yes. My client is ready to enter a nolo plea based upon an agreement with Mr. Hogan."

Judge Porter then asked, "Can either of you recite that agreement," as she looked down over her glasses to avoid her bifocals and peered at the two attorneys.

Upon recitation and agreement, Judge Porter said, "Mr. Larson. Do you agree to the terms and conditions as stated?"

"Yes."

"How do you plead to count one, attempted murder in the first degree against one Lisa Deagan?"

"No Contest."

"And how do you plead to count two, attempted murder in the first degree against David Deagan?"

"No Contest."

"Mr. Hogan, can you provide a factual basis for the plea?" Judge Porter asked.

"Your Honor, I would like the defendant, Mr. Larson, to do that."

"Mr. Larson, can you please describe the facts of what you did."

"Oh, Your Honor, can he be sworn in before he provides the factual basis?" Ton asked before Eric said a word.

"Madam Clerk, please swear in the defendant."

After being sworn in, Che whispered in Eric's ear as he said, "I live in Benton, California, and I planned the murders of the Deagans and then drove to their house on September 3, 1995. I went into their house with a baseball bat and attempted to kill them."

"Are The People satisfied with the offer of proof?" Judge Porter asked.

"Almost, Your Honor. I would like the defendant to describe the planning, preparation, others involved, and what they did in the victims' home."

Che started to object to the added factual basis as it brought in the guilt of the co-defendants but then stopped herself.

"Ms. Lopez, is there something you want to say?" the judge asked.

"No."

"Okay, Mr. Larson, please add the details of the crimes as requested by Mr. Hogan."

"I did this with Camille Deagan and Shane Summers. We planned it together. The goal was to get their money. Camille drove us from Benton to Mountain View. She let us in with a key, and I led them down the hallway to the room where her parents were supposed to be. Then I started swinging and tried to kill them with my bat...or billy club or whatever you call it."

"I accept your factual basis for the entry of plea and accept your no contest pleas. As part of your plea agreement, I'm sentencing you to fifteen years to life on each count to run consecutively for a minimum term of thirty years and a maximum of life in state prison. You'll get credit for time served in the Jefferson County Jail on these matters, and you will earn good time credits at no more than fifteen percent, as prescribed by law, while you are serving your term with the California Department of Corrections. The Sheriff's Department is ordered to transport Eric Larson to the California Department of Corrections in order to begin serving his term as soon as practicable," Judge Porter said.

Ton made an oral motion to dismiss the remaining counts against Eric Larson in lieu of the plea, gathered his file and his papers, and proceeded to walk out of the courtroom as Judge Porter began to return to her chambers.

Che turned to Eric as he said, "Thank you."

"You're welcome. Good luck, Eric."

He came into court viewed as a boy among his family, and he rose up as a man who did not rat on his friends and took some heavy charges without emotion that carried lengthy incarceration time. He would now work for his family "on the ins" instead of being an outcast "on the outs." Eric raised his head high as he got up from his chair and allowed the correctional officer to apply handcuffs to his wrists. He walked out with pride as he headed back to the county jail for a few more days and nights in Jefferson County, as he readied himself for a possible full-life term within the walls of a small city of men run by a government operation that dictates what you do, and when you do it.

*

Che was back to see Ton at his office after her client was led back to jail. She wanted to decompress a bit after the hearing and make sure that they still had a professional working relationship. As she walked into Ton's office, she immediately noticed the landscape art piece on the wall and started to laugh. She said, "I cannot believe it! I got Ton Hogan to do something that he didn't want to do! Unbelievable."

"You did! You weren't the only one, though," Ton said while looking at Che with a little smile.

While they talked and laughed, Che's eyes looked again at the art piece and then spotted the family photograph and said, "What the fuck! Is that your wife? You have a dog now? Wait. You fucking weirdo, that's not you! You sad little man. You put up the picture that came with the fucking frame?"

She saw the contentment on Ton's face as the reveal came off to perfection, and their friendship was sealed. Che wanted one more get as she built a relationship with the prosecutor when she said, "How'd you get your name, Ton? Is it a given name or a nickname?"

"Well, did you look it up on the State Bar website?"

"I did, which leads me to believe that it's your given name. We, the defense bar, want to know," she said with excitement while she leaned forward in her chair.

Ton did not like to talk about his first name but decided that a person like Che Lopez would tell everyone and that he could get it out of the way for good through her.

"I was born to parents who were raised in the forties. My dad had a job working for a refinery, and Mom was a housewife. They both enjoyed fitness and worked out with weights all the time. When their first child came along, it was a baby girl and they named her Barbie, and then when I was born, they named me Ton. Do you accept my offer of proof?"

She smiled like a kid on Halloween and said, "I got it! I got the story. I hope you know that I am going to share this gem."

Che flitted out the door with secrets to share, having forgotten all about Eric Larson and the moral dilemma that brought her in to see the man behind the curtain. Che then ventured back down the halls of the District Attorney's office. When nearing the exit, she mumbled, "Ton and Bar-bie," while smiling within a building that rarely saw such an event.

*

Word spread inside the jail about the guy named Eric Larson, who had just received two life terms. He had returned to the jail in proudful ignorance and a grin on his face. As the information was shared from unit to unit and cell to cell, it eventually made its way to Shane. Shane was stunned. He wanted Eric to hold out with Camille and him so that they had a better chance of fooling the jury with their united storyline. Now that Eric had pled guilty, he felt like he was done as well. Shane was taking the medication that he had been prescribed through the medical staff at the jail and was feeling better about his emotions and future until now. The three legs of the stool were now down to two, and he was scared. He drafted a letter to his attorney and wrote "Legal Mail" on the envelope to try to keep prying eyes out.

Since there was little chance of the female inmates being

able to communicate with the males in the facility, Camille remained in the dark about the news of her co-conspirator Eric Larson. However, the male population had a newfound respect for the guy who came in accused of attempted murder of an old lady and an old man. They now saw him as a guy who took two life terms with glee. Anybody who could eat that kind of time was either fucking crazy or an original gangster. Either way, such an action garnered respect and fear for the guy named Larson from Benton. Eric soaked it all in as he became one of the top dogs in the house. Life just became easier for him among the inmates as he awaited his departure via transport to the Northern California Reception Center for the Department of Corrections. There, he would spend several months being evaluated by the staff, as they would review his records, gang affiliation, and ability to follow directions while counselors checked his mental health and his suitability for rehabilitation. The results of these questions would eventually determine where he would primarily serve out his lengthy sentence. Ultimately, they would park him at the notorious San Quentin Prison next to the Pacific Ocean in Marin County, California.

*

Dean D'Pare received a letter marked *Legal Mail* from his client, Shane Summers. It stated:

> Help me. Eric Larson just got two life terms in prison.
> COME SEE ME.
> Shane Summers.

"What has happened now?" Dean blurted out loud as he tried to get up to speed on his current thoughts. He quickly sifted through the petabytes stored in his mind while trying to acquire a point of reference. He failed in gaining recovery through his random-access memory and asked his secretary for the case file for Shane Summers. A couple of hours of phone calls and other ventures brought him back to his client file for Shane as he saw Eric Larson in the caption of the charging document. He now understood Shane's issue and growled at the gut punch he received from Che in their endeavor to cause a whirlwind. But he may have just been given a break. Dean was going to blame all of the planning for the crimes during trial on Camille Deagan and all of the bloodlust on Eric Larson in the three-way scramble. Now, Dean could blame it on the empty chair. He wrote a letter to his client telling him to stay calm and to keep his mouth shut and that he would see him the next time he was in Mountain View.

When Shane received the letter, it did little to assuage the fears and anxiety that he was caught in. He was pulled from his cell and placed in solitary confinement in administrative segregation, where he could receive constant supervision since he was once again identified as a suicide risk by jail staff.

*

Weeks passed as the *Summers et al.* case was heard again on the pre-trial calendar. This time, there were only two defendants and two defense attorneys. It was getting more manageable for Ton and less so for Ting and Dean. As the case was called, Dean D'Pare asked the court if they could discuss the matter in chambers and then set a trial date. As they walked back to the judge's office, Ting said to Ton, "Son of a bitch! I can't reach this guy for weeks, and now he is gonna spring something else! I feel the knife coming...."

Judge Porter was pleasant but stern as she turned to Dean D'Pare and asked, "Okay, Mr. D'Pare, what was so important that we had to discuss it in chambers?"

"Sorry, Judge, but I want to plead my client."

"Oh, okay. We didn't need to come back here for that."

"I'm only pleading my client to counts five and six. Both misdemeanors."

Instantly, Ton Hogan figured out the strategy as Judge Porter asked D'Pare, "Are you only going to plead your client to two of the six charges against him?"

"He's still pleading not guilty to counts one through four. We would like a firm jury trial date on the remaining charges, Your Honor. I'll also be seeking an order for bifurcation of the trial and would like another date on the law and motion calendar for that."

Judge Porter turned to Ton and asked, "Any objections by The People?"

"Well, I'd like a plea to counts one through four instead, but I can't stop him from pleading guilty if he wants to. I do object to any bifurcation request but will make those arguments in the right framework."

Ting jumped in and said, "I wish that co-defendant's counsel was more communicative with me. That sure would be helpful," as he glared at Dean. "And yes, I'll also be objecting to the bifurcation motion."

Ting Bellows had been around the block as a lawyer more than once and was unhappy with the less-than-unified front. He already knew that Che Lopez was going to plead her client before she did, and now D'Pare wanted to separate his client out and try and leave Camille holding the bag.

Judge Porter re-called the case back into session as Dean moved to his left at the counsel table to allow for his client to be seated next to him. The court asked Mr. Summers if he wished to enter a plea while Dean whispered into his left ear. Dean then looked up and said, "Yes, Your Honor, my client is going to enter a plea of no contest to counts five and six. He will also continue to plead not guilty to counts one through four."

"As to count five: Evading a Peace Officer, a misdemeanor, how do you plead?" Judge Porter asked.

"Uh, No Contest, I guess," Shane quietly answered.

"I accept your plea of no contest. How do you plead to count six: Reckless Driving: a misdemeanor?"

"No Contest?"

"I accept your plea as to count six. Mr. D'Pare, would your client want to be sentenced today on the charges?"

"He does."

"Okay, Mr. Summers, before I sentence you on these two charges, is there anything you'd like to say?"

"I didn't do anything. I didn't know they were trying to stop me. I just wanted to see Tania," Shane said as he looked at the judge and then at his lawyer.

"Mr. Summers, I sentence you to three months in the Jefferson County Jail with credit for time served and three years of informal probation with the standard terms and conditions."

Judge Porter then set a date for the hearing of the bifurcation motion in two weeks' time. She then asked, "Do you want to confirm the existing trial date or seek a new one?"

Both Ton and Ting said that they were ready for the trial date. Dean ignored them and said, "I need more time to prepare my motion to separate the defendants for trial and so I need to get another date for jury trial."

"I'm vacating the current trial date and setting a new one on March 4, 1996, at eight-thirty. Does that work for everyone's schedule?" she asked as she again peered over her bifocals at the attorneys below.

In an unusual state of affairs, all three attorneys found that their calendars were open for that week, or at least not occluded, and agreed upon the date provided. Judge Porter nodded as she then called the next case on the calendar, looking for the following set of attorneys.

Ting Bellows turned to Camille as his client said with frustration, "Hey, old man, what do we do now?"

"Don't worry, this is how it works."

"Oh no, you ain't getting by with that bullshit. We were goin' to dump this on them two assholes. Now, Eric's out, and Shane is up to something. I'm not happy—understand?"

"Hey, why not? We're still gonna dump this in Eric's lap and Shane's too. Eric has now been convicted of attempted murder of the Deagans. That's really good for us. Really good."

"Really? One pled out and the other is going to have his own trial where Eric and I did it all. And why in the Hell did he just agree to those charges? What just happened?"

"They're going to try and hide that Shane ran so he doesn't look so guilty. They're trying to save their own skin and not yours, girl."

"That can't happen. You have to keep him in. You just got to."

"We'll do our best. Let's just wait and see what happens."

"And then what? I go off to prison, and you go home to whatever that is," as she heard a guard say, "Let's go."

"You come and see me at the jail. Now!"

*

Ting did not have a lot of time to spare since he was in a jury trial the next morning defending another client against Ton Hogan for a child molestation case.

He met Camille in one of the jail interview rooms about thirty minutes later, and she became hyperactive when she walked in. She asked, "What in the fuckin' A are you doing in my defense?"

"Wait, I thought you were running this ship?"

"I am, but you work for me. I got the jury. You gotta get me in front of them without lookin' guilty. I've got Eric to blame it on without him sayin' anything, but I gotta have Shane there to point to. Got it? Do you have anything? Anything other than, 'Let's wait and see girl. I don't have a fucking clue, but I will,' bullshit!"

"You need to calm down. Since things change, as you can see, I'll fill you in when we are closer to trial. I have another client going to trial in the morning. When yours gets closer, we'll work it out."

"I don't give a shit about your workload or your disgusting child molester client. This is your fuckin' job, dude."

"First, don't fucking talk to me like that! Got it? Next, they prosecute, we defend. We don't have to do anything. We prepare a defense, but a lot of our job comes along as the trial progresses, especially if we are screwed—and lady, you are screwed."

"You know what? You're the absolute shits. I want another lawyer!"

"That's fine. I'll file the paperwork for a hearing for ineffective assistance of counsel and the appointment of a new defense attorney."

Camille was not sure what all that meant, but she agreed because it sounded like something was going to happen.

*

Ting had his office file the paperwork as Camille had requested before his trial started at eight-thirty the next morning. By the end of the day, the court had adjourned the child molestation case a few minutes early so that she could hear the ineffective assistance matter.

Camille was brought into the cleared courtroom in handcuffs and leg shackles as usual.

"Miss Deagan, I see you want a new attorney. Tell me why," said Judge Porter.

"I want to fire Ting because I never see him, and he doesn't seem to know what he's doing."

When the confidential details of Camille's issues were completed, Ton was able to walk into the courtroom to see if Ting was going to stay on as Deagan's attorney. Just then, the Judge said, "Ms. Deagan, I have denied your motion for a new attorney. Mr. Bellows is still your appointed counsel. What I ask is that you both do a better job with your communication. This matter is adjourned."

As Camille was leaving and her chains rattled with her, she turned her head back and smirked as she said, "Ting, my boy, come see me when you can."

"I will," he said as he raised his hand toward her. Then, his head tilted downward, and his eyes met the worn carpet on the floor. "I will," he said quietly.

Ton waited until Camille was gone and said, "I'm sorry, my friend. Victims and witnesses can really be pissed with us sometimes, but your own clients doing this to you—well, you're a saint, my friend. I'll see you bright and early."

Ton went back to his office and worked on trial preparation for the next day until it was almost eight when he decided to leave and head home to try and get some needed sleep if he was allowed.

*

The trial for the man charged with several counts of child molestation had finally finished. The defendant was found guilty of all charges by the jury of his peers in a place that had little patience for felony-level behavior, let alone the sexual assault and abuse of children.

Now that the instant case was over, the repetition of the weekly court calendars resumed. Ton had no time to bask in the glory of his work, nor did anyone really care once the trial and the sentencing were concluded. It was always onto the next, or in this case, back to the next.

CHAPTER 16.

READINESS

Time can be a healer of wounds, whether they are physical or emotional. Improvement comes in layers, and one of those layers includes knowing that life must go on from setbacks and defeats—that a life well-lived must be meaningful and enjoyable in order to keep up the fight. Anything less invites decay and, eventually, a miserable existence.

*

Lisa and David Deagan had done their best to work through the trauma of the events of September 1995. Lisa sought professional counseling in town from a local psychologist, while David worked his "self-help program," mostly through internalization, talking with his wife, and the consumption of beer. Their friends were supportive and helpful, as were Lisa and David's mothers, who still lived in town. That was one thing that David and Lisa were grateful for was that neither of their fathers were alive to see this attempt on their lives by their own grandchild. They darkly joked, "Camille's attempt to murder us would have killed our dads if they weren't already dead!"

Lisa always wanted to go to Hawaii and now seemed like the time. The trial was a few months away, and it was winter in the northern California mountains. Lisa said, "I want you to take two weeks off and spend it with me. We're going to get out of here, and these are the dates...."

"You know that I like to save my leave time for emergencies and dedicated events, so I don't know if we can," David answered.

"Oh, we can, and we're going to. End of argument."

David sat silently as his face contorted in the struggle and then said, "Okay. I guess this is a dedicated event—let's do it."

A few days later, at the dinner table, David said, "I took the time off and am ready to get out of here for a while. I can't believe we're doing this!" David said as Lisa listened intently.

Lisa got up and ran into another room in the house and returned shortly with the roundtrip plane tickets she had purchased for a flight from Medford, Oregon, to Portland and then to the big island of Hawaii. David actually produced the semblance of a smile for the first time in months. He then said, "We're actually going to Hawaii? Are we gonna have to sleep in the airport, or do we have a hotel?"

"We have a room at The Tides Hotel!"

"Are you shitting me?"

Lisa handed him the itinerary as he said, "You're the best wife in the world!"

They were to leave in a week and try and relax away from Mountain View winters, and all of the ugly truth that was their offspring. That week went by quickly as the couple prepared their suitcases and informed Angelique that they would be gone for a couple of weeks to escape the madness.

*

As the couple basked in the glorious Hawaiian sunshine, they tried to release some anger and memories of their failures in life while they enjoyed the change of scenery. The pair did not prepare themselves for the sudden change in light exposure before their arrival, and they were sunburned on day one and had to protect the damage for the remainder of their stay.

The glow of pink and red skin gave every indication that they were mainland haoles from the backwoods.

Lisa wanted to try snorkeling, but David was not a great swimmer at his age and circumference. As they entered a dive shop, she said, "You can do it. Look at you. You're as fit as Mark Spitz," while reaching out to rub his abs that were hidden away like rocks on a high mountain in winter.

"Oh, now you are full of shit."

"You're round like a beach ball and should float just as good. Plus, that bald head of yours should cut through the water with hairless efficiency."

David laughed at the gentle ribbing as he looked at his wife in a new way. She was still shapely, she was still beautiful to him, and she was doing extremely well under the circumstances of the past year. His sudden emotional cascade reminded him that he was also grateful that Lisa Cooper married him in 1970.

He loathed the circumstances that they were in and that a great woman like Lisa deserved a loving and devoted child and not a demon seed. He now wished he had made more babies with her when they were young, as maybe he could write this one off a little easier if he had others to keep. David realized that judgment and decisions cannot be rescinded in the future from the past, as he still pondered the exception. The decision was made due to the desire to not add another handful of trouble to their hectic lives when, in retrospect, the addition of another child may have provided the return of love and respect that they desperately sought at this moment in time.

*

They were not ready for their departure from an island that lured to its beauty yet tricked from seeing its afflictions. As David and Lisa neared the airport, they became sullen as their raw emotions, which had been previously laid asunder in the allure of tourist traps, blue waters, and grey sands, were now starting to pulse with pain once again.

The wheels screeched as they hit the runway of the Portland International Airport. The pair let out a soft sigh of relief to be back on the ground and away from the magnificence of the ever-present Pacific Ocean below. When they got home from the airport in Medford, they arrived at their maudlin existence as the garage door opened to receive their car once again. As they entered their house, they could feel the heartbreaking and horrific invasion of their home, the violence that came with it, and the emotional abuse from its continuing aftermath. The internal walls came up to meet the affront as the scars hardened once again to remind hurting souls that they had never really left.

*

Dean D'Pare had a gameplan for trial. He had developed a motion for bifurcation, and he had his other motions prepared for trial as well. His client was still on suicide watch and was in decline, so he made the drive up to Mountain View on a Friday when he was free of court appearances.

Shane came into the attorney-client visiting room with his head down and his hair long and unkempt. He dropped into the chair after his handcuffs were removed by the corrections officer. Once they had the room to themselves, Dean said, "Shane, how are you doing? You look really good. Really good."

"I don't feel good," as his face fell to stare at his still hands on the table in front of him.

"We need to work on your acting skills, okay?"

"What now?" Shane said while he lifted his head and brought his eyes to meet Dean's.

"We cannot let the jury see this sadness and lack of care

for what happens to you. You have to act like you're innocent."

Shane was nonresponsive.

Dean quietly said, "You're doomed if you don't get out of this funk that you're in and help me in your defense. Do you understand that?"

"Yeah, I understand."

"Good. You need your hair cut and they provide them in the jail. Get one in the next ten days. And I want it short. Nothing goofy or weird, and no shaved head. I don't want them thinking you are some skinhead or something, and I also don't want them seeing that you really don't give a fuck about what happens to you, either. Look at me, Shane. I need your help, do you understand?"

"What's the use? I'm fucked," Shane answered as he looked at his lawyer with his face covered in graffiti of desperation and despair.

"Look. If we could just knock out a few counts, you'll still have a chance at life," Dean said as he looked into Shane's eyes with intensity.

Dean waited for responsiveness and then said, "Our main goal is to get all not-guilty verdicts returned by the jury, but that is going to be tough. If we get not guilty verdicts on the attempted murder charges, but you are found guilty on the assault or the burglary or both, it would still be considered a win!"

Shane remained inattentive as Dean resumed. "That kind of verdict would drastically reduce your exposure, resulting in your incarceration time being manageable. You'll still be very young when you get out of prison."

"How're you going to accomplish this when there was a video of the crime, and there are snitches willing to testify," Shane asked, in a flat affect.

"Remember that I had you plead to the misdemeanor charges so that those facts would be irrelevant at trial. I'm also filing a motion to limit the introduction of that evidence to only include you running from the house after things became violent. Look, you told me that you didn't do anything. I'm going to try and show the jury your defense. That you were only there on a visit as you had done before and that you didn't know that Eric and Camille were going to try and kill her parents."

"Will that work?" Shane asked as he looked up from having stared at the tabletop for the past few minutes.

"I don't know, Shane, but I do know that we have a chance with this argument and this maneuver, and you need to believe in it."

"Yeah. I hear ya."

"Keep your head up and your mouth shut. Believe in the desired result in order to help make it a reality. Understand?"

Shane nodded his head as he watched his attorney pack up his papers and briefcase.

"Shane, take care of yourself. No self-harm, okay? I'm working hard for you. I'll see you in a week or two."

*

Camille knew that she was not going to talk her way out of this mess with anyone but the jury. She was getting stabbed in the back by her co-defendants and needed Ting Bellows to help her. Ting had stopped by to talk with her at the jail after his other client interviews during the morning hours. Camille was reserved for once. "How're you holding up?" Ting asked.

"Well, old man, I want out of this shithole if that's what you're askin'. I got some inmates doin' shit for me now, though. I'm the boss again, so it's better. What do ya have for me?"

Ting's face was unpleasant in display as he looked her in the eyes and answered, "I had my investigator down in Benton to talk with some of your employees and other acquaintances to see if they could help as character witnesses."

"Now we're talkin'. Those people love me! Well, how'd

that go?" Camille said as she smiled and leaned in toward her lawyer.

"Well, I think the word love is a bit strong. You had a few employees provide statements as to your good character, but the friends and roommate were unwilling to help or even talk with our investigator."

"Those backstabbing bastards. I expected that from Sherry. Who did the guy talk to?"

"Like I said, your employees and Shane's roommates, Sherry, neighbors. Hell, we even asked the mail carrier. I would say those people may not understand love in the same way you do."

She sighed and said, "I see how you are enjoying this, old man. Yep, you're fuckin' me. I bet you're happy, huh?"

"Damn it! Focus on your defense instead of being a complete bitch all the time. Alright?"

"Yeah, yeah. Screw you! I need some people to help me, ya know?"

"Don't worry, we'll get help, and we'll defend in other ways."

"Yeah, right! What do you think Shane's attorney is gonna do?"

"Like I said before, he's going to put this whole thing on you and Eric. Eric won't be testifying since there is no reason to put him on the stand. He won't provide anything helpful, and he'll just muddy you up by association in the process. So, we're going to lay all the blame on Shane and Eric, just like you have been saying and tell the jury that you were forced into this by these two guys."

"Impressive! What in the Hell do you do? I gave you all that!"

"Just stop. Stop fighting me. I'm the only one trying to help you right now."

"That is true, and you're only tryin'. Will Shane and I have separate trials?"

"Look, kid, I've done this for a long time, and it does happen, but I don't anticipate that you'll be separated from Shane, and we don't want it to happen either. I'm gonna be frank here, you're looking at a long time in prison, and you need to quit fucking around. You need to get your mind right and prepare for such an event. Your chances of walking out of this unscathed are low. Actually, extremely low."

Her face soured with the news. Her eyes squinted as her eyebrows came together and her teeth clenched. The tension spread throughout her body as Ting observed the moment that the seriousness of the situation finally struck like a lightning bolt to the center of the earth.

Ting did not get any pleasure from this. In fact, he despised the delivery of unwelcome news. He became a defense attorney to help people, not to crush their hopes, but it came with the job, and he had built enough armor around his nerve endings to be able to deliver that message without wearing it home. In the end, he knew that there were ramifications for illegal behavior in a civilized society. His job was to make sure that the rules set forth by the Constitution, statutory law, and case law precedent were followed by the government.

*

The Law and Motion calendar finally arrived for Dean D'Pare to test his theories, his writing skills, and, most importantly, the persuasion of his oratory.

Judge Porter called the case. Since it was a defense counsel motion, they were to go first.

"I'm seeking a separation of defendants for trial, Your Honor. My client was the least involved in the matters that occurred on September 3, 1995. The culpability and overwhelming evidence against co-defendant Camille Deagan will compromise the fairness of the trial for my client. My client was, and is, a mentally damaged young man who was dating

Camille Deagan and trying to fit in with the group of people in their area. He was a meek young man who was not fully aware of what was happening around him as he traveled to Mountain View," Dean said while he sat and read from his notes in front of him.

Dean paused and stood, as he looked to his left at Ton and Ting with a smirk and said, "Ms. Deagan told my client to get a rental car for the weekend for a trip to visit with her parents. A trip they had taken before. Shane didn't have a credit card to obtain the car. So he got it through a friend, and he and Camille picked it up for their weekend trip. Shane didn't know that Eric Larson was coming along. He was surprised when Camille drove to Eric's apartment as they were leaving Benton on their way to visit Camille's parents. When they got to the Deagans' house, they went around to the back and Camille used her key and walked in. She then invited my client and Eric inside. It was then that he noticed that Eric Larson had a baseball bat and that he was being led down the hallway toward the bedrooms. He followed Camille into the bedroom, thinking that it was where they were going to sleep, when Eric started hitting the lumps in the bed with the bat. Camille then participated. As my client realized what was happening, he ran. He ran from the house and tried to leave in the car that was loaned to him. My client needs to present those facts to the jury without prejudice."

Dean paused again, but this time for theatrical effect, he moved behind Camille and then resumed, "I'm sure that Mr. Bellows has a plan to lay this on my client. I don't know how, but I'm sure that is their defense. Camille Deagan was seen attacking what she thought were her parents on video. What's not on video is an attack on the shapes in the bed by my client. He didn't do anything but have an epiphany that he was in the wrong place and wanted no part in what was happening. It also didn't capture the fear and shock that existed on the face of my client as he ran away. It couldn't because my client ran so fast that the video camera could not even capture his face as he passed. My client clearly will be muddied up by the story of Eric Larson and Camille Deagan's dastardly and despicable deeds. It would be unfair for my client to stand trial with the last culpable participant when he was duped into the trip."

"Are you finished, Mr. D'Pare?" the judge asked.

"Yes, Your Honor, but I would like a ruling on the bifurcation motion before we move on to the motion to dismiss."

"Mr. Bellows, do you have anything?" the judge asked.

Ting stood up and his face was red. This was one of the reasons that he did not like out-of-town defense attorneys since they were more inclined to shit all over the local co-counsel and other defendants in a co-defendant case.

"I appreciate counsel's enthusiasm for his client, but not his tactics. The case of *Maripol v. Texiera* from 1981 states that evidence of guilt or innocence presented by a defendant in a multiple-defendant criminal matter is an insufficient reason for a separation. Harm to the movant must be palpable and prejudicial, as set forth in *People v. Stone* 1974. For those reasons, I ask you to deny the motion," Ting answered.

"What sayeth The People?" the judge asked.

Ton stood and looked at the judge and then said, "Your Honor, defense counsel for Miss Deagan was on point. Those cases are current case law in California. Therefore, I concur with his argument."

"I'm ready to give my ruling. I find that the motion and argument of said motion lacks the requisite elements to meet the burden of bifurcation by merely showing fear of having a client associated with a co-defendant while seeking to escape any accusations from that same co-defendant. The Court's view is that the actions by all three participants in this case were exactly the same from the joinder in Benton to the attack when the police entered the room, and Shane Summers left it. Your bifurcation motion is denied. Mr. D'Pare, are you ready to argue on the remaining issues in your motion, or are you going to submit it?"

"I'll submit on the motion."

Judge Porter abruptly said, "Your motion is denied, Counselor. With that, are all counsel otherwise ready to proceed on March 3, 1996, at eight-thirty?"

Hearing that they were indeed ready, Judge Porter adjourned the session as the two defense attorneys each leaned in toward their respective clients and began the gift of gab.

Camille smiled at her lawyer and said, "Shane is such a loser. Nice job, old man!" She turned toward Shane and began to laugh at him as she said, "Hey, douche! Hey, where's Tania now?"

The bite from Camille pierced to the bone, and Shane's head dropped in defeat. Camille then said, "Now I'm ready to go back to the jail."

Shane, on the other hand, appeared to be getting more aggressive as he continued to assess the unwelcome news. The bailiff motioned to the two correctional officers that their inmate was tensing up. The judge, court clerk, and court reporter were now absent from the cavernous courtroom when Shane angrily leaned forward toward his attorney. Both defendants had been relieved of their handcuffs for the hearing so that they could write notes without restraints. Shane had a clear, hard plastic pen in his right hand and his thumb on the rounded end that opposed the ink tip. He did not need to go far to reach his lawyer since they were already facing each other while still seated in their chairs.

"I cannot stay here! You motherfuckers should rot in hell. This isn't right! I can't do this!" Now, in a panic, he subconsciously chose to fight this time around and was quickly out of his chair and on top of his attorney.

Dean's chair dispelled him into the sea of carpet in the fracas. His client grabbed his throat. Shane was choking his lawyer with his left hand as he brought his fist over his head, poised for the downward strike of the mighty pen that would appease his desire for real justice.

The bailiff was named Terrell Johnson. He was a seasoned cop who had been on the court assignment with Judge Porter for almost a year and a half without incident until now. He was already headed toward Shane when he initially yelled in anger. Terrell lowered his chest and hit Shane on the run as he started to bring the pen downward onto Dean's head. The velocity and weight of the bailiff were overwhelming for the thinner Shane Summers. He was taken horizontally from his previously vertical position of strength over his lawyer and pushed into a pile against a chair to the rear of where he was at a moment ago. Shane struggled as the responsive bailiff struck him a blow to the face and gained a control hold as he re-cuffed his hands behind his back.

The melee was over as quickly as it started.

"I'm fine. I'm good," Dean said as he stood and looked about the shocked faces with feigned calm while he pulled his tie back down from his shoulder.

While Shane lay on the floor facedown, still breathing heavily from his release of adrenalin, Dean approached, got down on a knee, and said, "Shane, I'm so sorry. It's going to be alright."

This was not Dean's first time that a client attacked him. Dean then rubbed the hair on Shane's head to try and soothe the savage beast. This ploy seemed to work as Dean whispered into Shane's ear, "Have faith in me and in the process. You're going to be okay."

At this point, Ton Hogan, who had been getting up to leave, asked, "Dean, are you alright?"

"Yeah, I'm fine. I'm fine!"

"Are you alright?" Ton asked Shane.

Shane growled back, and Ton was ready as he said, "I think you just picked up a new charge there," as he walked out of the courtroom.

Dean got up from the floor as the correctional officers took control in order to remove Shane back to his solitary cell at the Jefferson County Jail. Dean ran into the hallway to catch Ton before he was out of reach. Dean was hyperventilating at this point with adrenalin and anger. "You motherfucker! My client has mental health problems, and I was trying to calm him down when your stupid ass lit him up again! And for what? So you could have the power position? My client is already looking at life in prison! He's terrified, and you had to be a total dick!"

"Look, Dean, I'm sorry for the bad timing. He still may be charged with another assault, but I shouldn't have made that statement to your client under those circumstances."

"You don't give a fuck about me. You just want to add another charge for leverage and to show that you're the man in power! You're sub-human!" Dean said while the adrenalin began to subside.

Dean then turned away and walked back down the hallway to find the closest exit to get away from the turmoil that he lived within. To Dean D'Pare, the criminal justice system was like a tornado on the Great Plains. The people lived in the prairie landscape. Regular people living their everyday lives. Taking in the joys and hardships at their appointed time among the living. Criminals preyed on the people strewn among the prairie out of necessity or spite, like the unscrupulous locusts that they were, striking here and there. But the justice system—the justice system was a tornado that took everything in its path in an effort to be able to announce its powers in the settlement of disputes. It was indiscriminate and abusive. It tore apart families and homes all in the name of justice, with no repentance and rarely a reply.

*

Dean drove slowly out of the parking lot of the Jefferson County Courthouse and headed down Court Street, looking to make his way to the interstate. As he passed a gas station, he realized that he needed a nip of his friend and the miracle cure for what ails you, who, like the devil, went by many names. It was like the panoply of things that addicted the body to repetitiveness toward destruction, but that price was acceptable as it soothed the mind of angst, malady, and despair. Dean had come to rely on distilled spirits to adjust his own. Like many in the practice of law, Dean was overwhelmed by the stress of the job, and in his line of work, it included the wages of sin.

Dean pulled into the next gas station with a mini market before he hit the interstate. The yellow clamshell sign waved him inside with glee and fanciful allure. Dean grabbed a bag of potato chips and some gum on his way to his true target. On the wall behind the cashier were several of his faithful friends where the bottle caps called him in for a chance to ride. Dean spotted the whiskey that he liked the most, and the bottle began to scream and dance once its name was called as if it had won a universe pageant for most talented. Cash changed hands as the new passenger made its way into the paper bag disguise for the walk of dependence to the car.

As the Mountain View city limit sign exited Dean's tunnel vision seeking home, his old friend escaped its inadequate disguise, and the bottle tilted forward and laid its powerful medicine onto his lips. Dean felt the warmth wash through his body and into his face, as his nerve endings soon became numb. Dean put his 1996 Cadillac El Dorado into cruise control, rested his head on the seat's leather headrest, and listened to a Louie Prima album belt notes and instrumental harmonies from the four corners of his Caddy. One sip became ten and then more as he felt the weight of the world separate from his cares and worries. Dean slipped past the Cassell County line and neared the crossing of the big lake in the dark of night. About thirty minutes later he was taking the exit to head to his office, where he could clean up and wait for the impairment of his magic potion to somewhat subside.

Nobody was working at the Law Offices of Dean D'Pare as he waded through the darkness and found the comfort of his office chair. As he picked up his office phone, the numbers illuminated the darkness. Dean's fingers found the memorized single-digit numbers on the pad that matched his home. Shelly answered the phone. "Hey, honey, I just got back to my office from Mountain View."

"Are you okay?"

"Oh yeah, I had a long day, though. I have a few things to catch up on from today, then I'll be home."

Shelly was accustomed to long hours for her husband and the occasional slurred speech delivered her way. "Okay. Sounds like you've had a day so don't stay too long. I love you."

"I love you too, honey," he said as he hung up the phone and then turned on the television that he had in his office while he slipped into the numbed state from the mesmerizing satisfaction of intoxication.

CHAPTER 17.

TRYING TIMES

On the stage of justice, the unprepared and those lacking skills in courtroom drama will fail to inform and entertain, resulting in their client getting the hook.

*

On the afternoon of Friday, March 1, 1996, Ton Hogan and Ting Bellows appeared in department seven of the superior court for trial readiness. Dean D'Pare appeared by telephone. When Judge Porter was notified that Dean was on the phone in the courtroom, she got up from her desk, put her black robe on over her shoulders, and then zipped it up in the front. She told her bailiff, who waited patiently for her to get organized for the show, that she was ready to call the matter.

The two co-defendants were already in the courtroom. Shane sat near the telephone conference call speaker and Camille next to Ting. Judge Porter wanted to take the opportunity to see if there were any additional issues to be heard on the following Monday morning.

"I have one. I want any mention of my client's failure to stop for the police after he left the house to be off limits," Dean said.

"That is pretty straightforward, we will deal with that on Monday morning. Anything else?" Judge Porter said.

"No, Your Honor," was returned in a chorus. She reminded

241

them that they needed to be in court at eight and that they would start picking the jury at eight-thirty.

The organized robotics of court procedure was interrupted as Shane asked, "Hey, Dean. Hey, are you—still there?"

"I am. Please don't say anything right now, okay?"

"Dean!" his voice crackled with emotion. "Are we really ready for this? Are you? I don't feel like you are! I'm scared, Dean. Somebody help me!"

"Shane! Shane! Stop! Listen, please don't talk in front of others. We'll discuss this later when we're alone. Okay?"

"Okay. Okay—Dean, I'm so alone. Everybody and everything has gone away. I can't go to prison, man, they're animals in there. I just wanna go home to Tania. I just wanna go home. PLEASE!" he said while his mind ran away, and his stomach churned as he collapsed onto the tabletop, awash in helplessness as the tingles of fear and anxiety suspended movement, locking him down beyond the shackles of mortal men.

"You're such a loser. Ah, is da wittle baby scared? Yeah, drop your head, you piece of shit. Hey, it'll be okay. I'll visit you in prison...NOT!" Camille said, with her head turned, looking at Shane.

"For God's sake! Would you shut the fuck up! Dammit, this isn't a game," Ting said while leaning in toward Camille.

"Calm down, old man! You're gonna have a heart attack. You know you think Shane is a total douche...."

"You are such a disrespectful pain in the ass! Can you just shut up?"

"Damn, dude. You don't have to do all that."

"Look, I have some things to get done today, and you're fucking delaying it."

"Like what?"

"I have court and client meetings!"

"Do you know what I'm gonna wear for trial?"

"I don't know. Probably a dress, I would imagine?"

"Yeah, I would. I would like to wear one each day of the

trial in order to appear ladylike, ya know. I also need you to send someone over to do my hair and nails on Sunday evening."

Ting was grinding his teeth with a soured face when he said, "You could possibly do that with your own money and jail permission. The Public Defender's Office doesn't have a fund for that. We don't buy anything either. You'll be wearing a dress or two that have been donated to us or worn by previous women on trial."

"Gross! I want nice clothes and not some hand-me-downs, especially if those dirty skanks were convicted in those rags!"

*

Camille had spent many months in jail at this point and had made some friends and some enemies during that time. She also saw numerous people that she already knew from Mountain View. Some of the women went to high school with her at The Peak, and others from when she was at Mountain View High. Some of those people would not give Camille the time of day back in school, but now they needed allies, and they had seen her fight or had heard about it years ago. Most beneficial was that she was in the slammer for the attempted murder of her own parents. That scared all of the women housed in the female side of the jail.

Camille was one step ahead of her co-defendants in that she talked to her inmate friends who were going through the process and found out about the Public Defender's clothing line—it was used and out of date. She had a couple of people who were near release, and she asked them to get her some nice clothes in her size. Two of the women were eager to assist Camille since she had come to their aid in the jail on a few occasions and provided protection. But the real impetus was that if Camille did get a not guilty verdict, then she would be out, and they did not want her coming for them.

Shane was still in solitary confinement in the administrative segregation area and still a suicide risk, requiring twenty-four-hour monitoring. He did not see his attorney all of Saturday and Sunday, nor could he reach him by telephone. On that Sunday evening before the trial, Shane was told that he had an attorney visit. Shane perked up a little as he was escorted to one of the attorney-client meeting rooms. Dean came in with some clothing to see if it would fit his client. Dean laid the clothes against Shane's back and declared, "Close enough."

That was not exactly what Shane wanted to hear, but at this point he didn't have a lot of enthusiasm concerning his future, even if he was released. Dean worked with Shane on his courtroom demeanor. He said, "I need you to act and look serious and engaged. You can't mope or act like a loser, or you will surely be one. This is the most serious acting gig of your life."

"Acting? I don't know how to do that!"

"C'mon, Shane, we all do it every day. I just want you to act like the nice young man that you are and act like you care. You can do that."

"I'll try. What if I get convicted and Camille doesn't?"

"We can't worry about that. Look, I need you to stand when the jury comes into the room or when they get up to leave—and the same for the judge. You can remember that, right?"

"Can you remind me?"

"Oh, I will. I need you to keep your head up, look the jurors in the eye, and smile at them once in a while. Not a dumbass open mouth kinda fake smile, just a closed-lipped one, okay?"

"Like this?"

"Yeah, like that. If you testify, look serious. Be calm and look those people in the face when talking."

"I don't want to testify!" he said when he was hit with another panic attack, and he got up from his chair.

"Don't worry about that. If you have to, you will. This is your life and your liberty—it would be good for you to remember that. Now, the prosecutor cannot make you testify. Ting won't have you testify, and I will not be calling Camille, so relax. Okay? Sit down, it'll be alright."

"Dean, you know I'm scared, right?"

"It's normal to be worried about yourself in this situation."

"No, I'm really scared."

"I know. Most people are. I know I would feel like you do."

"Before you leave, I want to tell you that I'm really sorry about jumping on you in court. I feel bad about it. It was because I was scared, and I felt like I was livin' somebody else's life. I can't handle it sometimes."

"I'm so sorry, Shane, but it will be alright. Lots of my clients go through this. It's terrible, but they overcome it, and you will, too. Trust me."

*

Camille had a delivery at the jail of four dresses that same evening. They were all the correct size, brand new, and stylish. Her girls had come through for her. She had her former cellmate coming in the morning before she had to be in court in order to work her war paint for the battle of her life. Camille reviewed her clothing options and said, "They only brought one pair of fucking shoes? I'm gonna beat her ass!"

Worse yet, there was no underwear, so she would have to wear the standard issue, well-used jail underwear underneath her nice dresses.

After an hour of tactical planning regarding adornment for the big show, she settled in for some practice on her presentation in the courtroom when she spoke and, more importantly, when she did not. As the night dropped upon her, she had a moment of clarity brought about by some unusual second-guessing of her abilities to communicate, to persuade, and to win. She realized that she had mostly lost in life. Her few wins included getting the manager's job at Rusty's in Benton. She had lost at education, friends, boys, family relationships, her recent decision to commit a crime, and even trusting other people who were like her.

Camille began to delve into her feelings. It was not sorrow in the desire to seek forgiveness but in her ill-fated life and how she wasn't able to navigate such a shitbox on her own. The evaluation brought her to the brink of sanity. To a place where she could assess her future. Her real future.

Her cellmate noticed the internal upheaval and said, "Hey, are you okay?"

"Mind your own fucking business, bitch!"

*

The morning came early as she was awoken for breakfast at six-thirty with the other inmates who would commence their trials that day in other courtrooms. Camille didn't eat much and was already ready for court in a colorful floral dress with a belt and her brown heels. She was about to get her makeup done when her attorney arrived at seven. As she waited to be moved out of the cafeteria, she was suddenly told to pick up her tray and clear it at the garbage cans. She was ready within a couple of minutes and was soon headed to see her attorney and her friend Vera.

"Good morning, Camille. You look very nice. I like the dress. Just to keep us on schedule, you have ten minutes—tops," Ting said as soon as he saw her.

Ting then sat and reviewed his notes and readied himself for jury selection and opening statements. Vera was just about to add her finishing touches when Ting looked at his watch and said, "That's it. We're leaving."

Camille protested as Ting said, "We need to get to court." The request brought no compliance as he said, "Vera, you have to leave. Now!" He then called one of the correctional officers to escort her out. Camille started to bitch out her attorney for the interruption when he sternly said, "You're going to trial, not to the prom!"

Ting laid out his pre-trial advice and preparation the way he did with every client. "We're going to defend this case. We don't have to prove anything. If we need you to testify, you will. If I choose not to have you testify, you won't. We have limited witnesses, so I will be trying to poke holes in the prosecution's case to cause reasonable doubt while I paint you as a victim. I have to head over now. They'll bring you to court. I'll see you there."

Camille was reluctant about seeing her mom and dad in court for the trial. She wasn't keen on sitting near Shane while he blamed everything on her, either. With those thoughts coming to a conclusion, Camille heard the word "Deagan." She turned her head as a correctional officer told her to face the wall so they could restrain her. Camille did as she was told. Two correctional officers walked her through the jail and out of the sallyport and secured her in a waiting jail van.

Camille climbed aboard and was chained to the seat by her right hand. The trip was short, and soon, she was making her way off of the van after having her chains removed.

It was a sunny, vibrant morning in Mountain View. She hoped it would remain that way. She had been waiting to meet vindication on the other side for long enough. Her escorts brought her into the courthouse through the private inmate access, and eventually, she made her way into the empty seat awaiting her in the courtroom.

As she entered, she was hit with that distinctive courtroom smell once again. This time, it included a combination of paper, sweat, fear, arrogance, and the faint whiff of lady luck. She was soon joined by her attorney. Within a couple of minutes, she heard a door open in the courtroom, and in came Dean D'Pare as he made his way to the attorney's chair to her immediate right. Shane was then escorted into the courtroom as Ton was taking a seat at the left of the counsel's table. With him was Detective Neal Ruffin on Ton's right side. The jury box was on the extreme left in the courtroom, and so The People took the closest chair to the jurors as they were the plaintiffs in the matter. As usual, the correctional officers sat in the first row of chairs behind the defendants so that they were in the sphere of influence for control of the defendants if disruption arose.

The bailiff said, "Will the three attorneys head to the judge's chambers."

Once in chambers, Dean D'Pare said, "I'm asking this court to bar the prosecution and defense counsel from asking any questions of any witness regarding my client fleeing the police at any point after he ran from the house."

"Well, what do The People say?" Judge Porter asked.

"I agree to refrain from doing so in any way. The conduct of Shane Summers will be out of bounds from the point that he entered the getaway car until his arrest unless Shane Summers testifies and he brings such conduct to bear, then he can be impeached on the entirety of the conduct," Ton answered.

Dean D'Pare did not necessarily like that caveat, but Judge Porter approved his motion with the modification.

Ton sought to have the two defendants barred from asserting that the crimes were all on Eric Larson since he would not be present for rebuttal. Both defense attorneys wanted the motion denied, and the Judge said, "Just because The People did not retain Eric Larson in local holding for the trial, in the event that such an issue may arise, does not mean that the defendants should be compromised in their defense. The motion is denied."

"I move to have all witnesses excluded from the courtroom until called to testify and an order that they cannot speak to one another until the conclusion of this trial," Ton said.

"Granted. Anything else?"

As Judge Porter looked at the clock, she then asked, "Are you ready to get a jury seated? The prospective jurors are waiting."

*

The Judge commenced calling in fifteen potential jurors from the jury pool to start the process of selecting twelve people for a jury and two alternates.

Judge Porter welcomed the bright-eyed and the irritated as she gave a dissertation on the American criminal justice system and a citizen's duty to it. She then proceeded to ask the potential jurors a series of questions as they talked about themselves and their beliefs. The attorneys could each ask follow-up questions and then accept each juror or have them excused.

The process continued on for two hours as the pool began to shrink to almost no one. The jury was finally accepted, with twelve members and only one alternate.

Generally, the prosecution was looking for law and order types. In this case, they were also seeking men and women who could understand that there were women in the world who could be horrible people. As usual, the defense was looking for people with bad experiences with the government, those with big hearts, or the naive. Ting was specifically looking for males with the aforementioned traits since they may tend not to believe that a woman could or would do such an act without force or fear. The court had its jury and broke for a late lunch as the participants headed for the exits to eat and make the return in a mere sixty minutes of time.

*

As they all returned and everybody was in their assigned places for the start of the trial, the judge asked the prosecution to make its opening statement. Ton was eloquent and down to earth. This combination allowed him to communicate on various levels, as he generally laid out the story in a sequential manner. Ton looked into the eyes of each juror as his story wove its web of greed, revenge, jealousy, and a lack of compassion for other human beings. His opening statement was an hour and a half. Ton spent that time in animated motions and movements as he acted out the story like a single thespian trying to capture a transient audience in an impromptu play in the park. Some faces looked back at him in shock and horror, as others smiled gently, while still others presented faces of stone. The only promises that he made were that the evidence from witnesses and experts would support the facts as delivered and that the only result would be a unanimous finding of guilt.

*

Dean D'Pare was next as he stood, buttoned his suit jacket, and walked toward the jury box. Dean said, "My client, Shane Summers, was a boy in love and was unaware of what had been planned by Camille Deagan and another person named Eric Larson. My client has longstanding mental health issues, and you will hear from expert witnesses about those health issues that he bore and the depth of despair that he traveled in and out of since his youth."

He staged a long pause and then said, "The police caught the culprits in this case. They caught Camille Deagan and Eric Larson but made a mistake in accusing my client of such terrible things as attempted murder, burglary, and assault with a deadly weapon. My client was in a physical—a sexual relationship with Ms. Deagan and with his mental health issues, unaware that the woman he trusted. That woman right there"—pointing at Camille—"was making a plan to kill her own parents. Her own parents! She did this while laying the groundwork to set up my client. It was all Camille Deagan's idea." He pointed at Camille again. "She is the evil ringleader and the one who wanted to kill her own mother and father for money and satisfaction. A devilish plan that she never revealed to my client. Tricking him into going. Once in the car, he could not get away for fear of being killed, making him truly a victim of kidnapping. Shane Summers didn't willfully or knowingly do anything against the law. The evidence will show that my client is not guilty of all charges."

*

Ting Bellows was last. He was calm and smooth. Because of that, he lacked enthusiasm and theatrics, but he made up for it in the way that he asserted reasoning into the damnedest cracks. He made a venture down a lonely road where the pied piper hoped to eventually collect an entourage.

As he moved away from the lectern and toward the jury, he said, "My client is innocent and just a pawn in the greed of men. Shane Summers was the mastermind, and former co-defendant Eric Larson was the muscle. They wanted Camille's parents dead for the inheritance that Camille would receive as the only child of her parents, David and Lisa Deagan. Camille was under the control of Shane and Eric through force, fear, and love. Camille loved Shane and wanted to please him, but not to this degree. Camille had her issues with her parents like most teenagers and young adults did, but she didn't want them harmed, and she certainly didn't want them dead! You'll see that my client was not a willing participant in this crime. Not whatsoever! You'll also see a video of the events of the crime, whereupon Eric Larson tries to beat the Deagans to death. In that video, you will see my client Camille Deagan act out some aggression toward her parents. This will be shocking, but the reality is that she did that as a show of allegiance to her captors, who were forcing her to act, and only after realizing that her parents were not really in the bed. When the prosecutor rests, you will see that my client, this young lady right here, is not only not guilty but innocent of all of the charges. Thank you, ladies and gentlemen."

*

With a few business hours left in the day, Judge Porter turned to the prosecutor and asked, "Are The People ready to call their first witness?"

"Yes, Your Honor, we would like to call Jake Angelo to the stand," Ton answered as he looked up from the sprawling paperwork laid out on the desktop in front of him.

Angelique was waiting in the public seating area with Jake in order to keep him up to the task, with guilt and flowery support. Jake was nervous, and the jury could tell. Ton pointed to the witness chair in order to guide him to the spotlight—the orator's chair in which all focus was given and all that remained.

Ton walked up to him and said, "Take a breath. How are you doing this afternoon, Sir?" Ton asked while Jake tried to comply.

"Oh boy, I'm nervous. I've never done anything like this before."

"You'll be fine," Ton said as he smiled and nodded his head as if he understood.

Ton began to lay the foundation of the crimes through the testimony that would erupt from Jake Angelo. His testimony followed what he knew, what he had witnessed, and what he had told Detective Neal Ruffin. It was damaging testimony right out of the gate. Jake put both Shane Summers and Camille Deagan in a conspiracy plot to kill her parents and why they wanted to do it. He laid out all of the other witnesses' names as well. When Ton was secure in the knowledge that he had a fitting foundation to start the ball rolling, he said, "No further questions, Your Honor."

"Did my client, Ms. Deagan, tell you that she wanted to

kill her parents?" Ting asked on cross-examination.

"No. No, she did not."

"Did Mr. Summers tell you that he was going to commit a crime with my client?"

"No."

"Have you ever seen your roommate, Joe Jenkins, use illegal drugs?"

"I don't know."

"Please answer the question, Mr. Angelo."

"Okay, yes, I've seen him use illegal drugs."

"What types of drugs have you seen him use?"

"Mostly marijuana."

"How about methamphetamine or opiates?"

"Yes."

"Which ones?"

"Both...and other kinds, but I didn't know what they were exactly."

"So, you didn't see anything and were only told about this story from a habitual drug user? Is that right?"

"I guess. Yes."

*

When it came to Dean D'Pare's opportunity to cross-examine Jake, he felt that he did not want to belabor the fact that Jake did not really have a lot to say and what was said did not have much value and was untrustworthy, so he passed on the opportunity.

*

Ton had contemplated calling Slob Jenkins, but they had not heard from him in several days, and the Benton Police Department could not find him, so Ton was going to have to move on. He called Sherry Burns to the stand. Sherry was dressed well and all smiles since she really wanted Camille to eat time, and she had an immunity agreement in her pocket.

She testified about knowing Camille in high school and what Camille was like at the time. Sherry was asked about the fight after school, which she described in great detail. She further explained that she saw Camille, who offered her a place to live when she really needed one after having just moved to Benton.

"Camille and Shane were the ones that planned the killing of the Deagans," Sherry said while looking at the faces lined up in the jury box.

"Do you know why?"

"Camille has been, um...I guess miserable—for as long as I've known her. She always said that the reason for her anger came from how she was treated by her mom and dad."

"Miserable? Can you elaborate on that?"

"Well, she can be a real mean dude, if you know what I mean. You know, like a sour puss and an asshole. Especially to her parents. Like I said, she told me a thousand times that her parents were the reason that she was unhappy in life."

"Did she ever tell you specifically what it was that her parents did to deserve this hostility?"

"What wasn't it? She blamed them for everything she couldn't do, and the few things she was good at, she took all of the credit."

"Did she ever tell you that she wanted her parents dead?"

"Many times. Shane wanted the money, and Camille wanted Shane. She wanted her parents killed for her inabilities and to seal the deal with Shane."

*

Ting Bellows worked hard to show that Sherry really was out to get Camille after the fight in high school. He focused on the idea that Sherry could not get a place of her own but had recently taken over the lease of Camille's apartment and already had another roommate who was also a stripper at Prancers.

Dean D'Pare went after Sherry on the same points and then asked, "Isn't it true that you have romantic feelings for my client Shane Summers?"

She laughed and said, "Are you being serious right now? I have no interest in Shane. I'm an exotic dancer. I have hundreds of men wanting me sexually every night, and men are attracted to me in other areas of my life, too. With all those choices, why in the Hell would I want a lowlife dumbass like Shane Summers? Tell me that, counselor!"

*

On re-direct, Ton Hogan worked on supporting her credibility and burgeoning the accuracy of her testimony. When he finished, Dean D'Pare asked Sherry, "Have you gotten any deals from the prosecutor for your testimony today?"

Sherry proudly said, "Not for my testimony, no."

"Did you get an immunity agreement so that you would not be prosecuted?"

"Like I said, no. Not from Jefferson County. I did get an agreement in Cassell, but they gave it to me because of my attorney. I wasn't actually involved in any of this mess, but my attorney is good at what he does."

"Is your attorney one Darnell Howard?"

"Yes, that's my attorney."

"Is he your attorney, or really on retainer for the strip club you work at?"

"Objection. What is the relevance?" Ton asked.

"Withdrawn your honor," Dean answered.

"The question is withdrawn. The jury will disregard the question as if it did not happen," Judge Porter said.

"Nothing further," Dean said.

Ton then asked, "Did the Jefferson County District Attorney's Office give you anything in exchange for your testimony here today?"

"No, they did not."

*

Five o'clock had finally come to the first day of trial as Judge Porter announced that they were at a good place to break for the evening. She then admonished the jurors, "I remind you not to discuss the trial or any of the information from it with anyone. Not with family members, other jurors, news media, or anyone else. Any questions? Okay, you are ordered to return at eight-thirty tomorrow morning."

"Well, that went very well," Neal said in a whisper as he leaned in toward Ton.

"It's early, but this should be a home run. I'll see you in the morning," Ton answered.

*

The next morning, direct examination by the prosecutor resumed on time as he wound his way through his witness list, including Detective Ruffin, Detective Wilson, Investigator Suarez, Investigator Kemp, STOs, a couple of police officers, Lisa Deagan, and finally, David Deagan. During the testimony, the videos of the crime and the interviews of the two defendants were played for the jury.

CHAPTER 18.

VERITABLE VERDICTS

The incarceration of the sinister makes them adjacent but not forgotten.

*

The People rested their case after seven and a half days of testimony, at which time the defense made an oral motion to dismiss based on the lack of evidence. The jury was removed from the courtroom and sent to the jury deliberation room with the bailiff as they were once again ordered not to discuss the trial.

"Your Honor, clearly there was insufficient evidence presented in The People's case in chief. Through the testimony of witnesses and the accompanying video evidence, it showed that my client was leaving the crime scene, not participating in the crime," Dean D'Pare said as he paced about.

"The prosecution did not make the requisite elements to meet the two counts of attempted murder against my client. Since she was forced into going, there was no premeditation," Ting added with a flat affect.

Ton argued that the defense was all wet and that there was more than sufficient evidence to meet the elements, jurisdiction, and identification to have the motions denied.

"The requests for dismissal are denied as The People made their burden, but you both can argue your positions to the jury. With that, both motions are denied," Judge Porter said.

The jury was called back into the courtroom to resume the defense's case if they chose to present one.

"Mr. D'Pare, are you ready? If so, call your first witness." Judge Porter said.

"The defense for Shane Summers rests," Dean answered after standing and looking at the faces of the jurors with defiance.

Ting leaned over to his client and said, "You're gonna testify now! Are you ready?"

"Now we're talkin'. Call me up, dude. Oh, and make it good."

Ting stood while looking at the judge and said, "Thank you. The defense calls Camille Deagan to the stand."

Camille arose from her chair in yet another new dress. She was calm and ready to make her pitch. Her mom and dad were seated in the third row of the courtroom with disgust in their eyes and intensity in their faces.

Camille raised her right hand and was asked, "Do you swear to tell the truth, the whole truth, and nothing but the truth, so help me God?"

"I do,"

Ting Bellows started by asking about her childhood growing up in Mountain View. Camille told of fond memories and her love for her mom and dad. She waxed and waned about the trips that she took with her parents and how they doted on her. Camille admitted that puberty and the social structure of school were hard on her but that her parents always supported her. While Camille testified, she could see the faces of her mom and dad, who were so focused and ready that they appeared as if they were cast in bronze.

"Did you take Shane Summers to Mountain View to meet your parents before the events of September 3rd, 1995?"

"I did."

"Can you explain what occurred during that trip or what it was like?"

"We had a good visit with my mom and dad. Everything went great."

"Did Shane make an unusual comment on the return drive to Benton?"

"Yes. I didn't think much of it at the time. I really didn't think he was serious."

"What did he tell you?"

"He said that my parents were rich and that we deserved some of that money."

"What did you say to that?"

"I told him that they worked hard for the things they had, but they weren't rich."

"What did he say to that?"

"He told me that we needed to kill my mom and dad in order to get their money and their house."

"That had to be shocking—what did you say?"

"Oh, it was. I told him that he was sick and that I would never do such a thing, and that he needed to drop it."

"Did he ever bring it up again?"

"Oh yeah, he brought it up every so often for a year or so, then he became serious about it."

"What did you do then?"

"I didn't know what to do. I loved Shane. I still wasn't sure he was serious, but if he was, I thought I could talk him out of it. Then, when Eric Larson was brought in, I knew he wasn't bluffing. Eric threatened to kill me if I didn't go along. I was so afraid that they would kill me. Uh, and my parents, too. Um, I'm sorry. I don't know if I can go on. Can I have some tissue, please," she said as she covered her face with her hands.

The bailiff brought a box of tissue to the stand and returned to his seat.

"Thank you," she said as she pulled tissues from the box and dabbed the corners of her eyes.

"I know this is very difficult, Camille, but can you continue?" Ting asked.

"It is. I will try," she said as she patted her eyes once again with tissue.

"What did Eric say to you?"

"He said. Um, he said, we are takin' that money. Your parents won't need it when we are done, and if you fuck this up or tell anyone, you're goin' to the bottom of the river in two pieces," she said as she leaned down into her hands and appeared to be crying.

"Judge, can we take a short break for my client to gain her composure so that she can continue to testify?"

"Yes. We will take a short break. Be back in your seats in five minutes."

Ting walked up to the stand to console Camille. As he arrived, he said, "Good job. Hangin' in there?"

"Dude, that was so good. You do got some skills."

"I figured you were acting. Well, don't lay it on too thick."

"You just keep following my lead. Now put your arm around me," Camille said.

*

The trial resumed, and Ting asked, "Are you able to continue?"

"Thank you, Mr. Bellows, I think I am."

"Did you hear the testimony of Sherry Burns?"

"Yes, she was incorrect about a lot of things. Sherry has always bent the truth if you know what I mean? I have always cared about her, but she can be a leach and has low morals. I think she could still be mad about that silly high school fight. That has been blown way out of proportion." As her voice lowered, she said, "That's for sure."

"Did you contact the police about the plans by Eric and Shane to kill your folks?"

"No."

"Why not?"

"I didn't think that even the police could stop them. I

went along on the trip in order to try and warn my parents and save them from being killed. I felt that if I didn't go, then even I couldn't save them."

"On the video recording that the police made, you were seen jumping on the bed while saying, 'Kill them.' Can you explain that?"

"I knew that my parents were not in the bed as soon as we entered the room. I was about to warn my dad so that he could get them when I noticed that it was fake, so I went along with the attack in order to not be killed by Eric or Shane."

"Do you expect the jury to believe you?"

"I made Eric and Shane believe it. I even made the detectives believe it, so I admit my acting was very good. But I did say immediately after the police entered that I knew that my mom and dad weren't in the bed. So yeah, I expect the jury and everyone else in here to believe me because it's true."

Detective Ruffin was watching the jurors, and he thought he saw a couple of heads nod slightly as if they believed this shit. Neal whispered his suspicions into the right ear of Ton as Ton was asked if he wanted to cross examine the witness by Judge Porter.

"Why again didn't you call the police before you went to Mountain View?" Ton asked.

"I don't know why. I didn't really think that they would do anything and thought it was up to me. I guess."

"Isn't it true that you didn't warn your parents in advance or even when you entered their bedroom?"

"They weren't really talking to me, and I didn't think that they would believe me, I guess. I thought I could do something about it."

"Like what? Encourage Eric and Shane to kill them and join in?"

"Objection," Ting yelled.

"Overruled. You may answer," Judge Porter said.

"I didn't encourage them."

"In the video you did. Isn't that true?"

"I already told you why!"

"You encouraged them, and you didn't do anything about stopping them either. In fact, if you looked at your own behavior, wouldn't you say that you participated in all of the crimes you are charged with?"

"I know it looks like that, but it wasn't like that!"

"How was it like then?"

"I don't know, you're confusing me!"

"You were so clear about your testimony when your attorney was asking you questions. Why are you confused now?"

"I don't know."

"Could it be that you put together your talking points over the last several months to prepare, and you don't have lies prepared for what I've asked?"

"No."

"No? Just, no? Can you elaborate on that?"

"Stop trying to make me look bad, you asshole!" Camille yelled.

"You seem to have some anger there. Wow! Are you mad?"

"Kinda. I don't like being accused of something I didn't do."

"Well, let me see. It seems that you are doing a lot of guessing here in the courtroom as you testify. Let me ask you this. If you were forced to participate and you were fearful of Shane and Eric, then how were you going to develop the bravery and physical capability to stop them from killing your mom and dad at that narrow point in time in your parents' bedroom?"

"I don't know. I just know that I would have done it."

"Really? Just you against two violent men?"

"I, I hoped I could've stopped them—I guess."

"I just want to know how?"

"I dunno. I never really thought that through, I guess."

"One more question. Do you have keys for your place of work?"

"Yes." She turned to the jurors and smiled as she said, "As

I told you before, I'm the manager there. I helped start the franchise."

"Since you run the place, you must have keys to open and close the store?"

"I do."

"A lot of keys, I suspect?"

"Oh yeah, there are about ten of them."

"Crime in Benton can be pretty bad. Do you lock your apartment when you leave?"

"I do."

"It sounds like you have a lot of keys that you need to carry. Where do you put them all?"

"I have a keychain that I carry."

"When you were arrested, you only had one key. Isn't that right?"

"Uh, yes."

"Why was that?"

"My parents gave me a house key when I was young. They trust me. I can come and go from our house, so I have a key."

"Camille. If that key is for your use, why was it separated from all the other keys on your keychain?"

"I didn't need my other keys."

"How did you lock your apartment, and how were you going to get back into your apartment?"

Camille's face reddened as she took a millennium to answer when she finally said, "Sherry would let me in."

Camille tried to blame it all on the ever-present parachute for crooked women: love and fear. Her credibility was damaged, and Ting Bellows knew it. In order to rehabilitate his client, he decided to call one of The People's witnesses back to the stand. As Camille was excused and took her seat back next to her attorney, Ting Bellows called Lisa Deagan to the stand.

Lisa and David were surprised when the request was made, and Ton whispered to Neal, "Crafty ol' bastard! I hope this doesn't work."

Lisa was tearful as she reached the witness stand for her second turn in the chair of all chairs. The one that carries the biggest spotlight, with the sharpest focus in any land or at any time. Ting asked Lisa Deagan about giving birth to her only child and the care that she took in raising her. He asked about the small accomplishments that Camille made on her way through her youth to adulthood, as well as the sorrow and remorse of having to testify against her.

Lisa was a mess after hearing Camille talk about her and David so lovingly from the stand—something for which they'd waited their whole lives. She also knew that Camille was a devout sinner and teller of lies as the turmoil of motherhood bathed the jurors in emotions that brought them to the sullen camps of the war-torn.

Maybe just winners and losers on paper, but casualties of trauma and despair, nevertheless, applied as scars on skin and spirit forever more. Ting made his point. That point was that Camille was a crapster. A child no one wants but many receive. A child, perhaps with the need for redemption from loving parents. Ton Hogan tread softly after the emotional turmoil that had arisen like a spat between young love. Vicious, thoughtless, and hurtful, resulting in remorse and sensitivity yet unknown, in the re-bonding of that which was always meant to be.

The prosecutor brought the mother of one back to her logical senses as he re-focused Lisa on the realities of dealing with her daughter on a daily basis beyond the myths and rarities of divining or creating perfect loving children. Lisa's countenance sobered to the opposite recollections of abuse and stunningly inhumane treatment by her own offspring, especially on the date of September 3, 1995.

As Ton finished his line of questioning on cross-examination, he returned to his seat at the counsel's table and looked at each juror with fury and strength as the faces met his scowl with somber recovery.

The defense rested, and it was now time for The People to bring any rebuttal witnesses to support their case in chief. It had been eight straight days of testimony from witnesses, law enforcement officers, expert witnesses, victims, and even one of the defendants. At that point, Ton did not want to beat a dead horse. He had done all he could, and he had made his case as to each count, beyond a reasonable doubt, but he had one more thing....

Ton arose and asked the Judge, "Your Honor, I have a certified copy of Eric Larson's entry of plea in this crime. Specifically, his offer of proof to substantiate his pleas to two counts of attempted murder. I offer them through judicial notice and as an exception to the hearsay rule. I ask that the clerk read it into the record."

"I approve the document's admission. Madam Clerk, please read the transcript," the judge responded as all eyes peered down from the jury box onto the accused.

*

The judge was pleased that the prosecution was wrapping it up and said, "We will break here for the evening and resume at eight o'clock in the morning. At that time, The People will begin their closing arguments."

*

As the room came to order the following morning, the judge gave a slight nod as she asked, "Mr. Hogan, are you ready to give your closing argument?"

Ton stood and met the eyes of the twelve plus one sitting in the jury box as he thanked them for their service and reminded them of the charges in the case before them. He proceeded to weave the facts into a summation that joined the elements of the crimes to complete the long and complex puzzle laid out before them over the past week. As he recounted testimony word for word, he could see jurors nod in agreement after checking their notes on paper or those registered in their memories forever more. He became animated once again while adding exuberance as he said, "Evaluate the witnesses' testimony. Who had a reason to lie? Did Lisa and David Deagan have a reason to lie? Did the police officers? What about the defendants' own friends? They told a different story than what Camille Deagan shared with us. How can that be? Lastly, did the video lie? Take that evidence and place it side by side, and then ask if that evidence was based on a lie, or were the only lies those that came out of the mouth of defendant Camille Deagan? Eric Larson pled guilty to the charges and admitted to them in doing so. He also honestly told the court and you folks on this jury that Camille and Shane were as equally involved in this murder plot as he was."

He paused for about six seconds and then said, "Next, we have Shane Summers. His attorney tried to blame it entirely on Camille and Eric Larson. They gave no other explanation other than he ran. Why do you think he ran? Was he duped, or was he scared? I would assert that he was a big man to do this heinous crime and then got scared as it unfolded. That does not relieve him of criminal liability. It was his idea. He did most of the planning and made it all the way to the bedroom as the beatdown commenced. The evidence in this case is overwhelming. Overwhelming in proving both defendants' guilt beyond a reasonable doubt on all counts!"

*

The defense closing commenced with Dean D'Pare arguing, "This disaster was not the idea of Shane Summers. The testimony that you heard calling him the planner is completely false. It's being used to frame him! My client was a mere pawn in a game of greed and revenge that he was completely unaware of before and during the trip to Mountain View. Once my client became aware of the reality of the situation that he was brought into, he left. In fact, my client ran for his life. He was so shocked by the barbarity of the acts before him that he could not stop as he wanted to get as far away from what Eric and Camille were doing as he could. Listen: Eric Larson and Camille Deagan were the culprits, the planners, and the only participants in this murder scheme, and with that lack of concern for humanity, they, too, did not care about the predicament that they put my client into. Dare I say it? Dare I say that this poor man here is a simple man, one with lots of trauma in his formative years and in his adult life? That simplicity comes from a lack of any worldview and a lack of sophistication. You heard his psychiatrist explain the tremendous challenges that Shane Summers deals with on a daily basis. Yes, we all have ghosts and darkness in our lives, but some more than others. Shane is one of those others. He's just a simple and, yes, gullible man looking for someone to care about him and to love him. That's something we all want. Remember that when you are assessing his part in this complete horror perpetrated by Eric and Camille. With that, I ask that you please find my client not guilty as to all charges."

*

Ting Bellows was outraged at this point. He had a co-defendant's counsel lay the crime on the one co-defendant who was not there but also onto the other one who was. The general rule was that you fought for your client and did all you could ethically, but as a defense attorney, you needed to be on the opposite team from the government. In this matter, Dean D'Pare had tried the whole case in order to finger Camille and Eric, while absolving his client. He could have laid it all on Eric Larson in the empty chair, but he didn't.

Ting was on fire as he said, "You've heard repeatedly that

my client is a productive citizen in the community. She's the full-time manager of a restaurant. She got that job when she was eighteen years old! Would business owners turn over their first and only franchise to an eighteen-year-old girl who was a mean and corrupt person? Hell no, they wouldn't. Sure, she has issues with her parents, but she's not the kind of person capable of constructing this type of crime and getting these men to commit it. It didn't work that way. Shane Summers used her to discuss it. He then recruited Eric Larson to help and forced my client along in doing it! She's a victim in this. You heard her very own mother talk about her and show great emotion that came from her loving heart for a loving daughter. My client had a key to the house. Not because her mom and dad forgot to get it back but because she was always welcome home. She didn't call the police because they wouldn't have done anything. They chase down events that have already occurred or are about to occur. Not those that could maybe happen somewhere and at some time in the future. Even in this case, the police waited until Shane and Eric were taking action. The only thing she could do was wait and comply. Could she and her dad have taken on Shane and Eric in the bedroom of their home? I don't know, and neither do you. What we do know is that she has NO reason to kill her mom and dad. None. It doesn't make any sense for her, but it does make sense for Eric who already admitted to all of it. Eric tried to include my client in this ordeal as he pled guilty. That was merely the rantings of a desperate man with vengeance still on his mind. He threatened to kill my client. He couldn't kill her now, but he could say she was completely involved so that she was still punished at his hand, or in this case, his mouth. Don't buy into this. Camille is a meek, kind, and productive person who does the best she can. She's not capable of this, and more importantly, she did not do any of this on her own. She did this because these two men made her do it, and she needed to save her mom and dad from them. She's not guilty of any of these alleged crimes."

Judge Porter elected to adjourn the jury for one last break before jury instructions were given on the ninth day of their forced commitment. On their return, all could see that the jury members were relieved that the matter was nearing a close. Soon, they could retire to come to a quick verdict or fight for days on end with differing opinions. The jury instructions were extremely important but were long and boring, most of which entered the ears of the lay jury and, after sticking to nothing, passed through and out the other. After the tension and doldrums, the instruction phase was completed.

The jury did not reach full verdicts by the end of that first afternoon and returned the following morning at an optimistic eight o'clock. By mid-morning, they had a couple of questions for the judge. The three attorneys were called to return to court as Judge Porter read the questions to them on their arrival. The questions were:

"Can we find both defendants guilty of some counts and not others?"

"Can we read the transcript of Sherry Burns?"

The defense attorneys started to smile and move about in their chairs, hearing the possibility of an exciting verdict. Ton Hogan felt the pain of question number one but liked question number two and felt that Sherry Burn's testimony might solve their problem.

That morning came and went. As the day neared its invariable end, the jury wanted to be done by five and not come back. Breaking for lunch or the end of the day makes for a powerful deadline in the jury rooms around the country's halls of justice.

The buzzer sound was finally made as the foreperson depressed the notification button to alert the bailiff of the impending decision. The bailiff confirmed that they were indeed ready and notified the Judge. The court clerk then, in turn, notified each attorney as the hopes and fears of gamblers revealed themselves in the courtroom jousters and in those with their lives on the line.

The verdict was finally at hand. The defendants and counsel were standing while waiting for the jurors to file in when Lisa and David walked in, escorted by Angelique Perez.

As the jurors came to rest in the jury box back in Department Seven, Judge Porter asked, "Who is the foreperson?"

A woman stood up to be recognized.

Judge Porter then said, "Ms. Julian, are you the foreperson?"

She responded that she was, as she stood patiently with her completed verdict forms as the bailiff worked his way over to get them. The bailiff then presented them to the judge, who took about a minute to review them for completeness. She then handed them to the court clerk and asked, "Will the defendants and counsel please stand for the verdicts? Now, please read the verdict, Madam Clerk."

The reading commenced, and the verdict was rendered as follows:

"As to Shane Summers: We, the jury in the aforementioned case, find the defendant:

Count One: Attempted Murder in the First Degree of Lisa Deagan: **Guilty**.
Count Two: Attempted Murder in the First Degree of David Deagan: **Guilty**.
Count Three: Burglary of a Residence: **Guilty**.
Count Four: Assault with a Deadly Weapon: **Guilty**.

As to Camille Deagan: We, the jury in the aforementioned case, find the defendant:

Count One: Attempted Murder in the First Degree of Lisa Deagan: **Not Guilty**.
Count Two: Attempted Murder in the First Degree of David Deagan: **Not Guilty**.

Count Three: Burglary of a Residence: **Guilty**.
Count Four: Assault with a Deadly Weapon: **Guilty**."

The Deagans were shocked and dismayed. Dean D'Pare was relieved that it was over, although his client was so distraught that he needed to be removed by force from the courtroom and taken to the hospital for sedation. Ton Hogan was a little miffed about the two NGs related to Camille, as he said to himself, "Hhm. Jurors and voters, they're an unpredictable storm."

Camille turned her face to look at Ting and said, "See, I told you! I'm walkin' on the murder charges!"

"Congratulations to both of us, girl. You did good. Real good, but don't get too carried away with yourself. I figure that you still might be going to prison on the last two charges."

"Damn, old man, you're such a drag. I bet you fuckin don't even orgasm, do ya?"

*

The day of sentencing had arrived. Camille was sans a fancy dress and in an orange jumpsuit, sitting at counsel's table. Her parents were seated in the back of the courtroom, still waiting for justice. Shane was brought in confined to a wheelchair since he was emotionally erratic and physically difficult to deal with.

Judge Porter weighed the probation report to that of the recommendation by the District Attorney's Office and the arguments of defense counsel. She gave the Deagans time to give a victim impact statement and then settled in to pronounce the sentence.

"Mr. Summers. I have empathy for you for the difficulties that you endured in your youth. I also feel for you in your struggles with the ramifications that are happening to you for your conduct in this matter. With that said, this Court believes that you were the leader of the murder plot. The one who set this whole thing in motion and the driving factor to see it to completion. I accept the fact that you ran from the scene once things got serious, but that does not relieve you of criminal liability. Therefore, I am sentencing you to two consecutive fifteen-to-life terms, plus four years on the burglary and two years on the assault charge to run concurrently for a total of thirty years to life in state prison," she said as she shifted in her chair and looked down upon Shane and Dean with determination and finality.

Judge Porter then turned to the young woman waiting for a break and said, "The testimony showed that Ms. Deagan had some real anger issues throughout her life that were hard for her to control. I think the most germane issue at hand is the amount of persuasion that was applied to her by her boyfriend, Mr. Summers, and Mr. Larson."

Judge Porter, now looking at Shane, resumed, "It did not appear as though Ms. Deagan was thinking about, nor plotting to kill her parents until it was brought up repeatedly by her love interest with whom she hoped to marry. It's the court's belief, as I mentioned a few moments ago, that Mr. Summers was the impetus to this series of crimes and that he engaged and maybe even forced his co-defendants into acting, even if it was only by the use of manipulation as he embellished the benefits of the financial gain."

Judge Porter looked down onto the bench and paused. She slowly looked up and then focused on Camille, who was awaiting her freedom and said, "With all of that said, I believe that you do have evil in your heart and that you need time to correct that if it is possible. As the facts showed in this trial, you participated in the planning in many ways, and it appears that your participation went beyond what a mere captive would do. I think that you should thank your lucky stars that you were not convicted on the first two counts. If you had been, you would have received thirty years to life just like your co-defendants. I do believe that you are a danger to society and to the victims in this matter, your parents. Therefore, I am sentencing you to the midterm on the burglary for six years and the upper term of four years on the assault. They will run consecutively for a full term of ten years in state prison."

Camille stared at the judge with eyes of fire and rage and immediately stood up from her chair. She spun halfway to her right and partially bent forward as she said, "Kiss my ass, bitch!" while patting her rear end. The open palm then turned to an upwards fist as she turned back to face the judge again. The fist eased open as she flipped up her middle finger into the air and yelled, "Whatever. You can go fuck yourself! You'll get what's comin' to you, bitch!"

CHAPTER 19.

THE TRIBULATIONS OF TRIALS

And so it goes, in the endeavor to live and to live with choices made. Big or small, they come with regret or rejoice. As the players move on to the next, those in the wake wrestle with the damage and destruction that comes from recklessness and evil. The victims are externally free but imprisoned by the impacts of criminality and the system that revolves around it, while the imprisoned pay penitence with a free mind.

*

Shane was transferred to the reception center at the High Desert State Prison for his initial evaluation and was ultimately sent to the dreaded California State Prison in Folsom. The prison sat on a lonely knoll overlooking the American River while being overlooked by lesser captives in the subdivisions that surrounded the hills next to the prison of ballad fame.

It was an old prison with lots of blind spots and dangerous people. Since he was difficult to deal with and getting worse week by week, he once again was placed in administrative segregation. Shane was lost. His life had gone from an existence of trying to use people, only to be used by them while living relatively free in the physical world, confined only by his skill, effort, and morality. He now found himself confined in his physical world, too. He wanted out. He needed out. He decided to rebel in his new life without Tania. He believed that freedom could come in the form of rejection by authority. Shane yelled and spat at the guards. He physically attacked them as well when the chance came upon him. He had worked to be one of the biggest pains in the ass the Department of Corrections had ever seen in order to get himself released. Instead, he was tamed and brought back to reality. They had all seen worse, far worse, and they had handled them, too.

Shane changed his game plan to seek release or a pardon through reformation. With his attitude adjustment, he made it to the general population. He hoped that in Gen Pop he could either find his way out or get some assistance in doing so. Since he was of no consequence and had nothing to offer, the other inmates were of no immediate help. Melancholy, loneliness, and heartbreak took its toll over the next month.

One day in the yard, he was walking with his cellmate Sal in the open sun. Sal said, "Listen, homie, you got a good rep acting like a crazy fool, but you gotta still watch your back. This is the jungle baby. Remember, don't trust no one."

"I know, I know. Not even you...." Suddenly, three men from the Mexican Mafia surrounded a prisoner near them. Shanks appeared out of nowhere and the insertion of modified toothbrushes tore into the single man, eerily similar to piranha on movement. Sal turned his head while Shane watched in horror. The victim was stabbed to death while fear and acceptance roiled throughout. As he stared at the dead man on the grass, reds and purples flowed onto the yard. He felt queasy and began to retch as the world looked on. Sal gave him a hard kick while he was bent over, spitting onto the grass. Shane stood up, turned, and said, "What in the fuck did you do that for? Did you see that guy get killed? Right there!"

"Dude, shut the fuck up. We didn't see shit! You're gonna get us both killed. Man-up mutha-fucker. Your weakness was just seen by everybody in the yard. Trust me—you just got marked."

In his hopelessness, he realized his path of escape in the aftermath of the shocking drama.

That night, Shane waited for his celly to fall asleep. He sat on his bed with his top sheet in his hands. In the dank little grey room with two beds, a toilet, and a sink, the determination to escape pushed sorrowful sensitivity aside. The illumination from the lights of the tier assisted in his clarity and vision. He made a noose at one end of the sheet and then slowly arose and looked through the bars to see if there were any guards lurking about. Seeing none, he tied the loose end to the upper horizontal cell door bar where it met the vertical. He wrapped the sheet around the cross in the door until it was secure and tight. He slipped his head inside and tightened the noose. When it was fully cinched down awaiting its duty, he grabbed the bars and kicked his feet up and was then hanging upside down from the top of the door. He then lodged a bare foot in the bars of the cell door above his head. Now inverted, the sheet was ready for his liberation. He said, "I'm sorry, baby. We'll be married in the next," when he began choking severely, and his mouth dried while the blood rushed to his head. His face turned purple as Sal awoke to the gentle commotion, peaking from a half-closed eye. The rush of blood caused Shane to pass out as he suffocated. Convulsions ensued as he rattled against the cell door until he made his great escape!

*

Camille was transferred to the California Department of Corrections Women's Facility in Chowchilla. Camille was a survivor and a manipulator. She quickly worked her way into a job in the prison laundry. With her job, she made a little money for canteen and worked away the boredom of her daily life.

As the years passed by, Camille was prompted by another woman in her pod to take some college-level classes with her in order to work toward a degree. She answered, "College level? How does that work?"

"I don't know. They have teachers come in, and we get college credits for passing the classes. There've been a couple people since I've been here who have gotten their two-year degree."

"Hmm, what are the classes about?"

"I'm gonna take accounting. I might be able to get a job after I get out, and Lord knows I need some help, so take it with me. C'mon."

Camille started taking classes and moving through the curriculum over the next four years at a snail's pace. She also started a women's group to help each other with the difficulties that had brought them to such a place. As she morphed into a different person in order to make the system believe in her, she actually did change some with the act.

*

In 2001, she sent her first letter to her mom and dad, apologizing for her existence and for all of the turmoil she had caused them. By the third letter, she actually admitted to trying to kill them and asked for their forgiveness.

Although she did not hear back from her parents, she found the writing and sending of the letters to be therapeutic. Camille realized that she had settled into prison life long ago and was now actually living life in a small town. She had friends and enemies, just like in Mountain View. She had the occasional sexual encounter with a couple of male guards who were a lot like the boys she was attracted to, some additional education, a job, and a hobby. The only thing that she didn't have was the ability to take vacation, but with each day she worked and survived, she moved her way toward captive retirement and maybe into a life somewhere else.

By 2003, she had written forty-two letters to her mom and dad. What she did not know was that they had read them all. Lisa and David Deagan were now retired and still living in Mountain View, but in a new home without the bad memories. At the fiftieth letter, the parents were starting to believe that their one and only child was finally maturing and had become a human being who cared about others in her quest for redemption.

In 2004, Camille sent them her final letter from prison:

Dear Mom and Dad:

I want you to know that my parole was granted by the CDC, and I am being released from prison. The law requires that I be paroled back to Jefferson County. I will be there in about four weeks from now. I am so sorry that I will be in the same county, maybe even in the same town as you. I know that I embarrassed you, humiliated you, and destroyed your trust in me. I have hope for forgiveness but do not expect it.

I would like to see you both. I miss you tremendously, and as I have stated in my previous fifty letters, so sorry for what I did. You are the best parents a child could ever hope for.

Your loving daughter, Camille

*

Their daughter was now coming home. Coming home as an adult, and they were no longer scared to see her. More importantly, they were no longer scared to be around her. The couple penned a letter and placed it in the hands of the post office for delivery. That letter was headed to the prison as Camille was headed home.

Camille arrived back in Mountain View courtesy of the state. As she rode into town on the bus, she marveled at the lack of change over those many years away. They pulled into the Sunset Bus Lines station for those destined for Mountain View. She grabbed her duffle bag from underneath the bus and was immediately met by her parole agent. He said, "I'm Agent Crump. Terrence Crump. I'm your parole agent and the agent for Jefferson County. I'll be taking you to the halfway house, where we'll go over the rules, and you'll get your papers."

"Okay, where's the halfway house?"

"You'll see."

"Mr. Crump, do you have any jobs set up for me to do—that pay?"

"Yup, you'll be cleaning motel rooms at the Clark and the Vacation Stay to start with."

"Oh. I can't wait."

"Listen, get this straight, I don't give a fuck. Ever. If you're unhappy, that's on you. I only care that you do what I fucking tell you and that you work your program. You re-offend, and you're headed back to the joint on the bullet train—got it?"

"Oh yeah, I got it. Yes, Sir, boss man!"

As they arrived at the halfway house, Terrence pulled to the curb in his plain white state-owned sedan and said, "Here's your first test. Get your shit and meet me inside."

Camille sat for a few seconds as she waited for her new boss to give her some free air. As the door to the parole palace closed, she stepped from the car and took her time to get her things. Halfway to the halfway house, she stopped and looked out into her hometown. Memories filled with joy and pain erupted in those moments as she shook it off and went inside.

*

The morning found her being startled awake once again to meet the scheduled government breakfast. She had been given some clothes to wear that she abhorred but put on anyway. Soon, she was in the van with the other parolees, headed to their various jobs around town. Camille was the last drop at the two motels on the south edge. She was paired with Molly Seasons, a former addict and newfound convert to Christianity. She looked like Hell but had Heaven in her heart. Camille did not know her from her former life and took an immediate liking to her as Molly showed her the ropes.

As the first two weeks rolled by, the leash became longer. When it did, Camille finally saw a familiar face standing in the line at the grocery store on a Friday afternoon. A face from her days in the county lockup. Camille said, "Hey, bitch. I know you!"

The woman looked back as her face soured in recognition. "Camille? Is that you? How long's it been? Wow, you're finally out of prison."

"Long time. Long time. Yeah, I just got out. Feel like I missed a lot, you know. How you been, Tina?"

"Good. Got married and had a kid."

"Oh yeah? Good for you."

"Got divorced, too. The kid is good, though. She's livin' with my mom. Hey, have you seen your parents yet?"

"No. Kind of afraid to, ya know."

"I bet they want to see you. You know, you did your time and all."

"I was writing them."

"Do you need anything? Why don't you come by, and we'll kick it."

"Where you at?"

"Apartment nine at The Shadows."

As Camille left the store to walk back to the halfway house, Tina pulled up to her in the parking lot, rolled down the window and said, "You look like you need a ride."

"Thanks, girl, that'd be great," Camille said as she opened the front passenger door and sat down.

"Hey, have you seen all the changes in town?"

"Not really. Looks like it hasn't changed at all."

"We got a new liquor store, another Mexican restaurant, a woman's boutique, and two outlet stores. Oh, and another gas station and gym. That's a lot, right? Wanna see 'em?"

"Actually, I need some clothes. Can we stop by that boutique?"

As Tina was driving Camille back to the halfway house, she said, "Hey, let's swing by your parents' new house. You haven't seen it before. Whaddya say?"

"Yeah, I'd like to see it," she said while turning to look out the side window awash in sudden uneasiness.

"There it is! Nice, huh?" said Tina as she pointed.

"Yeah, it is. Really nice. That's a lot nicer than the old one. I'm ready to go back," she said, now angered at the sight of her parent's affluence compared to her predicament.

"Are you okay? You look like you've seen a ghost."

"No, I'm good."

*

As she cleaned toilets, sinks, and bedding the following day, she soured into jealousy and anger. It was all she could do to keep it together before her lunch break.

That evening, the couple's phone rang, and Lisa picked it up. A seemingly familiar, deepened yet still feminine voice slowly delivered a chilling message. "Hey, Lisa, I'm here now. I've waited for so long. So, so long. It's now your time to be locked away forever. No one can save you or Dave. No one will know when, and no one will hear. I'm always in your head, and soon, I'll be cutting that head from both of you for all that you've done to me. I will enjoy the glory of sweet revenge as I replay the memories and watch your guts sliding out onto the floor of your new fancy little house for the rest of my life as you both rot away in your forever box!"

ABOUT ATMOSPHERE PRESS

Founded in 2015, Atmosphere Press was built on the principles of Honesty, Transparency, Professionalism, Kindness, and Making Your Book Awesome. As an ethical and author-friendly hybrid press, we stay true to that founding mission today.

If you're a reader, enter our giveaway for a free book here:

SCAN TO ENTER
BOOK GIVEAWAY

If you're a writer, submit your manuscript for consideration here:

SCAN TO SUBMIT
MANUSCRIPT

And always feel free to visit Atmosphere Press and our authors online at atmospherepress.com. See you there soon!

ABOUT THE AUTHOR

JASTROW HILL is a retired attorney who spent 27 years in the practice of law. He worked in wildland firefighting, private security, corrections and as a police officer prior to receiving his Bar license. As an attorney, Jastrow was a prosecutor, before eventually working in other areas of law practice.

He loves the outdoors, the study of history, philosophy, sociology, and psychology. The author holds an associate's degree, a bachelor's degree, and a juris doctor degree. He and his wife reside in Wyoming.

www.ingramcontent.com/pod-product-compliance
Lightning Source LLC
LaVergne TN
LVHW091546070526
838199LV00024B/558/J